Eine Kleine Murder

A Cressa Caraway Musical Mystery

Kaye George

Barking Rain Press

Eine Kleine Murder

Copyright © 2013 Kaye George (www.kayegeorge.com)

Edited by Julie Spergel

Cover artwork by Stephanie Flint (www.sbibb.wordpress.com)

Barking Rain Press
PO Box 822674
Vancouver, WA 98682 USA

www.barkingrainpress.org

ISBN print: 1-935460-64-1
ISBN eBook: 1-935460-66-X

Library of Congress Control Number: 2013936588

First Edition: April 2013

Printed in the United States of America

9 7 8 1 9 3 5 4 6 0 6 4 0

DEDICATION

To Mom, Grandma, and my Alpha cousins
(who are nothing like Cressa's cousins)

ACKNOWLEDGEMENTS

I owe thanks to so many wonderful friends for getting this book where it is. I'm deeply indebted to and grateful for the following people. In the beginning, Valerie Wolzien read an early version and gave me encouragement. Rosalie Stafford broke me into print back in 2005, and the staff at FMAM awarded me my first contest prize.

I got help from Mary P. Walker and my Guppy critique group members, Lonnie Cruse, Peg Wyse, Peg Cochran, Cheryl Rivers, and later from Peg Silloway and Judy Dailey. Mary Buckham gave me good insights. The Alpha Police Chief took time to explain the workings of his office to me, but I've misplaced his name. Captain Steve Dooley of the Henry County Sheriff's Office also gave me valuable insight and information.

Recent readers, Gale Albright, Marilyn Levinson, and Daryl Wood Gerber gave me help with a later version. The Plothatchers not mentioned above are big boosters: Krista Davis, Janet Bolin, and Janet Koch. My daughter, Jessica Busen, came up with my title. Isn't she clever? I owe the staff at the actual Crescent Lake Club a shout-out for their kind cooperation.

I also must thank my editor, Julie Spergel, who has done wonders for this book.

Finally, all musical definitions are from *The Columbia Encyclopedia*, Sixth Edition. Copyright © 2003 Columbia University Press except *Kyrie Eleison*, which is part of the standard religious mass; *Eine Kleine Wassermusik*, which is my own play on *Eine Kleine Nachtmusik* by Mozart; *Water Music* by Handel; and the original title of this work (which most people thought was a bit inaccessible).

KAYE GEORGE

PLAYLIST

CHAPTER	TITLE	COMPOSER
1	Night on Bald Mountain	Modest Moussorgsky
2	Eine Kleine Nachtmusik	Wolfgang Amadeus Mozart
2	La Mer	Claude Debussy
3	Funeral March	Frederick Chopin
6	Funeral March of the Marionettes	Charles Gounod
8	Scarborough Fair	Traditional English folk song
10	Jesu, Joy of Man's Desiring	Johann Sebastian Bach
13	Plink, Plank, Plunk	Leroy Anderson
16	Thus Spake Zarathustra	Richard Strauss
17	The Chicken Dance	Werner Thomas
18	Theme from Jaws	John Williams
23	Song of the Volga Boatmen	Traditional Russian Folk Song
43	William Tell Overture	Gioachino Rossini

For links to these songs on YouTube, visit:
www.barkingrainpress.org/products/eine-kleine-murder

PROLOGUE

Stinguendo: Dying away (Ital.)

What was that sound? A foot, snapping a twig in the woods? Ida knew she shouldn't be swimming alone at night, but she'd been antsy all day. She needed to get her mind off Cressa's visit. Grace usually swam with her, but her friend had taken relatives to the Quad City airport tonight. Besides, Ida was a strong swimmer. She knew every inch of Crescent Lake. And she thought she knew every sound. But there was that snap again. It prickled the hairs on her arms.

She stopped stroking and listened, straining toward the trees on the opposite bank, just ahead. It didn't repeat. *Must have been a night creature in the woods. A raccoon out foraging?*

Ida cupped her hands and pulled herself through the caress of the cool water, creating tiny ripples and almost no sound. The moon, a mere sliver tonight, laid a shining path across the silent ridges in the inky liquid. Bullfrogs boomed from the shallow end of the lake and the wind rattled the oak leaves on the shore.

She neared the bank and stuck her toes into the soft mud, turned and stood waist deep for a moment before her return trip. The scent of the night woods was verdant, lush. She breathed in the familiar fishy smell of the dark water.

There was that sound again—*snap*, then a footfall. She tried to whirl around as a dark form—*Dear God*—sprang with a splash from the darkness, grabbed her from behind, shoved her under the water. Ida clawed, scratched. Strong fingers pressed her down. Into the muck. Ground her face into the bottom. Her nose and mouth clogged with silt. No air.

She twisted. Kicked. Her bare feet struck strong legs. Unmoving legs. She scratched, tried to pry the iron grip from her shoulders. It only tightened. Her arms went limp. Her legs stopped flailing. Those hands, always those strong hands, forced her down, into the mud. No air. No breath. Mud. Only mud.

She knew this shadow, these hands. She stopped struggling. She was dying. Regret mingled with the peace that took over as she collapsed and gave up.

Oh Cressa, my dear, dear Cressa.

-1-

THE NEXT AFTERNOON
Alla Diritta: In direct motion (Ital.)

I drummed my finger faster on the steering wheel. *Stop that, Cressa.* It was an old nervous habit that just made me more anxious. The CD in my car stereo was beginning to rattle me. Moussorgsky's *Night on Bald Mountain*'s spooky, ominous strains were too much like my surroundings: mile after mile of identical, disorienting Illinois cornfields, interrupted only by dark clumps of trees huddled on stray hillsides.

And now I had a tailgater. It was time to admit I was lost. It was getting dark and if I didn't reach my grandmother's soon, I'd... well, what would I do? I hadn't passed a motel since leaving Moline. Pull over and sleep in the car?

As I rounded a curve and the road straightened, the headlights of the car behind me flashed in my rearview mirror, blinding me for a second and yanking a cuss word out of my mouth. The jerk had been on my tail for at least twenty miles and wouldn't pass me. A sudden thought stilled my dancing fingers. Was it my ex-boyfriend Len? The thought was too unsettling, and I was already starting to lose it. I needed to concentrate on getting there.

Because I'd ridden to Alpha dozens of times as a child to swim in the lake where Gram always kept a membership, I assumed I'd just magically know the way there. Wrong. *Where the hell was I?* My gut clenched. Time to phone a friend.

I reached into my purse on the passenger seat and felt around for my cell phone. Dammit, that idiot behind me had just flashed his brights. Why did he do that? There was no way I was going to pull over to see if there was something wrong with the car.

Where was that cell phone? Had I lost it again? I dumped the entire contents of my purse onto the seat and grabbed the cell. Its name was Peter the Mediocre. He wasn't a Great cell phone. I punched in the familiar numbers. The phone buzzed twice. Neek answered on the third ring. *Thank God.* My shoulders relaxed a notch.

"Hi, Cressa. Wait a minute." She panted a couple of times. "I gotta catch my breath. Doing... extreme yoga."

"Extreme yoga? I see how that's something that would appeal to you, Neek."

"You should try it, Cress." Another pant. "What's up? Where are you now? Hey, I have good news."

"I don't know where I am and I'm being tailgated. That's why I called you." I tried to take the tremor out of my voice. "These cornfields go on forever. Why can't I ever win the lottery and get a GPS for my car?"

"Don't whine, Cressa." She chuckled. "And be patient." She told me that a lot. "When the omens are right, you'll win."

I felt better talking to her. Neek was my best friend and lived in my apartment building. I'd asked her to handle my mail and plants when I'd fled Chicago earlier that day.

"I don't think that latest 'if-I-can't-have-you' note from Len was a good omen," I said. Those notes, slipped under my door at night, were getting more frequent—and more frightening.

"He'll never find you in Alpha, don't worry. And, speaking of omens, this one's divine." Her little-girl voice squeaked with excitement. "Listen, Cress, I found a quarter outside your apartment door right after you left. You know what *that* means."

"No, I don't. This is your good news?" Neek was a sweet person and a true friend, but she tended to find omens in the strangest things. Last week she'd been foretelling the future by the clouds.

"Yep. A quarter. That's big stuff. Big changes for you. Oh, Cressa, this fits right in with you finally going to visit your grandmother. I'm *so* glad you're doing this."

I eased my foot off the gas. The car behind me slowed, too.

"Are you near your computer?" I asked her. "I need you to tell me if I should go through Ophiem or just drive on past it? Nothing has looked familiar since the Quad Cities."

I had driven across the floor of a wide valley, then climbed a gentle hill. The name of the town, Ophiem, was so familiar I thought I should drive through it. I turned onto the smaller road toward the town. But that soon felt wrong. And the car still trailed me.

I made a sudden U-turn on the local road into Ophiem and headed back toward Highway 150. That should shake him.

A glance in the rearview mirror told me no one was following now. I let out a relieved breath.

I would breathe even easier if I knew what kind of reception Gram would give me. I had tried calling three times to tell her I might be coming, but I hadn't been able to reach her. Preferring anyway to see her face to face for our first real conversation, I was relieved and left a few brief messages. She would be glad to see me, wouldn't she? My burst of self-congratulation, at being the first to capitulate and end our feud, was fast giving way to doubt.

"I can't wait to see her face when she realizes I'm actually at her cabin," I said. "Unless she doesn't want to see me."

"You're her favorite grandchild. She'll want to see you. Promise me you won't mention the piano."

"Okay. Not at first, anyway."

"Hey, I'm just glad you're going to see her."

I swallowed a lump in my throat, put there by her soft sympathy. "So am I. So am I."

"That's what this quarter must mean, a *good* surprise. And, by the way, that ficus of yours is dying of thirst."

I wanted to kill two birds: get away from Len's harassment and surprise Gram. Well, maybe three birds. A quiet, rural lake should be a good place to finish this piece of music. I'd been stalled on it for weeks, and my teaching job this fall depended on it. I hoped Gram would once again serve as my muse.

"Did you go through Orion?" Neek pronounced it like the constellation.

"It's ORE-ion," I remembered from years ago, "and yes, that was awhile—"

"Yep, the highway goes right past a town called Ophiem. You're almost there."

"Past, not through, right?"

"Right. A straight shot down Highway One-Fifty. Unless you're on the interstate?"

"No, I'm back on track. Thanks, Neek. I'll call you tonight."

"Tell me all about her new cabin when you get there."

"Her 'cute' little cabin?" My lip involuntarily curled into a sneer.

"Yes. And give your Gram a big hug from me."

A glint caught my rearview mirror. I flinched and blinked. Then I saw headlights close behind me. The hair on the nape of my neck raised. Was it the same car? I slowed again to try to shake it.

"I'll give her hugs from both of us. You know, Neek, I think a car really is following me. It's been behind me ever since I passed the Quad City airport. I hope it's not ..."

"Len?"

"I don't know. The car kinda looks like his, but how could it be? He has no idea I'm here."

"Well, I saw—"

"Neek, are you there? Neek?" I'd lost her. I tossed Peter the Mediocre in the direction of my purse. Cell phones were so useless. Mine was usually either lost, or out of juice, or dropping calls.

-2-

*Nocturne: A piece of a dreamily romantic
or sentimental character, without fixed form (Fr.)*

Sure enough, I soon passed the town limit sign of Alpha, Pop. 550. The car that looked like Len's—a blue two-seater convertible—slowed for the town, but when I pulled into the parking lot of a bowling alley, it went on by. I gave a sigh of relief; I didn't trust the restraining order to keep him away. Then I backtracked to the turn-off for the lake and rattled down a rough road until a sign told me I was entering Crescent Lake Club. It directed all visitors to "Please stop at the first yellow house on the left, past the swimming area."

I'd turned off the music, but Moussorgsky's ominous tones that had still been playing in my head gave way to the merry strings in the beginning movement of Mozart's much more cheerful *Eine Kleine Nachtmusik.*

The warm June sun was finishing a peaceful descent behind distant rolling hills as I bumped along the gravel road, past the yellow house. A sign directed me to check in, but, figuring I wasn't exactly a visitor, I turned and aimed my trusty Honda up the hill. Gram had described her new country place and, after I reached the crown of the hill, I recognized it from the huge blue spruce standing guard. It *was* cute: a white-trimmed redwood cabin perched on the side of the hill leading down to the water.

It made me think of Goldilocks coming upon the Three Bears' cabin. Gram had called it her little dollhouse. The sharp tang of window-box geraniums greeted me, a sure sign this was Gram's place. She couldn't live anywhere without planting flowers.

I knew I should be happy that she'd been able to buy this cabin. Like most of the locals, she'd always had a membership to the club and used it for swimming, boating, and fishing. Unfortunately, for most of her life, she hadn't been able to afford a second home here while living in the Cities. She was returning to the place she'd grown up. I should have understood that.

I didn't see Gram's car, and no one answered my hollow banging on the wooden door. I peered into one of the two front windows and glimpsed a wagon-wheel light fixture and black pot-bellied stove in the middle of the room. But nothing stirred.

It had been… how many months since I'd last seen her? There had been a rift between us ever since Gramps died. Our latest, terse phone conversation made it obvious that rift had widened since she bought this cabin. Surely she still lived here? Had she moved without telling me? *No, Cressa, don't be ridiculous.*

"Hi," chirped a light voice behind me. I whirled. A woman about Gram's age, wearing a comfortable-looking sweat suit, came across the grass, her smile as warm as the one last ray of sun that glinted off her wavy silver hair.

"Are you looking for Ida?"

I nodded.

"I haven't seen her all day. Didn't talk to her yesterday, either. I had to take our kids to the airport last night. My name is Grace Harmon." She stuck out a worn hand that was soft when I shook it. "My husband and I live right over there." She waved at the cabin across the gravel road. "I think Ida must have gone into the Cities. She talked about going a couple days ago. Ida usually leaves her car there." Grace glanced back at my car, ticking while it cooled beside the road, and gestured. "Doesn't look like she's around."

"I guess I should have let her know exactly when I was coming. But I wanted to surprise her."

"So, you must be Cressa."

"Yes, her granddaughter."

"Oh, I know all about you. She's been hoping you'd come."

"Yes, well… " I wasn't going to get into that stuff with this woman I didn't know. I wondered if what Grace said was true—I hoped so.

"You can get a key from Toombs, down in that yellow house. He's the manager. He keeps extra keys, just in case. I'm sure he'll let you in. Tell you what, I'll go get it for you."

I started to thank her, but she was already halfway across the grass. After Grace came back and gave me the key, I hauled my suitcase and piano keyboard into the cabin, sat for a good ten minutes, rehearsing what I would say to her. My cell phone beeped that it was low and I plugged it in.

It was almost dark and I knew from our phone calls that Gram liked to swim in the lake at dusk. Maybe, if I went down for a dip, she would return and come join me in the water. I scribbled a note, propped it on the countertop, and took off. Gram and I had always loved to swim together.

The water wasn't warm, but that would never stop Gram. So it wasn't going to stop me.

As I stroked through the dark lake she had grown up with, hoping to see her soon, the ripples of Debussy's *La Mer* accompanied me in my mind. Gram had made sure I learned how to swim, but I still hated putting my head underwater, so I usually swam either a sidestroke or a backstroke. She had passed her love of swimming on to me, though, and being in the water connected me to her. She hadn't liked to put her head underwater, either.

In the cool of the June evening, having frog-kicked and sidestroked halfway across the lake, I rolled over onto my back and watched the light show—fireflies sparkling on the eastern shore where I had started. A peace fell over me that I hadn't enjoyed for a long time. The fireflies competed with the far-flung stars overhead, and all were accompanied by the lazy creak of crickets.

When I had left my beach coat and sandals in a heap on the sandy shore, the lake hadn't looked this wide. I was tiring, but, backstroking through the water's cool embrace, I figured my outstretched hands would soon hit the mud bank, or maybe a tree root, on the west side. I didn't remember how deep it was there, so maybe, if I couldn't touch bottom, I could pull myself onto the bank and rest a bit before starting back. This side of the lake was inky black. Nothing but trees here: no cabins, no road.

I was sure I was in the general area Gram and I used to swim to when I was a child. Sometimes, when I was very young, and if I tired midway, she'd tread water and support me until I regained the strength to continue. I could almost feel her strong hands under me, buoying me up and propelling me gently through the water.

It was neither the mud bank nor a tree root I touched, though, and not with my hand. My toes met something oddly soft. I stood up in the shallows, reached under the water, grabbed some cloth, and more of the squishy stuff. A set of tympani roared in my head and I knew. Somehow I knew.

-3-

Soffocato: Muffled, damped; choked (Ital.)

I tugged Gram's body up the mud bank and left it under a tree, sobbing at her bloated face and those beautiful, brilliant blue eyes, now disfigured by hungry fish. The earth shifted, tilted beneath my feet, and I plopped down beside her, losing my balance.

Reaching toward her, I shook her shoulder—was I trying to wake her? Her cold skin burned my fingertips and I jerked my hand back. Even in the darkness I could tell the skin was not alive and no longer bore the color of life.

I reached over to touch her hair. Usually soft and snowy white, the curls now escaping from the flowered pink bathing cap were dank, clotted with lake weeds. We would never again brush each other's hair. Never rub each other's feet. Never hug, kiss. Never resolve our spat. My arms ached to hold her, but this thing beside me wasn't her. She was gone. Gram was gone.

My hands went to my face, but the stench from the body that clung to my fingers stopped me before I buried my face in them.

I made it to my feet stiffly, searching in my panic for what to do next.

I had to tell someone, had to—what do they say on TV?—notify the authorities.

The only thing I could do was swim back to the eastern shore to call for help. The return trip felt twice as far. I began to fear I might not make it. My hands shook badly as I stood dripping on the beach and tried to dig my cell phone out of the pile I had left on the sand. The tympani still beat in my temples, almost blinding me.

My cell phone wasn't there. I'd lost Peter again! No, I remembered I had left it charging in the cabin. I stood for only a few seconds, still in shock, then swooped up my things. After casting one last glance across the water where Gram's body was, I realized I had to get help in a hurry.

The only thing I could think to do was run up the hill to Grace Harmon's. A tall man I took to be her husband answered my frantic pounding.

"Gram," I blubbered. "She's… she's …"

Grace came up behind him. Warm light spilled around them into the darkness where I stood. "What is it, Cressa? What's the matter?"

"You're shivering." The man reached a long arm around my shoulders. He guided me to their couch. Grace shook out an afghan from the back and wrapped it around me.

I took a couple of deep breaths. "I found Gram." Tears sprang to my eyes again. "She's dead. She's drowned."

"Drowned? Ida? Here? In the lake?" Grace's blue eyes grew huge. She threw a glance at the man.

The genial expression on his face disappeared into a frown. "What happened to her? Were you swimming together?"

"No, no. I went for a swim and she was on the other side. Underwater. Drowned."

"Oh. My." Grace sank, dazed, into the rocker behind her. It gave a couple of feeble rocks, then settled. The kind man sat beside me on the couch.

"Cressa, this is my husband, Al." Grace murmured. "This is Ida's granddaughter."

"I'm so sorry to finally meet you under these circumstances. Where is she now?" he asked, his voice somber.

"I pulled her onto the bank. On the other side of the lake. I had to leave her there. We need to get her. I need to call nine-one-one, but I left my cell phone in the cabin." I was dizzy. The world spun off-kilter.

"I'll call." Al got up and walked to the kitchen where I heard him dialing and speaking softly, much calmer than I could have been. After he hung up he said they were sending an ambulance.

The cup of tea Grace handed me rattled in the saucer and it warmed me up a bit. Al accompanied me down the hill, just in time to see them load her body, zipped into a dark bag, into the back. They had commandeered a boat to get her to this side of the lake. From the looks of the dripping EMT, he had done more than a little wading in the process.

My legs threatened to give way. I swayed and Al caught me.

"Where are you taking her?" I asked the technicians, barely able to talk through my chattering teeth. I wasn't cold—on the outside at least—but couldn't stop shivering.

The young female driver walked over to me as the EMTs slammed the back door of the ambulance.

"That's my grandmother," I whispered.

"I'm so sorry. We'll take her to the funeral home here in Alpha. That's the usual procedure until she can be looked at."

"Can I come?" I asked, not wanting to let her go with these people. It was a struggle to understand her words, to make sense of what was happening around me.

"There's really no need. There's nothing you can do tonight." Her voice was gentle, handling me like I might break. "You can go in tomorrow to make arrangements. The coroner ought to take a look at her, but he's out of town until the day after tomorrow. We'll have the doctor in Cambridge pronounce her tonight. I'm surprised. No one has drowned out here for a few years."

"Yes, but—" My voice caught, unable to finish my thought. It would have been a denial that she drowned, but I was looking at the evidence in that horrid bag.

The ambulance driver reached out to touch my arm, hesitated, then gave me a pat and climbed into the driver's seat.

Debussy had long ago given way to Chopin's ponderous *Funeral March,* the stark piano version. The one Gram had encouraged me to practice over and over for a recital. I watched my beloved Gram disappear with the taillights as they bounced along the gravel road, then faded to nothing.

⚬⚬⚬

At last I was alone in Gram's cabin. All the things I had wanted to say to her jumbled together in my mind, whirled round and round, and ceased making an iota of sense.

Al and Grace had been wonderful. They'd even offered to let me spend the night there, but I wanted to be alone in Gram's place.

My note to Gram sat where I'd left it. With more force than necessary, I grabbed it and wadded it into a tight ball.

"Oh, Grammie, I hope you know …" I couldn't finish the thought. The incomprehensible echoed in my mind: *she drowned.* The impact of those two words was simply unbearable. And how could a mere two words describe the fact I no longer had a grandmother, that she was lost to me forever?

One of the supports of my life, my Gram, was gone. A chasm was opening under me and I teetered at the edge of it.

I needed to talk to someone. Neek.

⚬⚬⚬

I had met the person who became my best friend only a year ago. Even though we lived in the same apartment building, and I knew her by sight, we connected in a yoga class given at a nearby high school. We were as different as a bass viol and a flute. Neek was definite about everything and always knew her place in the world, whereas I would probably always be tentative about my abilities, despite Neek's assurance that I was talented, smart, and not too bad-looking. She later said she predicted we'd be friends the first night of that class.

My cell phone wasn't in my purse. I remembered it was plugged in. Peter was charged now, but had zero connection bars. I took it out onto the glassed-in porch, built out over the hill on the back of the cabin. It held cheerful-looking white wicker furniture, a rocker, a settee, and tables, as well as a brass daybed where I knew Gram sometimes slept. I stopped. It hit me that the afghan I had crocheted for her in seventh grade was draped prominently over the foot of the daybed.

She kept it all these years.

The workmanship was nothing to brag about, but Gram had taught me to crochet and that was my first finished piece. I realized tears were racing down my face.

I fingered my afghan, then punched Neek's number into my cell phone and it leapt to life. There was only one bar, but maybe it would be enough.

She answered on the fourth ring, as I was about to give up.

My hello sounded weak to me.

"Are you okay? You sound like you have a cold. Can I send you something? I have a great new cold cure. It's a powder and you mix it with orange juice."

I wasn't masking the thickness in my throat. I steadied my breath.

"No, I'll be all right." I didn't really believe that. "But Neek, that big change you talked about earlier today?" My voice was still trembling.

"Was it not a good one? I was afraid it might not be."

"Oh, Neek. She's dead. Gram's dead."

For once Neek was speechless. I told her about swimming across the lake and finding the body, then about the Harmons, and about the ambulance taking her away. My voice became steadier as we spoke.

"She was so tough, Cressa. I didn't think she'd ever die. So where are you now?"

"I'm here, in the cabin." I sniffed, feeling a little more human. "It really *is* cute. I like it, even without the piano. I wish I could tell her that."

Neek was silent for a moment. "You're not going to stay there alone, are you?"

Where else would I go? "I... I think so."

"Are you sure? Will you be okay? Should I come down?"

"I want to stay, Neek. There's no place else to go. And I have to make *arrangements* tomorrow. And I guess," I was thinking ahead of my words, "she'll be buried here. Next to Gramps in the Alpha Cemetery. No reason for you to come. I'll probably be here for a few days."

I pictured her name carved next to his. The only thing missing on her side of the stone was the last date. Now it could be filled in.

"But, Cressa. How did she die? Did she get caught on something under the water?"

"No, I don't think so. There's nothing in the lake but fish."

"Do you really think she drowned? You've told me what an expert swimmer she was."

"Yes, yes she is... was." Neek had a point. How could Gram have drowned? "But she had to have drowned, had a cramp or something. That's the only explanation. Isn't it?"

-4-

*Pastorale: An instrumental piece imitating in style and
instrumentation rural and idyllic scenes (Fr.)*

Peek and I talked more about the funeral and about the possibility that the blue car behind me had been Len. She was concerned he had followed me; I didn't see how he possibly could have.

This long day had started in another town, another world. I had received another nasty note slipped under the door of my apartment from Len. He couldn't quite get it through his head that he was now a stalker, under a restraining order—no longer a romantic interest.

For days I hadn't been able to concentrate on my composition, the symphony I had to finish by the end of the summer. It was the only hurdle between me and my master's degree in music. I was specializing in composition, and this was my thesis. My university teaching job required the degree. And the job was my stepping stone onto a podium.

I was going to conduct.

There was nothing I'd rather do. I'd known that since I was four. It was a hard profession to get into, but I was determined to do it.

Lately, my fear of Len had been blocking my concentration. So had the emotional distance between me and my Gram. One rift had festered for a couple of years, and I had caused that one, too. But the conflict over the cabin was more recent. This morning I had decided it was time to do something about it.

When Gram had sold her house in Moline to buy the cabin, I'd mourned. That house had been the only stable home I could remember. My musician parents had stuck me on stage as soon as I could warble a tune and bang a piano, hauling me all over the country until their deaths when I was eleven years old.

For years, I was so shy I could barely talk to people. Moving constantly, everyone seemed like a stranger. I was always the new kid in school—when I went. The only time I felt confident was when I was on stage. All stages were alike, not changeable like the people in each new place.

After they died, I went to live with Gramps and Gram, my mother's parents, in Moline, where they'd just moved to from Alpha. It was there that I finally learned to feel secure after my nomadic childhood. I still had trouble forming friendships, but I felt much safer being in one place with my grandparents.

Now I traced the fine filigree of the locket around my neck, one of my most precious possessions, to soothe myself. The jagged thought of Len ran through my mind like background music to a horror flick, but my mental foreground was filled with a keening dirge for my lost Gram.

The shimmer of moonlight on the water below the cabin shone through the tree-covered hill like the glint of brass. That damn treacherous water.

What was I going to do?

I didn't want to go back to Chicago. Could I stay here for the summer and write? I noticed that no music ran through my head at the moment, a rare thing. I couldn't see the future clearly beyond Gram's burial. It was blanked out by the abyss in my soul that kept widening.

Gram had been so pleased about buying the cabin, I shouldn't have become upset with her. I shouldn't have refused to go see it. She'd been thrilled to be going back to Alpha, where she grew up. And she told me over and over on the phone how much she loved her new place. She had never let anyone's opinion stand in her way. Including mine.

Back inside the main room, my suitcase and portable piano keyboard still lay where I had plunked them down when I first carried them in, on the wooden floor next to one of the pair of couches flanking the front door. Those couches must have been the indoor bedding for nights when the daybed on the porch was too cold; there wasn't an actual bed anywhere.

My trembling started again and my knees gave way. I sank onto the soft cushion of the other couch, unable to take another step.

The evening's grisly events, plus the presence of Gram I sensed in this place, picked that moment to overwhelm me. My returning tears stung, but not as acutely as the stab in my heart.

I pictured Gram zipped into that body bag, all alone. It was a gruesome image, but I couldn't shake it. She had been such a strong swimmer. I didn't understand how she could accidentally drown in this lake she knew so well.

My tears blurred the room. This rustic one-room cabin, with its friendly looking black Franklin stove smack in the middle of the room, was so much like her, I could picture her here.

I had been relieved to see indoor plumbing, a tiny bathroom walled out into the main room. Especially now that I was stuck here, at least until she was buried. Gram used to insist that a large house and modern conveniences were unnecessary. She had grown up with an outhouse.

I sniffed, looking through my purse for a tissue. The cabin smelled like my Gram.

A small TV sat on the countertop. I smiled to see a remote control by the couch. If I could, I'd tease her for having a remote. A tool, she always said, for lazy people. One more tear trickled down and I wished she were here to tease.

6⤫9

Realizing I hadn't eaten for hours, I finished unpacking and rummaged through the cabinets in the kitchenette that occupied a back corner of the cabin. Her blue metal coffee pot sat on a burner, ready for her Swedish coffee. She made it the old-fashioned way, boiled on the stove with a whole egg cracked into the pot to clarify the brew.

I stared at the peanut butter and crackers I had brought along, then at the apples I'd put into the square refrigerator tucked under the counter. I picked one up, but put it back. I couldn't eat.

I tested the lock on the door and inspected all the windows to make sure I would be safe as I slept. Turning back to the porch, built up on stilts over the sloping hill to make it level with the rest of the cabin, I opened all the louvers to let in the pleasantly cool air. The glass slats were inside sturdy screens. If someone, someone like Len, tried to get through them, the clattering would wake me up. Deflating with fatigue, I lay down on the porch's brass daybed.

I wanted to sleep on the porch because Gram had once mentioned to me it was her favorite sleeping place when the weather was fair enough.

At first I thought the trauma of the day's events would keep me wide awake, but the journey, my long swim, and emotional exhaustion soon overcame me. I carefully laid my afghan on the rocker and snuggled into the old pink and green quilt, one I recognized from Gram's house in Moline, deeply inhaling the clean, cool air, and dozed off, hoping Gram wouldn't appear in my dreams.

She didn't turn up, but I had nightmares anyway.

Visions of igloos and howling winds. Huge, hollow-eyed creatures that snarled with low, rumbling roars over a great cold abyss, a sort of hell frozen over.

I roused myself. The one thin quilt, which had been fine at nightfall, now let most of the cold air filter right on through to my freezing flesh.

An echoing boom rolled uphill to the daybed. Another boom, then another—a chorus of demonic monsters down at the lake, I thought, through my half-asleep haze. A chorus with a really scratchy percussion backbeat. I bolted upright, wide awake, when an owl hooted next to the porch, inches from my head.

I tried to call out. Fear paralyzed my throat. The croaking I made sounded like the monsters in my dream. It took a couple of minutes for my breathing to become regular. I cleared my throat—my voice was back, though still taut.

The acrid smell of brimstone from my lingering nightmare became the pleasant smoky smell left over from the wood fire I had noticed at the Harmons' earlier. The monsters, I realized, were bullfrogs croaking across the water.

Reluctant and groggy, I realized I was going to have to get up and get more blankets. My childhood afghan wouldn't keep me warm; it had more holes than thread. I vaguely remembered the location of the large armoire in a corner of the inside room. All I had to do was find my way there in the pitch black. Why hadn't I thought to put a flashlight by the daybed before I went to sleep? *Tomorrow*, I thought, *I will for sure.*

I swung my frozen legs over the side of the bed and searched with my toes for my slippers. They were in my apartment back in Chicago. All I felt was a cold wooden floor. The bushes beside the porch rustled, but I ignored them.

I felt along the painted clapboard wall to the doorway, searching the rough wooden planking inside the cabin for a light switch, but couldn't find one. I came at last to the armoire. It was so dark in the cabin I couldn't have seen a monster if one had leapt at me and grabbed my neck with its slimy claws.

I groped inside the cabinet, foolishly thinking a flashlight might be conveniently stashed there. Grabbing several thick pieces of fuzzy cloth, I made my way back to the daybed and settled in. But didn't sleep. Not yet.

The wind sighed ever so slightly through the leaves of the dense growth as the grotesque bullfrogs continued, and crickets and cicadas provided backup. Vermin and scratching noises inside the cabin? I'd think about those in the morning. The bushes rustled again. Was someone out there?

-5-

Reveille: Signal for rising (Ger.)

It was a short night. Before the first light of dawn glimmered through the trees, the birds started up. First, there was only one, shrill and insistent. Then others joined in, one at a time, initially sounding sleepy, even peeved that the early bird woke them up. Quickly, however, they gathered strength and numbers until the forest rang with joyous song.

I groaned, irritated with their exuberance. How could they be so happy, so alive, when my Gram was dead inside a black bag?

Here I was, in her bed, alive and warm. In the cabin that had been the root of the coldness between us for the last months of her life. If only I'd known they would be her last months, I wouldn't have refused to visit her here.

I missed the Moline house Gram had sold. My home. Still, I had to admit, I had become uncomfortable there after Gramps died almost two years ago. Every time I returned for a visit, I ended up driving back to Chicago in the middle of the night. I would wake up breathless and terrified in my childhood bed and want only to get out of there.

He died because of me. I knew that, no matter how hard Gram tried to tell me otherwise.

I'd been home on summer break from my second year of college. Gram had asked me to replace the burnt-out light bulb on the basement stairs, a treacherous flight of steep wooden-slat steps that led to a solid concrete floor. I was busy playing the ancient upright piano that presided over the dining room, an instrument that was an old friend to me, and I put the chore out of my mind. Playing that piano reminded me of the old days, performing with my parents. It made me forget how shy I usually was, how awkward I became around my college classmates. Especially the boys. I'd barely dated in high school and it had looked like I wouldn't ever be kissed, even in college.

Later that day, Gramps headed to the basement to work on the elaborate model train set he loved. He slipped at the top and tumbled, fracturing his skull on the cement at the bottom. The vision of his wispy, thin, gray hairs sticking in the glistening red blood haunted me still. Gram and I had been outside picking cherries in the yard and didn't find him right away. The blood was starting to dry by the time we came in and found him. My guilt was so great, I could never completely explain to Gram what I'd done.

After all they'd done for me, I had failed both my grandparents. Gram and Gramps were the only ones who approved of my choices. My parents thought I should stick to popular music and make more money. Gram was the one who paid for classical piano lessons from the talented neighbor, lessons that taught me how to read music and laid the foundation for the career I wanted.

Under my heap of blankets—one of them looked quite a bit like a tablecloth—I lay, unable to stir. A squirrel skittered across a bough next to the porch, did an athletic twelve-foot leap to the next tree, then turned around to scold me for watching him. I couldn't help but smile, and his antics broke my mood.

My mind filling with ways I could use the early morning sounds of the woods in my music, I stood and stretched, stiff from being in bed too long. The leaves rustled, the birds hopped, the waves lapped below. Everything was so alive; the air smelled vibrant.

Drawn by the awakening wildlife, I stepped outside and inhaled the clean air. Then I saw them. A couple of fresh footprints, right outside the porch. Had someone stood and watched me sleep? Was there a Peeping Tom at the lake? The thought sent a jangle up my spine, like a trembling tambourine. I'd have to make sure no one could see me tonight when I went to bed.

As I started to turn away, I spotted a cigarette butt, ground into the dirt. I kicked at it to see if I could tell whether or not it was the kind Len smoked. I looked for the brand, stamped above the filter, but it fell apart when I poked at it. I stared at it. That tambourine shook harder, rattling my whole being.

I told myself that Len was *not* here. NOT here. Maybe I could recite it in my head enough times to make it true, like Dorothy repeating, "There's no place like home." Yeah, right.

I retreated back into the cabin to shower.

I knew I had to go into town to see about Gram, but it was too early for any businesses to be open. What I wanted to do was crawl back into bed and cry. I forced myself away from the porch and the bed.

After my shower, for distraction if nothing else, I spread my music-writing materials onto the kitchen counter, a sort of breakfast bar which jutted out from the wall. I arrayed my equipment, my midi keyboard, my laptop, and a pad of lined clef paper I used for jotting quick inspirations. Could I manage to write something? I was surrounded by enough ideas for an entire symphony.

⧼⧽

The knock at the door brought me back. I had spent a couple of hours staring at my work, getting nothing done.

Grace's sunny smile was a welcome sight.

"I've brought you sandwiches and brownies, dear."

She read my expression correctly. "I know you may not feel like eating, but you need to try. Have you talked to the funeral home yet?"

I shook my head. How would I be able to face that?

"If you'd like, Al and I could go with you sometime tomorrow. I'm driving in to Alpha in a minute. While I'm there, do you want me to set up an appointment for the afternoon?"

Still mute, I nodded my thanks. I could put it off one more day.

"You know, Ida and I were a couple of compatible old Swedes. We swam together, used the same hairdresser, and the same lawyer. I can call him for an appointment, if you like."

"Lawyer?" I couldn't think why I'd need a lawyer.

"Yes, the one that has her will."

Her will. But those are for *dead* people. Oh. Dead people like Gram. It was so hard to consider all the ramifications of her being dead. "Okay, sure."

She thrust a wrapped plate into my hands, gave another quick smile, and bustled off to do her errands. Gram had had good friends in the Harmons.

I put the sandwiches in the fridge, but, tempted by the chocolatey aroma, left the brownies out. As soon as I could eat, I would have one.

After staring at my music manuscript a little longer, I quit fooling myself that I could work and wandered back to the daybed on the porch.

I pulled the tablecloth that I'd mistaken for a blanket off the bed and returned it to the armoire. Feeling for an empty spot on the high shelf, I felt some little round things. Mouse droppings. Ugh! I shoved the tablecloth onto the shelf and dislodged a thick envelope onto the floor. I stooped to pick it up, turned it over, and saw my name written on the front in Gram's familiar, precise hand.

-6-

Stile osservato: Strict style (Ital.)

I plopped to the floor, caressing the envelope, holding a little piece of Gram between my fingers. For a long moment, I stared at the envelope, willing myself—commanding myself—to open it. I couldn't. Not yet. My fingers flew to my locket and traced its comforting filigree.

I was pretty sure one of two things would be in that envelope. Either a note trying to patch up our stupid quarrel, or—*please God, no*—a continuation of it. We were both stubborn, and our disagreement could have gone on for a long time. I hadn't even gone to see her at Christmas. How could I have been that angry over her selling a stupid house? For the rest of the day, until bedtime, I pretended to compose music.

The next morning I awoke stiff all over. I squatted down on the porch and did a few minutes of yoga to loosen up. Regular yoga, not Neek's extreme variety, whatever that was. In the middle of a half-candle I heard Grace's soft voice at the door.

She apologized for bothering me when I greeted her. "You look much better this morning, Cressa."

I was surprised by how much better I felt.

"That old bear, Mr. Toombs, was around this morning, right after we got back from church. Why he's badgering us and not you, I don't know, but he does want to see you."

"What for? Who is he?"

"He's the manager of the complex, a stickler for regulations. There's a rule about signing in with him. I explained your grandmother just died—he couldn't have missed all that commotion—and asked him if he could leave you alone for a bit. But he went on and on."

I had to get out of the cabin, so I agreed to go "sign in" at his house, the yellow one I had passed on my way in. How long ago had that been? It seemed like weeks.

The envelope in the armoire reproached me when I walked past. I couldn't see it, of course, but I knew it was there. And knew I should read the contents. But I couldn't yet. Maybe later.

I pulled up the shades I had drawn over the louvers in defense against the person who may have spied on me the night before last. In the clear light of day, I admitted that the footprints and cigarette butt were most likely innocent. They had probably been there before I arrived. Nevertheless, I would throw the sturdy deadbolt on the front door again that night, like I had the night before.

The outside air drifted in through the small front windows as I dried off after my shower and dressed. The air was as fresh as yesterday. Today I could appreciate it more.

A small shed, painted red to match the cabin, sat near the road. I walked across Gram's front yard, bordered by lilac bushes, the smell of the last of their lush blooms floating across my face, and reached the gravel road leading down the hill.

To my left, the land sloped up. Beyond the Harmons' cabin was a playground in an open area.

To my right, the road led down the hill to the swimming area and the entrance, and the manager's yellow house. The route led me past several cabins on my right, the lake shining below them. Just before Toombs's was a space big enough for another cabin, but it held only a cement pad. The growth around the slab looked cold and stunted. Tangled growth surrounded strangely lopsided trees. I shivered and hurried past.

A stepping-stone walkway, bordered by tidy flower beds, led to the front door of the neat house. I lifted a brass knocker, engraved with the name "Toombs" and let it fall. A paddleboat and a shiny row boat bobbed next to a freshly painted dock below, at the water's edge. From a nearby oak, a robin serenaded me, telling me to *cheery-up, cheery-up.*

The door opened a crack and a woman with her hair in pink foam curlers peered out.

"Yes?" She kept plenty of door between us.

I smiled to reassure her. In case that's what she needed. "Hi. Grace Harmon mentioned I should sign in here? I'm Cressa Carraway, staying at my grandmother's cabin."

"Oh, you're Ida's… yes… well, come in."

I had passed some sort of test, because the door swung wide and she stepped back for me to enter, although the worried expression didn't leave her face. After I was inside, she was unsure of what to do with me. I glanced around and took in a shag-carpeted room with out-of-date everything, cheap early American furniture, heavy wood paneling, but everything orderly and clean. The smell of lemony furniture polish almost masked the odor of cigarette smoke. One bookshelf held newish books that gave no signs of having ever been read. One big comfortable chair, flanked by several artificial plants, faced the television. Almost every surface held a clean ashtray.

"I'm so sorry about Ida," she said. "Such a terrible thing. And such a nice lady." She lingered uncertainly in the middle of the room. "I'm Martha Toombs. My husband

and I manage the lake. Are you staying on for awhile?" She gave me a tentative smile. If anyone personified the musical piece "Kitten on the Keys," it was this flighty, skittish woman. How could she "manage" anything?

I took a breath and thought about how long I should stay. "Maybe. At least for a few days, until the funeral. If it's no problem."

"No, no, it's no problem. I think. Are you her only grandchild?" Mrs. Toombs looked around vaguely as if searching for the answer to her oddly off-topic question. Maybe she wondered if she would have to put up with any more intruders.

"No, I'm not." I looked around too, but the room hadn't changed. "I have cousins on the West Coast, but I'm the only one she was close to." The robin's song came through an open window. "It's so peaceful here, isn't it? A big change from Chicago. Gram used to bring me here to swim when I was younger, but I haven't been out of the city for ages."

"You haven't been to the cabin since she bought it, have you?" She sank onto the couch and motioned me to a chair. She must have been relieved to have thought of seating me.

"No, I didn't get here while she was alive." I knew these people probably all wondered why I had never visited Gram. I perched on the edge of a sofa cushion; I didn't want to settle in and stay long.

"Her death was so sudden. That must be hard for you."

"Where's the chips I bought yesterday?" yelled a strident male voice from an inner doorway. Mrs. Toombs looked fondly toward the sound. The man poked his handsome head, topped with dark wavy hair, into the room. He flashed me a dazzling smile and walked in from the kitchen, lighting up the room like a fanfare. He stubbed out the tail end of his smoke in the nearest ashtray and approached me. I tested the smell and tried to determine if it was the same kind I'd smelled outside the cabin. Not being a smoker, I couldn't tell.

"Hi, I'm Mo Toombs. I'm her son." He nodded backwards. "And you're?" He stepped closer and offered his hand. His handshake was warm and strong.

"Cressa Carraway," I said. "Ida Miller's granddaughter."

"Oh." His face sobered, not nearly so handsome without the smile. "We're sorry about what happened to her."

"Thank you. I'll miss her terribly." I was surprised I could talk about her without bursting into tears.

Another young man emerged from the kitchen. He looked about Mo's age, mid-twenties, the same as me, with coppery-red curls and a camera slung around his neck. He nudged Mo to prompt an introduction. His entrance didn't bring a fanfare to mind, more like a nice overture.

"Cressa, this is Darry Johannson, friend of mine."

"How do you do? And it's Daryl, not Darry." His glance at Mo held a slight frown. His green eyes widened then. "Oh, you're the one whose grandmother died a couple of nights ago. I heard you came to see her, and you... Well, I'm so sorry."

Yes, well, we're all sorry, I thought. That's official.

"You're only the second person I've ever known with one green eye and one blue eye," Daryl said.

It's odd how few people notice that. I decided I liked him.

"Is your father home, Morris?" Mrs. Toombs asked her son, her pinched eyebrows pleating her forehead.

"Yeah, he's coming in a minute. He had to check something down on the boat." Mo squinted at me. I figured he was trying to see my mismatched eyes.

"Oh, there you are." Mrs. Toombs stiffened in her seat as an older man joined us. He was a more mature, shorter version of Mo, but with a narrow fox-like face.

"I went to get beer. I told you where I was going," he said to his wife, his high voice sharp and petulant.

"Again?"

The glare he gave her chilled the warm room. It made me think of Len, for some reason.

"This is Ida Miller's granddaughter." Martha popped up. "She's going to stay at the cabin for awhile." She gestured toward me with tightly clutched hands.

When he saw me, his manner changed from petulant to oozing and oily, all in an instant.

"How do you do?" he said formally, bending forward and shaking my hand, sheathing the sharpness he had shown his wife.

"I was going to register her," his wife said with a sickly smile.

"Well, did you?" He scowled at her.

"Uh, no, not yet."

Poor woman, I thought. I wondered if he did more than verbally abuse her. Her eyebrows twitched together and she sank back onto the couch, deficient and defeated.

He turned to me again. "Me and the missus does all the managin'. It's a big job. Lots of responsibility." He cleared his throat with a moist sound. It didn't help. His squeaky tenor still grated on my ears. "No noise after ten o'clock on week nights, now. Garbage is picked up once a week, on Wednesdays, at the foot of the hill. You need to haul your own trash down there. The upkeep of your cabin, your boat, and your dock is your responsibility. You get your own yard mowed, we mow all the common ground. You got any problems, you come see me about it." At this he thumped himself in the chest with his thumb. I pictured him sticking his hand inside his shirt and striking a Napoleon pose. He did look a bit like the French emperor.

"And watch how you drive with all this gravel. The teenagers sometimes go berzook, 'specially on the weekends, we gotta watch 'em. They drive like crazy, tearin' up and down the hill. Throwin' gravel all over the place."

Berzook? Was that a version of berserk? "Did you know my grandmother well?" I asked, changing the subject.

"Sure, I knew her. Knew her from way back." He quit talking for a moment and the silence was conspicuous without his whining, raspy voice.

Toombs got some papers out of a corner cabinet drawer, rustled them a bit, and wrote down my name, address, and phone number in Chicago as I dictated them. He opened a door in the upper half of the cabinet. The inside of the door held rows of hooks, each with a neatly lettered label above it. He looked at the hook under the name Ida Miller, from which one key swung.

"Oh, that's right. Gracie came and got the other key." He gave me a sharp look. "You still have it?"

"Of course." Did he think I'd lost it already? But, prone to losing things as I am, I was glad to see a spare.

"Guess you're all set, then." He dusted his hands together with an air of self-importance.

"I need to run errands. You stay here," he ordered his wife. She pulled in her head, turtle-fashion, and sank further into the couch, like a dog responding to a "sit" command. Would I have turned into a person like Martha if I'd put up with being beaten by the man in my life? Once was all it took for me, but with a different upbringing, a different outlook... who knows?

"Be back later." His departing strut needed to be accompanied by Gounod's comic *Funeral March of the Marionettes,* the song Alfred Hitchcock used as the theme song for his television show. The room breathed a sigh of relief after he left.

"Mo, dear," said Mrs. Toombs, brightening. "Poor Cressa doesn't know anyone here. Why don't you take her to lunch at the bowling alley and show her around?"

I wasn't sure I was up to eating yet, but Mrs. Toombs looked so pitifully hopeful, so proud to have had an original thought, I agreed to meet Mo in a couple of hours. I felt some kind of a kinship with Martha. There but for the grace.

"Just so I'm back in time for my appointment at the funeral home," I said, not looking forward to that meeting or the lunch all that much. Mo stood there staring at me, making me increasingly uncomfortable.

-7-

Trio: A piece for three voices (Eng.)

Back in my cabin—I was already beginning to think of it as *my* cabin—I phoned my own personal oracle, Neek. After mentioning the funeral home and the lawyer visit for later today, I told her I wasn't sure if I should go to lunch with Mo Toombs or not. There was no good reason for my feeling, I told myself, but a tingle in my gut told me something was off about him.

"I think it'll be okay," she said. "I found a penny this afternoon. It's got your birth year on it, so you should be fine."

I groaned. "You-You," my name for her when she annoyed me and I wanted to annoy her back, "you are crazy. You know that, right? Listen, I'll have my cell with me and I have you on fast dial. So if anything happens I'll call you. If I don't say anything, call the cops." You-You was long for UU, which was short for her real name, Unity Unique. Her parents were hippies. She'd told me they were upset by her latest job, working at home taking calls for an internet catalog business. I thought that job was probably what made her slightly nuts.

"You think he's an ax murderer or something? Or just your usual poor choice in men?" she said.

"No, I just, I don't know, humor me."

"Don't worry, it'll be fine. And I'll be around all day."

"Thanks, girlfriend. Oh, one more thing. You should probably forward my bills out here. I know I haven't paid the cell phone or cable this month and I'm thinking, maybe, of staying on a bit."

"Okey-dokey. What's the address?"

"Um. I guess I don't know." I hadn't seen any mailboxes. "Gram had a post office box. I guess I'll have to get one if I stay. I'll let you know."

After I flipped my phone closed, I searched the cabin for a land line. Gram had called me several times after she moved here, so there had to be a phone. I found it, but it seemed to be disconnected.

I'd been impatiently checking the clock for the last thirty-five minutes when Mo finally drove up in his rattle-trap car and honked, long and loud. He gave me what I'm sure he thought was a cute grin when I got in the car. I didn't say anything about him being late. He pushed the last bit of a cigarette into the ashtray on the door as I reached for the seatbelt.

Mo's old Ford would be good material for a demolition derby. It was large, well dented, and gave off a faint, peculiar smell—a mixture of oily rags, dirty socks, and, of course, stale cigarette smoke.

When I turned to reach for the seatbelt, I was surprised to see Daryl in the back seat. That hair of his glinted reddish in the sunshine. I mumbled a surprised hello.

"My car's in the shop," he said. "I'm hitching rides with Mo today. I had some shots I wanted to take at the lake this morning." He gestured to the camera still hanging around his neck.

"You look great," Mo said to me. "That's a pretty cool necklace." He ran a hand through his thick black hair, then reached over and fingered my locket.

What the hell? I flinched and jerked away. I didn't like him handling it. Maybe it was because his hands looked faintly grimy. Or maybe because his wavy hair was oily and he'd just run his hands through it.

That locket was one of my most prized possessions, a delicate filigree antique that Gram had given me for my birthday the year I came to live with her. Mo knew something about jewelry.

It turned out he knew a *lot* about hamburgers.

They were thick and juicy, with an aroma that overpowered the usual bowling alley mix of sweaty feet and decades' worth of cigarette smoke. I piled on lettuce, tomato, pickles, and mustard and carried my plate to the booth where Mo had put two drinks. Daryl, sitting beside Mo, was evidently joining us for lunch.

I slid in across from them, relieved that this wasn't turning out to be a date between Mo and me. The guy bothered me a little. He gave me small cymbal shivers in my stomach.

"I work here," Mo said, looking around with pride of ownership.

"Part-time," added Daryl. He gave me a slight smile before his look turned frank. "How are you doing with your grandmother's death? You okay?"

"Well, I do wonder about her drowning like that. She was such a good swimmer, and she swam there almost every night."

I took a bite. Surely these burgers would await me in heaven.

"No kidding," said Mo, smoothing out the ketchup he'd slathered onto the top half of his bun. "Why do these old ladies swim at night, anyway?" Mo frowned and chomped down on his burger.

Daryl and I both grimaced at his lack of tact.

Mo said something else I that missed because of the *thunks* and *clunks* of the bowling pins. We all continued eating without speaking, but, since I had been reminded of Gram with Mo's coarse remark, the burger had lost its flavor.

"Are the police looking into it?" asked Daryl. If I looked closely, I could see a faint sprinkling of freckles across his nose and cheeks. I couldn't tell if I was attracted to him. Neek was right. The last thing I needed was another boyfriend. The memory of Len was too fresh.

"I don't think so. As far as I know, it was an accident. It's just that... I'm going to the funeral home this afternoon. Maybe I'll learn something there."

"Sure is strange." He shook his head, then resumed his meal. No one spoke again for a couple of minutes.

"Do you live here in Alpha?" I asked Daryl, to break the uncomfortable lack of conversation.

"Darry and I are housemates," answered Mo, his mouth stuffed with fries. "We rent a house a couple of blocks from here."

"You rent a whole house? Aren't there any apartments?" I stared at the two-thirds of a burger on my plate, but watching Mo eat had completely turned my stomach and I couldn't poke another bite in.

"They're scarce here," said Daryl, taking over for Mo, whose mouth was now completely full. "But we're not exactly housemates. We each rent half of a duplex. We don't live together. And no one has called me Darry for years, except *Moey*." He directed a dark look with his light green eyes at Mo, who frowned, perplexed. "Moey" didn't have quite the same ring as "Darry."

"Moey?" asked Mo.

"Darry," snapped Daryl. Irritation shimmered between them.

When Daryl got up, I let out a puff of tension I didn't know I'd been holding in. He returned after a few minutes with a Coke and asked me if I wanted to bowl, but I declined. I needed to stay away from men.

"You sure?" asked Mo, reaching for more ketchup.

"Yes, I'm sure."

How could Mo be so cavalier about my grandmother's death?

And Mo's attitude toward Daryl? His momentary pique at being called Moey had evaporated and he was chums with Daryl again.

I supposed I should be grateful for his friendly gesture in taking me to lunch, even though it was probably just an obligation to his mother. But I mildly dreaded the ride back to the lake alone with him. What would we talk about? He wasn't holding up his end of the conversation at lunch.

To my surprise, Mo chatted all the way back over the sound of his loud car, mostly about his plans to open a jewelry store someday in Moline or Rock Island. I revised my estimate of his intelligence upward a notch. Just one notch, though.

He pulled up in front of my place and asked if I'd like to take a dip. Could I even go into that water again? It took Gram's life, but she had loved it. Loved swimming. She'd won a competition swim meet in her sixties. I could feel my tough Gram watching me, waiting to see if I could do it. I didn't want to let her down.

It was still over an hour until I was due to leave with the Harmons, who were taking me to the funeral home. The weather was sticky and my clothes were damp after the ride in Mo's unairconditioned clunker. And going swimming wasn't a date, either, any more than the lunch had been.

I nodded my consent and met him on the beach in ten minutes. After drizzling cool lake water over my shoulders I lay face down on my towel in the fine white sand and let the sun melt the tension out of my shoulders. Maybe I would just sunbathe.

Mo splashed in and out, diving down and shooting up, spouting water out of his mouth like a whale, seeing how far he could get it. I shuddered, as usual, at the thought of being underwater.

When we were kids and my West Coast cousins, Trygve and David Dahlberg, would visit us at the lake, they thought it was hilarious to hold me underwater just to watch me splutter and cough. I couldn't hold my breath and would usually panic and inhale some water. It took at least a half an hour to cough it all out of my lungs. Since then, I always swam on top of the water.

The sun lay like a soothing film of deep softness on my shoulders, my back, my—

"Whatcha doin' lazybones?"

I startled awake. I hadn't realized I'd nodded off.

"Hi, Mo. I guess, I guess I fell asleep." The trace of a tear running down my cheek surprised me. Vague memories of a dream floated, wraithlike, just out of my grasp. In it, Martha Toombs and I were on a hike together and, somehow, depended on each other, but I couldn't remember any more than that. And why the tear?

"Wanna go in, or are you just gonna lay there?"

I hesitated. I knew I didn't want to, but felt I should immerse myself in the water, the last place Gram ever was, to prove to myself I could.

Sweat dotted my face and arms, so I made up my mind, splashed into the water with him, and followed as he challenged me to race out to a large wooden diving deck about halfway across the lake. I stroked through the cool water, keeping my head well out of the water, fighting frissons of fear. I let him go on ahead.

I watched my hands disappearing, over and over, soon after they entered the murky water as I glided through the ripples. Realizing I was on the opposite shore from where Gram had died gave me some confidence; I was in the water where she'd last been, but not exactly *that* water. I realized I'd lost sight of Mo. The water was so nearly opaque, he could be anywhere if he were swimming underwater. I turned to head back the way I'd come.

Then I stopped moving. Something gripped my feet. I stroked hard. Kicked harder. It pulled me down. I struggled, grim with determination, my teeth tight, trying not to swallow the water. It was useless. Daylight dimmed above me. Down I went, toward the muddy bottom.

-8-

Eine Kleine Wassermusik: A little water music

A face loomed next to mine through the dusky water. It was Mo! His hands gripped my ankles like steel bands.

A vision of Gram flashed through my mind. Had Mo killed her? Would he kill me, too? My head was swelling, ready to burst.

I was going to die. Soon. Needed air. I gulped the dank water into my lungs, panicking under the water, as I always did. I was surprised when my life didn't flash before my eyes.

One more tremendous kick.

And I was free. Paddling with frantic strokes, I burst through to the top and slapped the surface, treading water, sputtering, choking, and gulping huge quantities of sweet, sweet air. Mo surfaced beside me.

"Sorry," he said, flashing his fabulous smile and supporting me by my arms. "Guess I shouldn't have held you under so long, huh?"

"What," I shouted, choking and gasping for breath, "were you… trying… to do?"

"Just foolin' around. I thought you'd think it was funny. I said I was sorry." He sounded like a little kid caught at the cookie jar. He dropped his hold on me and I stabilized myself, still coughing and spitting out foul-tasting water. How could this stuff support life?

"Forgive me?" he grinned. "I won't do it again. Promise."

"Damn right you won't!" I ignored his surprised expression and swam back to shore. I gathered my things, looked at my watch, and realized with a jolt that I needed to hurry to get ready for my trip into Alpha. I didn't know if Mo was just an idiot, or if he had a cruel streak like my cousins.

I gave Mo a look I hoped was fierce and hurried up the hill past the dark, empty space with the shriveled trees. The place reminded me of the sad, sweet ballad, "Scarborough Fair," set in the ancient Dorian mode, with its allusions to the medieval Black Death. I climbed past a cabin with blue shutters that had a tent camper parked in front. I moved past another smaller one until I reached my yard and heard a loud, grating voice behind me.

Toombs had just burst out of the blue-shuttered house. He turned back and shouted in his high, whiny tones, "You better remember what I said! There's such a thing as decimation of character!" He slammed the door furiously, rattled those shutters, then turned and saw me.

"Hello, there," he snapped and strode stiffly away for a couple of steps. Then he stopped abruptly, turned back, and stomped over to face me. I took a step back.

"That's what comes of higher education." He pointed at the cottage. "Higher education is overrated, let me tell ya. Me, for instance, I'm self-educated. I never got no degree, and I got a lot of responsibility here. Like I always say, it's a big job, keepin' all these folks happy."

I shifted over a few inches in an attempt to get upwind of Toombs's hair oil. And his beer breath.

"That girl has high school and a bunch of college. Her mom always told her she 'had to have an education.' Ha! What do you need an education for to lay around gettin' dirty ideas from soap operas all day long? She has the guts to accuse me of …" He sputtered to a stop.

"I love those girls," he droned on at a lower volume. "I would never really hurt 'em. Sorry to take on like this in front of you, Miss Carraway. Hayley's got me so upset, I can't spit straight."

He disproved this immediately by arcing a glob directly into the grass, then crunched angrily down the slope. I wasn't sad to see him go. *How violent could Toombs get?* I wondered.

Two small girls made their way from the back of the cottage, one stealthy step at a time, peered around and watched until Toombs disappeared, then scampered in my direction, stopping at the cabin next to mine. Were these the girls Toombs would "never really hurt"?

I walked toward them, trying to be careful and not scare them away. They looked skittish.

"Hi," I said. "My name's Cressa. What are yours?"

The smaller one looked at the ground as if something very absorbing were there. She had thin straight hair and a pinched, homely face. A half-dressed Barbie doll was clutched in one hand. The older one put her arm around the little one and answered me.

"I'm Rebecca. And this is Rachel."

Rebecca was a bit cuter, but also had the same wispy, thin blond hair.

"That's a pretty doll," I said gently to Rachel, trying to get around her shyness.

She whipped the doll around behind her.

Rebecca's thin cheek was disfigured by the purple smudge of a large bruise.

"It looks like you've hurt yourself," I said, unconsciously reaching toward her little face.

Rebecca pulled back. From what I'd just heard, it sounded like Mo's father didn't treat them well. I had to find out if these children needed help.

"How did that happen?" I persisted, gesturing toward her bruise, but being careful not to touch her.

Shy Rachel mumbled, "Uncle Mo."

I was seething inside. "Is Uncle Mo mean to you?"

Rachel remained silent while her big sister took over. "Not very much. He was more mean to the other lady."

"Who was that, honey?"

"The other one, the one that lived there." She pointed to my cabin. "The one that died." She spoke so softly, I could barely hear her.

"That was my grandmother." I questioned her with a look.

"Down there," she pointed toward the lake. "Uncle Mo was there."

The hair raised on my scalp. I needed to learn a lot more about Uncle Mo—from a distance. "At the lake?" I asked.

She nodded.

"When?"

"When she died." Rebecca looked down and kicked at the gravel. "I saw her die." Then the little girls ran to the nearest cabin and pounded on the door.

That wasn't where Toombs had come from. Maybe they weren't the girls he was whining about. The screen door opened and they disappeared inside.

-9-

Repercussion: In a fugue, the regular reentrance of a subject and answer after the episode immediately following the exposition (Eng.)

The Harmons were exactly the right people to have with me at the funeral home. They had attended the Alpha Lutheran Church with Gram and knew what hymns to pick for her service. They also suggested donations be made to a summer camp for underprivileged kids where Gram used to teach swimming. Grace and Al helped me write the obituary notice, and—the most painful for me—guided me toward a casket that looked decent, but didn't cost half the town budget of Alpha.

The funeral director told us the coroner hadn't looked at "the deceased" yet, so we set the funeral up for the next week, which would give him plenty of time to do whatever it was he needed to do. The director suggested having the service at Gram's Lutheran church instead of the funeral home. I thought she would want that.

They also accompanied me to the lawyer's office and waited outside while I conferred with him. He informed me Gram's will left almost everything to me. "Everything" consisted of the cabin and cash in a bank account back in Moline.

"That's all the money she has?" I was astounded at how little it was.

"Your grandmother was a generous woman. She had income from her late husband's retirement, and from Social Security, but she kept only what she needed."

"Where did the rest go?" It occurred to me I might sound greedy, but I was curious, more than anything else.

"She helped out whatever cause or person happened to come to her attention. Are you in a difficult financial situation?"

"Oh no, not at all."

"Good." He settled back in his leather chair. "I consider it a compliment to you that Ida didn't think you would need her money."

That gave me a warm feeling, too. It was a vote of confidence from beyond the grave. Not that Gram had a grave yet. It surprised me, given my initial reaction to Gram's purchase, that I liked the thought of owning the cabin. The lawyer concluded by saying he was obligated to contact my cousins, as they had been bequeathed a small amount of money.

On top of everything the Harmons had done for me so far, Grace asked me over for dinner while we were driving back. It was hard to hold back my tears of gratitude. "I don't want to impose any more."

Al waved his long fingers. "Don't be absurd. Our kids and grandkids left just before you came and it's suddenly too quiet over there."

"Besides," Grace gave me a wink. "Al's looking forward to telling his stories to someone who hasn't heard them yet. Just come around to the back."

I found myself looking forward to it, too. And I needed to ask someone what was going on with Rachel and Rebecca.

As soon as I was inside the cabin my cell phone rang.

"Well?" It was Neek. "What about the lunch?"

"I didn't have to dial you, did I? At least not from the lunch. The lunch was weird, but that's not all that happened."

I told her about going to the bowling alley for hamburgers and about Mo's rude ducking, trying to make light of my terror. My stupid problem of inhaling water was embarrassing and Neek hadn't known anything about it. In retrospect, I had probably overreacted to being pulled underwater. It wasn't like I hadn't been dunked before. I didn't mention Daryl being there for lunch. I don't know why.

"Cressa, you're going to have to start picking men some other way. Your track record isn't good."

"Well, it wasn't a date or anything." But I knew what she meant. My boyfriend history was bleak. After being on exactly three dates in high school, I guess I hadn't known how to handle myself in college. My first serious guy there, a fellow music student, dropped me just as I was falling for him. I thought my heart would break like a shattered violin. He was my first love and I thought it would last forever. I lost all sense of direction. After that, I dated two druggies, one philanderer, and a couple of guys who wouldn't let me go. Len, right after Gramps died, was the latest of those.

"So what are you doing tonight?" Neek asked.

"The neighbors invited me to dinner." I just realized I was starving; I'd left most of my hamburger on the plate at lunch. "They drove me to the funeral home and the lawyer's office. I'm so glad they're here. They're much better company than Mo's family."

"What's wrong with them?"

"Mo's father is an abuser if I ever saw one. I don't know about actually beating on his wife, but she *is* scared to death of him."

"Poor thing."

I related the details of the will to her and we talked about the irony of my ending up owning the cabin.

"I'm still not sure Len isn't around here somewhere." I told her about finding evidence of a Peeping Tom.

"He's not there now," she said. "He might have been a couple days ago, but I caught him trying to sneak another note under your door this morning. He gave me a dirty look and left when he saw me. How long are you going to stay there?"

That was good news about Len. Maybe he hadn't been here at all.

"At least until Gram's funeral. We've set it up for next week, five days from now. I want to give my cousins a chance to get here. That's as far ahead as I can think. Do you think you can come down?"

"I'll be there for the funeral, you bet. Glad your lunch date was okay. No danger, right? I knew you'd be fine—remember that penny?"

I had to laugh. "Yes, I suppose your prediction was good today. For a change."

"What do you mean, a change? Is that a pun?"

"No. Well, maybe." I laughed again.

"You know I'm always right. It's just that sometimes you have to reinterpret events a little."

"Or a lot. Love you, Neek. Talk to you later."

After my dud lunch with Mo, I was ready for dinner with the Harmons. I warmed toward them for offering me their easy friendship. As I walked around the corner of their cabin to the back, cheery light spilled into the night through the screen door. After knowing me only a few days, their embracing welcome was as warm as their small kitchen.

The meal was ready to dish up, so we started in as soon as I arrived. Grace served the catfish Al had caught that morning. Grace knew exactly how to bread and fry them: a little light cornmeal, a sprinkle of oregano and thyme from her herb garden, she told me, then quickly sear in the flavor. We also had delicious sunfish in an onion and garlic sauce, plus corn on the cob, dripping with butter.

"I'm grateful you were Gram's friends," I told them both as our flatware clanked merrily on pretty china plates.

"Well, gracious, she was *our* friend, too," said Grace.

"She never really wrote about anyone except you two. Do you know who lives next door to me?" I recalled the two children, one with a bruised cheek, slipping through the door. "Do two little girls live there?"

Al gave me a blank look. "Little girls? No, they don't live next door to you. They live in the next house." That was the one with the blue shutters that Mr. Toombs had come out of.

"Eve lives next door to you," said Grace. "She's at least our age, no little girls."

"And she's *not* good with children," Al broke in. His voice lowered and his face reddened. Grace turned to me and changed the subject.

"You'll have to see my herb bed another day," offered Grace. "I'd show it to you tonight, but it's too dark. You'll have to come back and see it in daylight."

Al glowered and lowered his head.

"Maybe tomorrow." The tension between them puzzled me. It was the mention of Eve that set him off. I wondered why.

Grace nodded, smiling. "I hope you'll be able to enjoy at least some of your time here. We love it. And our grandkids do, too. We have twin boys, one in Wisconsin and one in Minnesota, but they always send our grandsons to visit in August."

"I wonder," said Al, "if any of them will ever want our cabin, since they didn't grow up around here. If Grace and I should ever leave …"

"Leave? Are you moving?" He sounded sad. Was he going to get upset again?

"There's a chance. If my condition—"

"Al," interrupted Grace. "Remember?" She gave him a cautionary look over the top of her wire-rimmed glasses.

He nodded and returned to his meal. That condition was taking a beating. The storm had passed again, gone as quickly as it flared up. I didn't dare mention the little girls again.

-10-

Crescendo: Swelling, increasing in loudness (Ital.)

Fat, lazy June bugs, drawn by the yellow light washing into the yard, crashed against the screen door in their silly spring ritual. I hated to ruin the mood, but I had to ask some more questions about Gram's death, so I swallowed my last bite of catfish and dived in.

"You were my grandmother's swimming buddy, weren't you, Grace?"

"Usually. We'd been in together the night before she drowned."

"Are there any undercurrents in the water?"

"No, just underground springs. They keep the lake from freezing completely in the winter. The springs aren't very warm, not warm enough for me. I can't swim in the winter." She shivered thinking about it. "But Ida would swim sometimes when it was too cold for me. She was so stubborn about things. I used to call her pig-headed to her face. She had the idea swimming in cold water is good for you." I knew about that. "Really, she could swim in anything. She was such a strong swimmer, but, well, we all get older." Grace shook her head. "I sure wish I'd been home …"

She set her empty ear of corn on her plate and wiped the butter and salt off her hands. "I feel so guilty about her death. Not being there. Maybe if I had been …" Grace snatched her glasses off and swiped at a tear. "She must have tired out."

"I have to say, though," put in her husband, "I was shocked to hear Ida drowned. I never would have thought that she …"

I wouldn't have, either, I wanted to scream.

"What a character your grandmother was." Al sipped his iced tea, then rose and paced while he talked. "Right after she moved in, her water line started leaking and her water had to be shut off for a couple of days before someone could get out to fix it."

"Oh, yes," said Grace, watching her husband walk back and forth in the small kitchen. "I remember that. We offered our shower to her, and the sink to wash dishes. She could even have slept on the couch if she wanted." She threw a glance at Al, who still paced. "But she insisted on staying in her cabin. She hauled water in a bucket from the campground shower across the road. Bucket after bucket. She was tough."

"Yes, she was," I said, feeling anew the raw void she had left. A dark space. Would it ever fill with light? "I wonder what happened to her telephone? It doesn't seem to be working."

"That's strange. I'll look at it tomorrow," said Al. "You live in Chicago, right?" He scraped his chair back to lower his long body and resume his seat, and his sweet corn.

"Near Fullerton and Racine." I had to have one more ear and busied myself buttering and salting it.

"That's quite a ways from here," he said. "Do you think you'll keep the cabin?"

"Gram left it to me. At the moment I think I'll keep it. It's lovely here and would be a good place to do my work."

"What kind of work?" asked Grace. "I thought you were in school."

"Yes, I'm teaching piano and working on my master's degree at DePaul University. I write music, too. In fact, I'm composing a piece for my degree. This would be a good place to finish it."

"Al is a retired English professor," said Grace. "He used to teach at DePaul several years ago."

"Quite a few years ago," he added. "It was one of my first teaching jobs."

We chatted about the changes at DePaul for awhile and I learned the Harmons were both avid readers and made weekly trips to the library in Moline. He had become hooked on fishing since his retirement, and she had recently taken up studying wildflowers and herbs, and was doing experimental cooking with them.

As I ate another ear of sweet corn, the Harmons talked of local happenings for a bit. The way they picked up on each other's conversation, Grace and Al went together like a violin and bow. I caught a phrase Al used, "before the lake."

I licked some salty butter off a finger. "Hasn't it always been here?"

Grace told me it was man-made. "This lake is a strange phenomenon in this flat cornfield country, isn't it?"

"I sure remember the stories about when they made it," Al said.

"And the controversy," added Grace. She leaned forward over the table. "There was a regular feud between the factions. It lasted for years."

"Toombs's father," Al said, "was totally against it. Now Toombs makes his living off it. The idiot." Al's face mottled at the thought of Toombs. His sudden, hot anger alarmed me.

"Yes, there was bad blood between his whole family and the Greys."

"It was built," said Al, "when they made the highway that goes through the middle of Alpha. That small two-lane road doesn't look like much, with all the interstates and cloverleaves they build today, but it was a nice road when it was first made. The stream was dammed up to provide water for mixing concrete. That's what created the lake."

"Ah, so the half-moon shape is because of the shape of the valley, then?" I asked. He'd calmed down again talking about the lake. I'd keep in mind that was a safe subject.

"Yes," said Grace. "The water backed up around the bend and made a crescent. Beavers used to dam this valley up before that. I remember my grandmother telling of skating in the winter on the beaver pond when she was a girl."

I pictured a young woman who looked like Grace, gliding on the pond, then pictured two very different little girls, the ones I had met today. Rachel and Rebecca, going into Eve's place.

"Al." I didn't want to set him off again, so tried to phrase my question carefully. "I'm curious about my neighbors. What did you say about Eve, the one next door to me? About her not being too good with children?"

"Did I say that? Not too good? That's an understatement. She's disastrous with children."

"Al, you shouldn't say that," scolded Grace. "It was her husband." She turned to me. "Their children were both killed by poisoning."

"Poisoning?" I exclaimed. "How awful!" A shiver gripped me in spite of the warm room.

"It was horrible. Mr. Evans was convicted and sent to prison for murder. Some people think Eve may have done it. But her husband is serving the sentence. I'm pretty sure he did it, not her."

My heart thumped, pumping cold blood through my veins. *What a horrific thing to happen.* I closed my eyes and tried to picture losing two children... and at the hands of their father. The poor woman.

"I don't think a responsible parent would let their kids associate with her," Al said. His face was flushing again.

"Oh, she's all right, Al," his wife disagreed. "Eve is just a different sort of person. She's always nice to me."

It looked like I'd have to make my own mind up about my next-door neighbor.

-11-

Con Fiero: With fire; wild, fierce (Ital.)

I t was so homey at the Harmons' home. *Jesu, Joy of Man's Desiring* by Bach was even returning to me. The dark event of Gram's death had silenced my old favorite. When nothing else is running in my head for background music, Bach usually is, and it's almost always *Jesu.*

This time it was Al who broke the mood. "Well, dear," said Al, rising with a smile. "Isn't it about time?"

"You go get started, Al. I'll just put these dishes to soak."

Grace shooed me outside with Al, refusing to let me help with the clean-up, and soon a leaping blaze from their patio fire pit was sending sparks into the cool night sky.

Grace brought out a basket with some knitting and clicked her needles as she sat glancing from time to time at the flames. Al stood poking at the logs with a long stick for a few minutes, then brought over straightened wire hangers from a hook by the door and handed one to me.

Just then a familiar-sounding car that badly needed a muffler roared past at the bottom of the hill.

"That dolt must be visiting his idiot parents again," he muttered. "He might as well live with them. He's always out here."

His hands shook slightly as he threaded two marshmallows onto his own wire.

Grace saw his difficulty and stirred in her seat.

"Al, dear, don't get so upset about it."

I stuck two marshmallows on my wire and held it over the flames, pretty sure I knew who the dolt was.

Al's face clouded. "No one's allowed to make noise at night, we agree on that. But all you have to do is be related to Mr. God Almighty Toombs." The veins in his neck stood out as he struggled to repress his emotions. "Then you can do whatever you want …"

"Al, please," Grace pleaded. She set her needles and yarn down in her lap.

"It's true, Grace, and you know it." He whirled toward me. "He even complains about our having a camp fire every night."

His eyes blazed in the firelight. They scared me. The homey feeling had gone up with the smoke. "He says we shouldn't build one so often. Makes the air too smoky. It isn't the city, for God's sake. There's enough air here to go around."

He lowered his face and peered earnestly into mine. I cringed slightly and tried to avoid his fiery eyes by peeling my browned marshmallows off the wire and stuffing the sticky mess into my mouth. "Did you see that camper trailer in front of Hayley's?" he asked.

"The house with the pretty blue shutters?" I mumbled through my marshmallows.

"That's where the two little girls, Rachel and Rebecca, live," said Grace. She had started knitting again. It appeared to be a sleeve for a sweater. "Their mother is Hayley."

So they did live in the house I'd seen Toombs coming from. They were the girls he "would never hurt."

"Ask Toombs if you could park a camper in front of your place," snarled Al. "Go ahead. There's a 'rule' about it. No one is allowed to park trailers at cabins here. They all have to be put up on the campground. The regulations apply to everyone but his relatives."

"Al, she doesn't leave it there very long. She'll move it soon. Your ulcer." Grace reached into her basket for another skein, pushed her glasses up as she shot him a warning look, then tied the yarn on. If Grace was the bow to Al's violin, she was lifting up, lightening the pressure, trying to stop his strings from vibrating so forcefully.

"All right, all right, I'll quit talking about him. Cressa will think I have an obsession. It's just that he's such a Neanderthal. I surely feel sorry for Martha. She's a better person than he is."

I'd ask them another time about Toombs and the girls. Right now he needed to cool down. Would talking about Mo set him off?

"What's his son like?" I ventured, wanting their opinion of the "dolt."

Al sighed and they exchanged a glance.

"Tell her about your earrings, Grace."

She looked up, then gave me an abashed smile. "I'm not really sure I didn't lose them myself, that's the trouble. Just like Ida and her rings."

"Rings?" My voice came out gravelly. The smoke was starting to burn my throat a bit.

"Ida lost her wedding rings and we always thought Mo took them. Then, a few weeks ago, my good diamond earrings, Al's gift to me on our twenty-fifth anniversary, went missing. Mo has a bad reputation for stealing jewelry. But enough about problems. Would you like another marshmallow, Cressa?"

"No thanks, two is plenty after that fabulous dinner. It's fun, though. I haven't roasted marshmallows for years."

Mo said he wanted to open a jewelry store. With stolen goods? The subject of God Almighty Toombs seemed to be, thankfully, dropped. But Mo—did he steal Gram's rings *and* kill her?

"I'd better get going," I said. "I'm about to be yawning in your faces."

"Let me show you my garden on your way out." Grace got up and stuffed her work into the basket. "What you can see of it in the dark. I'm experimenting with edible plants. Herbs and such. I've learned so much about what to eat. And what not to."

"What do you mean?" We strolled away from the patio.

"There are so many things in a regular garden that are poison. You'd be amazed. A daffodil bulb will kill you if you eat it. Of course, who'd eat a daffodil bulb?" Grace laughed, her bright gray curls bobbing in the moonlight.

She squatted down and pointed to the edge of the bed.

"See these cute little things?" she continued, pointing to a clump of small tan mushrooms with white spots on the tops, just visible with the light of the fire behind us. "They're called Death Angel. Never pick a mushroom with white gills."

"I would never pick any mushrooms. I don't know anything about them at all."

"Well, some are tasty, but these can make a person very sick, even kill you. And you don't start to get sick until hours after you've eaten them. Sometimes the next day. They pop up all around here, too. I have to dig them out almost every week."

Grace offered to walk me part of the way back.

"You don't really need to," I told her.

"That's all right. I was getting stiff sitting. I need a short walk. And I think I'll take my evening dip shortly."

"You're going swimming this late?"

"Oh yes. This is about the time Ida and I have always loved to swim."

"But you're going alone?"

"Don't worry, I'm very careful and I don't swim when it starts getting chilly out. It's cool tonight, but not too bad. Would you like to join me?"

I shuddered. Could I go into that water again? Do the get-back-on-the-horse thing? "Maybe not tonight."

"I understand."

When we were out of earshot of her yard, she started apologizing for her husband's earlier tirade.

"It was Mo roaring around here tonight in his car that got him started."

I ducked my head, glad I hadn't mentioned I'd gone to lunch with him. That might have set off another rant.

"It's mostly," Grace continued, "that Al hates the way Toombs sets himself up as such an important personage and lords it over everybody. I think he resents having such an illiterate person in a position of authority over him. Al is used to being the professor, you know. In charge of things and looked up to. Toombs is really ignorant. You should see some of the notes he writes."

"Well, I've heard him talk. He has strange ideas about the meanings of some words."

"He has *no* ideas about the meanings of some words." She tossed her curls. Even in the darkness, anger distorted her round face. She was free to express it away from her husband, whose rage she had to keep in check. "He'll be the death of us. He would rub Al the wrong way even if we only saw him once a month. I think Toombs knows that, and I think he takes pleasure in objecting to almost everything we try to do." She pounded one fist into her other hand. "I'm convinced the reason they stopped keeping up the footpath around the lake is because Al and I used it so much. It was weedy and buggy the last time we attempted it."

Grace sighed as we crossed the gravel road in the pale moonlight, sadness on her usually placid face, worry on her brow. The crunch of our shoes was becoming a familiar sound. "I can't really blame Al for disliking Toombs so," she said, "but I wish he wouldn't let it get to him. It's bad for his health."

"I'm getting the idea Toombs isn't very popular. Couldn't the members get someone else?"

The dewy grass in my front yard was so tall we were almost wading through it. I would have to get it mowed before Toombs complained about me.

"It wouldn't be that easy to get a new manager. They have to live here, to be on hand all the time. We complain a lot about the Toombses, but I don't think anyone else around here would want the job. By the way, we'd love to have you join us for lunch or dinner any time. Al's been catching so many catfish we can't eat them all."

"Your catfish is wonderful. I'll probably take you up on that."

We had reached my front door and I thanked her again for dinner and for walking me to my place.

"See you tomorrow," she said as she turned back.

-12-

Lagrimoso: "Tearful," polic plaintive, like a lament (Ital.)

For the second time, I pounded on Al Harmon's door in panic. "I found her in the same place I found Gram." My voice was screechy. He looked past me, not comprehending. His body stilled and I had to shy away from his hollow eyes.

When I had looked out my front window at Grace's dark form heading for the swimming area, a large towel draped over her arm, I realized I couldn't let her go alone. I could hear her flip-flops' *twup, twup* as she went. Her step was springy for someone her age. A beam of moonlight glinted off her bifocals. I knew I really should join her; she was as vulnerable as Gram. So I stuck my cell phone in the charger and started to gather my things. My bathing suit from last night was still wet, but I dug my spare out of my suitcase, grabbed a beach towel from the armoire, ignored the envelope with my name on it again, and put on my beach shoes. I lifted my locket over my head and threw it onto the couch next to the door.

When I had reached the beach, Grace was nowhere in sight, so I'd headed across the lake to find her. Looking back, I suppose, somewhere in the dark part of my mind, I expected to find her body there, on the west side, but it was a shock nonetheless.

Now I led Al to the couch and gently sat him down, much as he'd done for me after I'd found Gram's body. But I wasn't sure I should wrap the afghan around his shoulders, as Grace had done. Thinking it might remind him too sharply of that night, I sat and rubbed his thin hands instead.

"I called nine-one-one already," I told him.

I'd run to the nearest phone when I'd found her, immediately after throwing up that wonderful meal Grace had cooked, complete with marshmallows. The mess had floated on the water, then dissipated as I retrieved her lifeless form and dragged it onto the far shore, as I had with Gram. The nearest phone, since mine was on the charger back at my cabin, was at the Toombses' house.

Martha had opened the door wide at my frantic pounding. I noticed Mo's car was there. If he left while we were eating, he must have come back.

"Oh, it's you, Cressa," she had breathed, and let me into the living room.

"The mister is out," Martha confided, confirming my thought at seeing the one big comfortable chair empty. Her perpetual worried expression made her look distraught over the fact that he was gone. I would have been relieved, myself, if I were her.

There was no sign of Mo in the house, either, thank God.

As she did at my last visit, she stood in the middle of the room, looking like she couldn't decide what to do next. I decided for her this time.

"I need to use the phone. It's an emergency."

"Oh dear." Her eyebrows tented higher and she clutched her worn hands together. Her pink rollers shook with her head. She took in my bathing suit and beach coat. "What seems to be…?"

"I'll tell you in a minute." I used the phone on the corner desk to call it in. The operator made it easy, asking what my emergency was (a dead body), what my location was (Crescent Lake), and telling me to stay put until an official arrived. I said I'd be at the Harmons' place, then left Martha standing agape at what she'd heard me say, and made my way up the hill to be with Al.

Now Al stared around the room. The cottage bore Grace's touch on almost every inch. Her framed needlework adorned the walls, her unfinished knitting sat on an end table, and books on herb gardening and cooking stood in piles on the kitchen counter. Her gardening gloves were flung onto a shelf by the door.

"What am I going to do?" he asked me. All I could do was grab his hand again. There was no answer I could give. I brought him a glass of water, but he set it down in front of him, shaking his head back and forth in his own private rhythm of grief.

"Is there anyone I should call? Your sons?"

"Yes. Their numbers are over there." He motioned to the spindle-legged desk under a side window. I rifled through the top drawer and managed to find a cloth-bound address book with the sons' names listed under H.

I patted his long gnarled hand and went into his kitchen to make the call.

Not ten minutes later, an extremely tall dark-haired man in uniform knocked on the door. His name tag read Kyle Bailey, and I led the Alpha police chief down to the beach area and pointed toward the far shore where I had found Grace's body. Al didn't want to come with us. I had to scurry to keep up with the chief's long strides. The man must have been six and a half feet tall.

The ambulance had arrived and the EMTs were already setting off in Al's boat.

Chief Bailey stared across the lake for a minute. The water lay peaceful, the boat's wake barely rippling in the moonlight.

"It's the same place I found my grandmother." My voice came out as a whisper.

"Your grandmother was Ida Miller?" He peered down and gave me a quick look, his face shadowed in the darkness.

"Yes. I'm staying here in her cabin until the funeral." I screwed up my courage to give him my opinion. "And I don't see how they could both have drowned. Do you think that's likely?"

"You'd better go back to that cabin. I'll need to get a statement from you, in light of the two deaths being so similar, but I can do it tomorrow. We'll work on getting the body recovered tonight. See what it looks like."

He said he would be around the next morning, then turned and strode toward his car. I was officially dismissed. So I did as he asked and started my trudge up the hill to sit with Al, but he hadn't answered my question. I wasn't at all sure my Gram, or Grace, had died accidentally. And Bach had again deserted me.

I looked toward the heavens for some answers. A shooting star arced in cold brilliance across the sky. Its trail split the blackness surrounding it. Was that an answer?

-13-

Berceuse: A cradle song, lullaby (Fr.)

I sat with Al for awhile, but, after a long hug and thirty minutes of both of us mostly staring straight ahead, swiping at our tears, Al told me he'd rather be alone. When I left, he was stroking the unfinished knitting Grace had left on the end table.

I opened the door of my place and stepped in, realizing I hadn't locked it when I went down to swim with Grace. After I locked up, I moved through the cabin with caution, turning on all the lights as I went. Nothing looked disturbed. My purse was right where I had left it. Still, the cabin was different. No longer safe. Somehow... out of harmony.

The air was stuffy and stale in spite of the one tiny side window I had left open. I picked up one of Grace's brownies from the counter and wandered out to the porch and cranked open the louvers. Grace's and Gram's deaths were weighing me down, pulling at my every movement, my every thought.

I finished the brownie, then went back into the cabin and pulled my cell phone from the charger. Nothing happened when I entered Neek's number. I checked the battery icon. It was charged. I shook it and dialed again. Still dead. I didn't see any connection bars on the phone's screen. Stupid Peter the Mediocre. Maybe I'd rename him Ivan the Terrible. A new cell phone was at the top of my wish list. I'd try Neek later.

That made me think about what day of the month it was; my phone payment would soon be due, and I still didn't have a forwarding address so Neek could send me my bills. I could call her from the Toombses' or Al's tomorrow, if I still couldn't connect, and have her cover the phone bill for me. Since I did have my checkbook with me, I could mail her a check later. On second thought, I decided I'd use the phone at the yellow house tomorrow, but only if Martha was the only one there.

I spread the beach towel, dry by now, on one of the daybed couches, showered, and changed into my nightgown, then sat on the brightly lit porch, pondering my future.

Did I want to stay here longer? I was torn in two directions. Go or stay? Go back to Len's stalking or stay with Gram's ghost?

Maybe I would leave straight after Gram's funeral. No, I should stay for Grace's, too. Was there really any way those two women could have both accidentally drowned in the same spot, at the same time of night?

Then a horrible thought hit me. I gasped. Would Grace be alive if I had gone with her? Or would I be dead, too? I desperately wanted to talk to Neek. The dark windows reflected my unhappy face back at me. I couldn't see anything outside with the inside lights on.

But someone else could see in. Remembering the evidence of a peeper, I knew I was too exposed on the porch. I turned off the lamps, went inside the cabin, and closed the door to the porch. There sat my composition, on the breakfast bar.

An idea hit me like a flash, *sforzando*. I would dedicate this piece to Gram. I would fill it with life, with her passion, her fascination with just about everything. Above all, I would fill it with the sounds of this place she loved. I had a vague sense of making something up to her, of atoning for her death.

A sweet melody came into my head and I jotted it down. I tried to imagine if Gram would like it or not. From an early age, probably as a result of having had musicians for parents, I started making up ditties on Gram's piano whenever we weren't on the road. Sometimes she recorded them and played them for other people. She thought I was a genius and I never tried to talk her out of that idea. Really, all I was doing was composing melodies, but she loved them. I eventually learned there's a lot more to composing than that. She grew more proud as my music matured.

I decided she'd like this one. Then I found myself wondering if my mother would have liked it. Or my father. Putting away such unproductive thoughts, and satisfied I had the bare bones of something I could work with tomorrow, I made up one of the daybeds and climbed in.

I could hear the night sounds through the small open window above the bed. The sounds were of last year's dead leaves being disturbed, of live leaves riffling with the passage of animals, and of the peculiar woody scratching sound I'd heard my first night.

I raised both ears off the pillow to hear that last one better. That last noise was definitely not coming from outside. It came from inside the cabin. And more clearly than ever. Right across the room. It must be in the kitchen area. It had to be a mouse. The droppings atop the armoire had told me mice had been here. The scratchings told me they were still here. Shoot! The cabin was far from airtight. I'd seen places on the porch where daylight peeked through the chinks.

For a moment I thought I smelled cigarette smoke coming through my window. I fought my panic and tried to convince myself Len wasn't here. Neek had seen him in Chicago. But Mo was a smoker, too. Should I look out the window? While I was still paralyzed by indecision and fear, the pure, clean country air replaced the odor.

Now I had a new worry. Was Mo lurking outside my cabin at night?

-14-

Agitato: Agitated (Ital.)

My eyes flew open to blankness and dark. My heart rattled like a set of castanets. I was sure I'd heard a gunshot. Was Len shooting at me? No. The trees were singing? The leaves were speaking? Ah no, listening more closely, I could tell it was rain swishing through them. I turned over to resume my sleep but was interrupted again by a terrific flash and a thunderclap that sounded like it struck two feet from the front door. My heart hammered like a snare drum for several minutes.

How does anyone ever get any sleep around here?

The storm continued. I jumped every time the lightning struck and the thunder boomed—until the storm moved off into the distance and was only a faint rumble. Then silent lightning flickered on the walls. Eventually the rain settled down to a soothing sigh coming steadily through the arbor and lulled me into a deep, deep sleep.

The rain had stopped by morning, but the day dawned sunless. I put on blue jeans and a T-shirt and went across the road to check on Al. He had dressed and fixed himself breakfast, but didn't want company this morning. His sons weren't able to come for a couple more days, but he said he was fine with that. Would everyone be so casual if the authorities weren't calling the deaths accidental? I offered to go with him to pick out Grace's casket. He said he wanted to get it done before his children arrived.

I was worried about Al, but knew there was nothing more I could do for him. I walked back to Gram's cabin, *my* cabin. It squatted on the hill like a toad. For some reason, the anxiety I felt last night returned and I wasn't able to go in, even though my symphony beckoned.

I peeked inside the red shed in Gram's yard, next to the road. So far I hadn't paid much attention to it. I guess I expected it to hold storage items. And it did, but Gram's car was also there. A blackness composed of more guilt enveloped me. When I first arrived and didn't find her, it hadn't occurred to me to check if her car was there. Would it have made any difference? Could I have found her sooner and saved her? My conscience ignored the fact that she'd been dead long before I arrived. The blackness was deep and silent.

A scent of lilacs wafted by that brought Gram's smile before my eyes. It went with a mental picture of her sitting at her vanity with the round mirror, brushing her hair out… then the scent was gone, but the blackness lifted an inch or so.

A movement beside the house caught my eye. The phone line dangled beside the pole. No wonder Gram's phone didn't work. I wondered if the chattering squirrel halfway up the pole was responsible. There was something to add to my task list; I certainly couldn't bother Al with this now.

Before I went inside, I searched for the footprints of a possible nighttime lurker in the mud under the window. The ones outside the porch from the day before were gone. If any had been made last night before the rain, they were already washed away.

I walked around the cabin, at loose ends, and came to a stairway that led down to Gram's dock. The steps leading to the landing were probably muddy, and I figured the thick grass down there would be sopping wet from the rain. With that and this pea-soup weather, there wasn't any point in going to examine Gram's boat. Her overturned rowboat near the dock displayed its gaudy bright red bottom. It looked inviting. Some other time.

The sound of tuneless humming caught my attention as I turned back. It was coming from the cabin next to mine. A woman's face appeared in the window and she called out.

"Hi there! Come on in for a minute."

Well, I sure don't want to go back to Gram's cabin right now. This is the woman Al and Grace talked about, the one whose husband murdered their children. I wonder what she has to say about what's going on?

She was taking a batch of cookies out of the oven and talking a mile a minute when I walked in through the screen door. The cookies smelled like chocolate chip. I was a sucker for those.

"Just sit down while I get another batch in." She waved toward a wooden chair and drapes of tan, wrinkled skin swung from her thin upper arm. She moved with quick, sure movements, working just as rapidly as she spoke.

"I'm Eve. It's really Evangeline, but that's too long." Her ancient, beaming face was creased and furrowed, her skin seemed too big for her and hung from her prominent bones. "Nobody has time to say that. Just call me Eve. I've had this cabin for years and years. Ever since my husband's been gone. You must be Ida's granddaughter. I miss having her there next door to me. Who have you met so far? When did you get here?"

She scraped the cookies from the cookie sheet onto the counter top. There were two pies cooling on racks next to them. What an odd woman. I wondered if she supplied a local bakery.

Her cabin was a lot like mine, consisting of one large room with a corner walled off for a bathroom. But it looked a whole lot smaller because it was crammed full of furniture. Instead of a countertop breakfast bar, Eve had a wooden kitchen table and chairs next to the small kitchenette. In the front half of the cabin were an L-shaped sofa set, two recliners, and several stuffed chairs, along with a hutch, a coffee table, and other small tables and chests. A large round-backed trunk looked like the only real storage space, since she had no wardrobe, and neither of us had any closets.

"I got here a few days ago," I said, breathing in the aroma of the pies. She didn't act like she knew about Gram's death. Or Grace's. "I've met the Toombses, and their son, Mo."

Eve plopped cookie dough onto the sheet with small rapid motions and sniffed in disdain.

"None of them are worth much. And what's your name, dear?"

I told her as she stuck the cookies into the oven and wiped her hands on her apron.

"Interesting name, Cressa. Is that short for something?"

"No, it's just my first name."

She picked up a huge knife and started hacking away at leaves that were lying on a cutting board. I could hear the frantic rhythm of Leroy Anderson's *Plink, Plank, Plunk* as the knife hit the wood. That's a *pizzicato* piece, where the string players pluck their strings instead of bowing them.

"You'll meet Sheila, I'm sure. She and her husband take care of the grounds. At least that's what they get paid for. Don't ask me what they do. They live in one of those campers over there. Kind of trashy people." The leaves were in tiny bits, but she kept cutting, the large knife beating a rapid staccato on the cutting board.

"Do you know my grandmother drowned the night I arrived?"

"Oh land sakes, yes. Tragedy. You poor dear. And then that nice Grace, too." She stood still for a moment, but her body hummed with suppressed energy.

"Did you know my grandmother well?"

"Oh, I don't know about 'well.' I knew her."

"Do you think it was peculiar she drowned where she swam every single night?"

She gave me a hard look. "Odd things happen, you know."

"It looks like you've been baking for days. There must be a bake sale somewhere soon," I said.

"Oh, no! I just like to bake." She dashed to the oven and peeked at the cookies. "The kids sometimes stop in for cookies. And these are rhubarb pies for whoever pops by. Mostly the children. Their parents stay away."

I recognized the leaves then. Gram used to bake rhubarb pies back in Moline. They were rhubarb leaves.

"I didn't know you could use the tops of rhubarb for anything."

"Oh, you can't. Not that I know of. I'm chopping them up to throw away. They fit in the trash easier that way. Would you like a piece of pie?"

How strange, chopping them up to throw them away. What an odd person.

"Thank you, but I have work to do." Watching her made me tired. "I saw two little girls come in here yesterday. Rachel and Rebecca, I think?"

"Those are the Blake girls. Poor things. Their mother is Martha Toombs's daughter, Hayley. Hayley's divorced and lives in the cottage down there." She brandished the knife with her long thin hand toward the next-door cabin as she chattered.

"Only Martha's daughter?" I asked. "Not her husband's, too?"

"No, Hayley is from Martha's first marriage. Hayley would never claim Toombs for her father. They don't get along. He's not too good to the girls, either."

A fleeting spark of light, reflecting off the knife blade from the overhead fixture, dashed hotly across her face.

"They like to come over to my place. Poor tykes. That's their house there, right next to mine. With the light blue shutters."

We said our good-byes, with me promising to return soon. For pie.

She put the knife down and followed me to her door. Eve pressed a small packet into my hand, fluttered a wave as she shooed me out the door, then darted inside to tend to her baking.

She had given me a sandwich bag with three of her homemade cookies in it, still warm. They might come in handy later, I thought. A person never knows when she'll need a chocolate chip cookie.

I went back to the cabin, not so loath to enter it this time. Since Gram's funeral was scheduled for tomorrow, and I had finished making all the arrangements, there was nothing more I needed to get done today. I could have sat down to work, but it was a confining feeling rather than a freeing one, since there was also nothing I really *could* do. I paced the cabin, restless.

Was I the only person in the whole world with an inkling those two women didn't just happen to drown? I wanted to shake Chief Bailey until he saw the urgency. If only we were in England, I could call Scotland Yard, or MI-something. I'd have to keep my eyes and ears open. I knew from reading mysteries and newspapers that criminals eventually slip up. Usually.

If I didn't know how to investigate Gram's death, there was at least one thing I knew how to do for her: devote my composition to her.

I fixed tea and toast, then spread my papers out on the glass-topped table on the porch. It didn't feel so exposed during the day. The notes I had set down yesterday weren't right today. A couple of the ideas were good, and some of the melodic passages had promise, but everything was bland. The piece should be full of life. Of passion. It should express the abundance of life and epitomize its goodness. If I wanted this to be a tribute to my Gram, it had to be exuberance itself. To capture the excitement of living, the thrilling sound of the endless choir of birds that awakened every morning, the almost sinister murmuring of the frogs at night, the mystery of the morning fog.

I got up and put one of Eve's cookies onto a paper plate beside my manuscript paper.

Maybe, if I captured Gram in song, I wouldn't have really lost her.

I sat. Nothing came. It was hopeless.

After I had munched half the cookie, I began to notice an odd tang to its taste. Maybe I shouldn't eat Eve's things.

I noticed all the crumbs I'd dropped onto my music and knocked them off, then thought maybe I should have just left them there and put notes where they had randomly fallen. That couldn't be any worse than what I already had.

I stared at the paper and my mood continued to darken. Misgivings trampled on my confidence. My struggle went on. Time passed. I wrote nothing.

I have no talent. Why the hell did I ever think I could be a composer? Or a conductor? I should forget about it.

Who cared if I got a master's degree anyway? Gram, my biggest fan, wasn't even here anymore. The thought that came to me in my darkest moments came to the surface: I had been the cause of my grandfather's death. There wasn't a soul who would be disappointed if I became a drunken bum. A complete fuck-up. Except maybe Neek.

Struck by this hard fact, I swept the papers onto the floor and stood up, immediately beset by dizziness and a pounding headache. A large rock had landed in my stomach. I need to clear my head, I thought. I reached my hand up to finger my locket in my distress, but I hadn't put it on.

I tore through the cabin, throwing the cushions off the daybeds and kicking up the throw rugs, but couldn't find my necklace. The day was still dark and cloudy and the cabin held shadows in all its corners.

Damn! If I've lost Gram's locket, I don't know what I'll do.

Okay. Draw a deep breath. Ugh. That makes my stomach hurt worse.

My heart hammered and the pain in my head was like a living being. Swallowing hard, refusing to vomit, I tore the place apart.

Hadn't I set it down somewhere last night, on my way to go swimming with Grace? On the daybed right inside the door? Yes. The cushions were already on the floor. I stripped the bed, then got onto my hands and knees and peered underneath. My panting breath disturbed nothing but dust. That necklace wasn't in this cabin.

I sat on the floor and sobbed. I'd lost my Gram and I'd lost the locket she gave me. I didn't need to worry about becoming a complete fuck-up—I already was one.

My precious locket. I had broken the chain soon after I started seeing Len. He had searched high and low to find the braided antique chain that matched so perfectly. He had given it to me the Christmas we were together. I wore the locket every day, since Gram had given it to me, but I'd replaced Len's chain the day after he put me into the hospital.

Added to the blow of losing the locket, was losing the pictures inside: tiny images of my mother and father. I climbed onto the rumpled daybed and wailed for a good ten minutes.

Had Mo, the alleged jewel thief, taken it while I was out? I remembered him fingering the chain. And the footprints, and the whiff of cigarette smoke late at night.

My stomach heaved. Had I been poisoned?

-15-

Tumultuoso: Vehement, impetuous; agitated (Ital.)

L paced the cabin until it could no longer contain me. I put on my tennis shoes, threw the rechristened Ivan the Terrible into my purse, and went outside. Wanting to go someplace new, I fled down the crude steps toward Gram's dock. The peaceful lake began to soothe me as I stood near the overturned boat and loosened up inside.

The silence was broken by the roar of a powerful motor from within the thick woods. When I looked back toward the steps, a tractor was making its way down the hill, using tire ruts I hadn't noticed before, a steep road that wound down the hill through the trees beyond the steps I had come down.

The tractor reached the bottom of the hill, a jiggling mower attachment raised up in the back. On the driver's seat bounced one of the most enormous women I had ever seen. Not the tallest, just the widest. Wreaths of chins surrounded her face, and a slim brown cigar dangled from her thick, loose lips. Her soft-looking body sagged around the tractor seat and wobbled with the vibrations of the motor and the bobbing of the vehicle as it made its way across the grass toward me. Her pink muumuu billowed out behind her like a parachute. I hoped I wasn't staring.

She saw me, waved, braked to a stop beside me, and struggled off the seat, dislodging a bright yellow cushion onto the grass.

"Hi. I'm Sheila Weldon." She extended her pudgy hand and I took it and introduced myself.

"Glad to meet you, Cressa." She shifted the thin cigar with her meaty lips as she talked. "Your grandmother was an old friend of mine."

"I do miss her. She died so suddenly."

"Yeah, that was strange."

"Were you there?" If an adult, as well as the two children, had seen Mo there, I might place more credence in what they'd told me.

"When she died? No. No one was, so far as I know. Especially not us. My husband and I do the work here. I do most of the mowing." She stooped with a loud grunt to pick up her yellow cushion.

"It's a beautiful place. You do a nice job."

"Well, we don't do everything we should. Toombs," she spit his name out the side of her mouth opposite the cigar, "should hire more help, but he don't do it."

Her ample bosom lifted and fell in a gloomy sigh. The thin smoke of her cigar hung in the air, giving the meadow a faint barroom smell.

"You know, this club ain't what it was back in the day," she continued shifting the cigar to the other side of her mouth. "It was pretty nice here then, but it don't get managed like it should with that snake doing it. Six people used to do what me and Wayne try to do." She climbed back onto the tractor with a great deal of grunting, arranged her muumuu, and clashed the gears with a swipe of her hammy hand.

Toombs had failed the course in "Winning Friends and Influencing People" when he self-educated himself. Didn't anyone here like him? She steered the mower across the small patch of grass. Then she muttered, "Guess I'll hang up the mowing for now. Grass is too wet, clumping up on my blades." She lifted the attachment and drove back up the hill.

I turned back to inspect Gram's rowboat. The red-bottomed vessel had been hauled onto the grass beside the dock and its oars were lying beside it. I tugged, but it didn't budge.

A soft footfall made me look around. Rebecca and Rachel were standing beside me.

"Hi, girls," I said tentatively, not wanting to scare them off. They gave me doubtful looks. Could they know I wanted to ask them questions?

Rebecca answered "Hi" and her little sister looked down, as usual.

"It's a nice day out," I prodded. "Did you see that tractor that was just here? I guess you know Mrs. Weldon, huh?"

Rachel kept her face averted, making me wonder if she had a bruise, too. They both nodded in response to my question. Progress, I thought. I decided to plunge right in.

"Do you remember the night when Ida Miller was swimming and your Uncle Mo was there?"

Two more nods. Rachel glanced up at me, then looked out at the water, her delicate eyebrows raised. Was her expression wistful or fearful?

"Do you remember where they were?"

"Down by the lake," answered Rebecca.

"On the beach," ventured little Rachel.

The beach was on this side of the lake, the shorter east side as the water curved around in its confining valley. Her body was found on the far side.

"Both of them? Together?"

"No. Mrs. Ida went in the water," said Rebecca. "Uncle Mo was watching her. Mrs. Ida didn't see him."

"Was it dark out?"

"Uh-huh," said Rebecca.

Rachel nodded.

"Did you see Ida come out of the water?"

"No, just Uncle Mo."

"But we ran away, Becca. Don't you 'member?"

Rachel sprinted away toward the steps. Rebecca turned to watch her little sister, then followed her.

I stared after them. It wasn't exactly an indictment of Mo. More like circumstantial evidence. Not chorus and verse, but at least a stanza. I wanted to ask them if they'd been around when Grace died, too, but maybe I shouldn't traumatize their little minds any further.

The girls disappeared up the hill into the foliage. Soon their light treads stopped and an angry voice accosted them.

"What in the hell were you doing?" It was Mo, yelling at the little girls. I couldn't hear an answer, but he continued at a slightly lower decibel level. I strained to hear.

"Were you talkin' about Ida Miller? I told you, don't talk about her. Stop spreading lies or you'll wish you hadn't."

The hair on the back of my neck tingled in anticipation of Mo's appearance. Maybe they had all continued up the hill. Now was the time to get this boat turned over and into the water, in case Mo showed up.

I managed to slide it down the hill and wrestle it right side up at the same time.

I clambered down into it from the dock, threw my bag onto a seat, and poled against the muddy bottom to get out of the shallows. Then I rowed north out of the cove. Still no sign of Mo. Good. A breath of relief escaped.

Being in a rowboat in the middle of a lake seemed like a good idea. I would be unreachable, for one thing, in case a killer lurked at the lake. A shiver rose up my spine at the thought that Mo might be the killer.

Maybe, if I could calm my mind, my stomach would stop aching so and my head would clear on my way across the lake.

Okay, clear your mind, Cressa. Concentrate on… On what? On rowing the boat, on the moment, on where you are. Use the yoga breathing you've been practicing with Neek.

The water trailed smooth ripples behind me as I sat backwards and aimed for the middle of the lake. I grew hypnotized by the slowly widening ridges of my wake, dissolving into the calm surface of the water. After I pulled completely out of the cove, I could see Al Harmon's tall form fishing in his boat, almost around the bend to the west, too far away to hail. I assumed he was taking his solace there and wouldn't want company. He fished like I wrote music: as an antidote. I would go to his place later and see if there was anything I could do.

I thumped the oars into the boat to rest a moment, the oarlocks jangling, as I reached the point halfway to the other side. My arms ached from the unaccustomed strain of rowing.

The fog had mostly dissipated and was lifting into the clouds where it belonged. The lakeshore looked even more beautiful from out on the water. The trees bent down and brushed the water where the woods were thick, and here and there, the wooden boat docks poked out into the lake with an air of solidity. The earthen dam, a solid grass-covered strip dotted with bushes and a few small trees, stretched from shore to shore at the eastern end of the lake, daring the captive water to go anywhere. Clumps of white and yellow flowers bloomed in the open spaces on the dam, spots of brightness among the green.

My mind decided to start working overtime, dreaming up more and more improbable scenarios. I went on to consider it possible Mrs. Toombs's daughter was abusing her own girls and Toombs merely trying to protect them. Yeah, right. Or maybe she had a boyfriend who mistreated them? Or maybe the younger one was just shy and the older one had fallen and hit her cheek.

There must be some way to get to the bottom of what Rebecca and Rachel are telling me. Their story of Mo being in the vicinity is the only indication, besides coincidence, that those two ladies didn't drown naturally. And I'm the only person who thinks so.

Would it do any good to ask Eve more about the two little girls, and maybe about Mo, too? As soon as I got out of the boat I'd call Neek to get her thoughts, if Ivan would cooperate. On the boat, our conversation would bounce off the water, like vibrations from a piano soundboard, ringing out to the whole place.

To think that the water I'm staring into is what took your life, Gram. What really happened that night?

A glance at my phone showed the connection bars full and a message waiting. I didn't recognize the number on the caller ID, but it was a local one. I listened, and the message was from Gram's lawyer, and unwelcome.

"Ms. Carraway, I've spoken with your cousins and they're not happy about the terms of Ida Miller's will. They say they're planning on contesting it. I wouldn't worry about this—there's no chance they'll win—but it will hold things up a bit. I suggest you occupy your grandmother's cabin, if you can, until probate is finished, in order to retain possession. As I said, they don't have any grounds, but it puts you in a better position if you stay there as much as possible. I'll talk to you later, Ms. Carraway. Call me if you have any questions."

The mention of a court battle brought my nausea back full force. I longed for Gram's homemade chicken soup, and her gentle touch to accompany it. Foul tasting bile rose in my throat. Those rotten boys! Would they ever be done tormenting me? One thing I knew, they would *not* get the cabin. It was mine.

Al Harmon's boat had gone around the bend ahead of me, out of sight.

I considered, again, who could have killed the women. Mo was my prime suspect. But what did I know about the rest of the Toombses, really? Only what the Harmons, Eve, and Sheila had related. Gram had said little about the Toombses. Al Harmon was harassed by him and Sheila Weldon also felt he didn't treat her right.

I jumped and my hand knocked an oar into the water when, just as I was thinking about him, Toombs's nasal tones came ringing across the water in a loud, clear whine. How creepy.

"And who do you think is in charge around here? This place is run on a schedule, damn it! And *I* make the schedule."

His voice sounded like an oboe played by a drunken beginner. Also a little like Mo, when he had yelled at Rachel and Rebecca. At a higher pitch, but with the same anger.

I recovered the oar, still in its oarlock, and peered at the shore, looking for Toombs. My gaze traveled to the top of the rise.

Toombs and Sheila Weldon stood in the road by the Weldons' trailer. It was quite a distance, but from their elevation, and with no growth of trees in the way, the sound carried across the water. They were two tiny silhouetted figures from where I sat, but I easily identified them both. The voice of the one was unmistakably Toombs's, and the rotund shape of the other was just as decidedly Sheila's. I probably imagined I could smell her little brown cigar.

Poor woman. Was everyone here a victim of this imbecile? I clenched my eyes to shut out an unbidden vision of Len's fist just before it smashed into my face.

"You women are all, are all ruled by hormones, or, or the phrases of the moon, or something. You can't unnerstan a simple sss, schedule." He was still shouting, and slurring his words. Phrases of the moon? More self-education. I wanted to belt him one, like I hadn't been able to hit back at Len.

Sheila spoke in lower tones and I couldn't make out her words. I saw him stagger and heard his answer, though.

"I don't care how wet it is! That hill gets mowed today! You're not gonna get your feet wet sittin' on the tractor. Just... Just mow the, the damn grass!"

He wheeled, lurched, then stalked away. Sheila's stout figure slumped a bit, then she slowly lumbered over the crest of the hill, out of sight.

❦

-16-

Subito: Suddenly, without pause (Ital.)

I t was time to resume rowing, to get as far away from these people as I could. I pulled and clanked until the boat bumped the other shore. In spite of my haste to cross the lake I had drifted toward the dam, almost right onto it, so I turned my craft and headed away, hugging the northern shore. Turning awakened more queasiness, but I wanted to make sure Al Harmon wouldn't see me from his boat. There was no sense in digging at his wound unless it became necessary.

When I rounded the bend, he was no longer on the lake. His boat was moored across the water, beyond the beach. I nosed into the shore on my side of the lake, grabbed a protruding tree root, and pulled myself onto the mud bank in the shade of a tremendous old oak. An exposed series of rough tree roots made a crude but useable stairway. I looped the boat's rope around one of the roots and straightened up. A cold tremolo ran up my spine. This was, as near as I could tell, the spot where I had found the two bodies. I didn't want to be here, but I had to see if there were any signs left by a killer.

It was too cool a morning for swimming. Not surprisingly, no one was on the beach across the lake, giving me total privacy. *It wouldn't be too cold for Gram. She'd be out there—if she were still alive.*

Okay. So, if she had been killed, it would have happened right around this place.

My cell phone trilled. It was Neek. The connection here was good and her familiar, calming voice came through clearly.

"Cress, I don't think I'm going to be able to save that ficus. Have you ever watered it, even once?"

Ficus. Oh yes. That stupid plant Len had given me.

"Maybe not. I don't like it much. Pitch it if you want." I hated to kill living things, but this was one more reminder of Len.

"Where are you? Whatcha doing?"

"Well, for starters, I haven't thrown up yet."

"Huh?"

"I feel lousy today, Neek. But right now I'm standing, well, I'm standing where Gram's killer must have stood."

"What!? What on earth are you talking about?"

"Oh, Neek, I'm more and more sure she was killed."

"And why are you in the place where she died?"

I told her how I had taken Gram's boat and just ended up there. "I vaguely remember walking around this lake with Gram when I was very young. Grace complained about the footpath that leads over here. She said it wasn't being kept up. I can see the path from here. And it's weedy, all right."

My dim memory focused slightly. My mother and father were leaving on yet another road tour, this one for four months. I was four years old, and Mom made me put up four fingers, thinking a time period of four months would make sense to a child that young.

The way I remembered it, I cried for days after they left. It may have only been hours, though, or minutes. The vivid part of the memory, surfacing now, was Gram scooping me up and driving me to this lake. We had walked on the footpath, the one I could see from the shore. I don't know if we made it all the way around the lake or not, but the memory of holding Gram's hand and the thrill of being in what I saw as wild woods was clear.

"Cressa, why did you go ashore?"

"I'm not sure. I want to see it again. The place Gram died. And... think about it: if someone stood here, waiting for her to swim over, let's see... Would she have gotten out of the water, or would she have turned around and swam back?"

"Well," Neek said. I could hear sitar music behind her. In addition to herbs and plants, she loved all things Eastern. "I'm thinking. Why would she get out of the water?"

"You're right. She wouldn't. Unless someone she knew needed her to. But why would they? It's not all that easy to climb up here in broad daylight and it was night. It's shallow here. So she stands in the water and, if she turns around to go back, she could be surprised from behind. From where I am."

"How did the killer get there?"

"The path is probably not totally impassible. I'll have to try it. And if Grace's killer is the same person as Gram's killer, they would've stood in the same place."

"Grace's killer?"

"Oh, I haven't told you." I sagged against a tree trunk. "Grace was killed last night, just like Gram, in the same place—right here."

"That's the lady that was so nice to you? Your grandmother's friend?"

"Yes, she and her husband have been super."

"I hope, at least, you didn't find... I mean, I hope someone else found ... They didn't did they?"

How did she always know? "No, no one else did. I'm the one who found her. Just like Gram."

"Oh, Cressa," she wailed. "I wish I had more days off. I wish I were there. I really do. This must be so hard for you."

"Well, it's not easy. But you're here on the phone with me. That's almost as good. Help me with this, Neek. The foliage doesn't look too dense to walk through, but it would make a good screen, especially at night." Treading with care, I searched the ground for anything telltale; I found nothing but sticks and leaves. "Maybe there's something that could tell us who was here. A footprint or something."

"But it's part of the club, right? If you *did* find a footprint here, what would that prove?"

She had a point. Lots of people had a right to walk around here. I slumped against the trunk of the oak and slid down to the damp ground, heedless of my jeans.

"Okay, you're right again," I admitted. "There wouldn't be any evidence here." I sighed into the cell phone. "So, you called to ask me about the ficus?" She wouldn't have called about a plant.

"Not exactly. I hate to bring this up," Neek said, "but you told me to get the messages off your answering machine."

"Yes?" I straightened up against the tree trunk. I hoped Len hadn't left any.

"Somebody named, uh, TRIGG-vee called. He sounded nasty. He said he and his brother were going to take you to court."

I groaned. "Oh damn."

"What's he talking about?"

"Gram left her cabin to me. My cousins must think there's a lot of money to fight over because they're contesting the will. Gram's lawyer says they won't win."

"Oh, Cressa, what a nuisance. And on top of everything else."

"Yeah. They're not my favorite people."

We said goodbye, then I saw it. A shiny metal something sticking out of the wet leaves. I lifted a soggy layer of vegetation and discovered a pair of silver-rimmed bifocals.

I heard, in my mind's ear, Grace's progress the last time I'd seen her out my front window, her dark form heading for the swimming area, a large towel draped over her arm, her flip-flops going *twup, twup* as she went, and the silhouette of her glasses—her silver bifocals—perched on her nose. But how did they get here?

I retrieved my bag from the boat and, being careful not to put my fingers on the lenses—who knows, they might carry fingerprints—nudged them into the bag with a twig.

Could I have actually found evidence? Excitement vibrated inside me. I had to show these to Al.

I set the bag down with more care, climbed in, rowed back to the cove as fast as I could, and headed for the dock. I glanced over my shoulder and thought I was lined up, but the next time I looked, the boat had drifted sideways. I tried it again. Missed again. It was a lot harder than I thought it would be.

I didn't need any more last straws. I slammed the oars into the water, but that didn't help anything.

Okay, take a deep, cleansing breath. I should be analytical about this. Maybe landing a boat is like working on a composition—the ending is the hard part. I stopped for a moment, drew a steady breath, and re-aimed.

I hummed Richard Strauss's *Thus Spake Zarathustra*, the piece that was used for the opening of the movie *2001: A Space Odyssey*, for inspiration. I hummed it aloud and I guess it worked, because at last my craft bumped against the big wooden post. I threw the rope to loop around it, grabbed the dock and pulled the boat over, then hopped out.

After the boat was secured, I dashed up the stairs to take my findings to Al's place. He was bound to be back home from his fishing expedition.

"Kisha, Kisha, can't get me!" shrieked a high, light voice. Others answered with shrieking laughter.

Curious to see what the commotion was, I slowed. Three children ran across Eve's yard playing tag, and two more stood near her cabin door.

"Everything's ready," Eve called from inside. "Come on in, kids."

They all piled onto the stoop and crowded through the door. Their small, piping voices continued from inside Eve's cabin. They were cute kids, all with shiny black curly hair, and close together in age. I wondered who they were, and whether they should be going into Eve's. Rebecca and Rachel seemed fine, though. And I was in a tremendous hurry to get to Al's.

-17-

Bellicoso: In a martial, warlike style (Ital.)

Now that I knew I wanted to dedicate my master's thesis composition to Gram, I was stuck on several fronts. My insipid melodies wandered around with no central direction, and no relation to each other. I couldn't find a trace of Gram in those stupid notes.

I was afraid of a life without Gram. I had pictured her so many times, sitting in the audience while I conducted this piece. Her face would beam, her heart would swell with pride. And I would bask in her love.

But there was no Gram.

I had fixed a small lunch, though I couldn't eat much of it. My stomach decided to play percussion for me.

The fact that a murderer might be near distracted me, as did the thought that Len or Mo could be lurking anywhere right now. Added to that was a popular melody stuck in my head. Not that popular, actually, but very catchy. And very stuck. "The Chicken Dance." Now, how did that get there?

The final reason I couldn't get any writing done this afternoon was the thought of those mice creeping around the edges of the cabin. They were probably running through the shadows inside the walls and laughing at me.

Admittedly, there was one more thing bothering me. After I showed the glasses to Al he was convinced that his wife had been murdered.

"I've been suspecting this," he had said, his voice low and dejected. "Now it looks like I was right." He had called the Alpha police station. Al told me the police chief, Kyle Bailey, had come out and looked at them, but hadn't taken them seriously.

"Chief Bailey didn't think he could use her bifocals for evidence, even if Grace met with foul play," Al told me after the chief had left. "He mentioned a couple of times the deaths are both being considered accidental until the autopsies tell him differently. He said something about chain of custody, too."

Al's thin shoulders drooped. "Since the evidence is tainted now, he said I can take them over to Henry County myself and have them checked for fingerprints. The chief promised to call and give them a heads up. If anything comes of this, it might point the police in the right direction. At least that's something."

Al said he would do that this afternoon.

It was discouraging that no one, except Al and me, thought foul play was involved, and I despaired of justice ever being served to Gram's killer. I didn't see how any fingerprints could have survived being buried in those damp leaves like that, but I was glad I had made sure mine weren't there, just in case.

I wandered out onto the back porch and sat in Gram's wicker rocker, creaking to and fro and feeling the comfort of the afghan in my lap. I could hear the five children still at Eve's.

"James, mind your manners," said an authoritative, but sweet, light voice. Probably an older sister. I smiled at the thought. They were doing fine at Eve's.

Sometimes I knew Gram had been killed, other times I talked myself into thinking maybe both women had drowned. But just because the police thought they were accidents, didn't mean they were. Police can be wrong, I told myself. And I was accomplishing nothing.

I had to get something done. Back inside, I looked at my work in disgust. The air hung like heavy draperies. As the day warmed, it got muggier, outside and in. Spotting a small oscillating fan atop the armoire, I thought it might feel cooler if I used it to move the sluggish air around.

The armoire was tall, the top of it above my sightline, so I had to stand on tiptoe to get the fan.

The door started to swing open, but I kicked it shut. I had to avoid dwelling on thoughts of that mysterious envelope inside. If it held an angry note from Gram, I would fall apart, lose my fragile hold. I would face it later.

But was anything else up there? I stretched up and patted around with my hand, and there was. Several hard, dark balls. I'd forgotten about those. Bile surged as I shook the hand that had touched the mice droppings, like a cat trying to get goo off its paw. I thumped the fan onto the counter and ran to scrub myself at the kitchen sink. I ran hot water over my hands, picturing mice running up my legs and over my face in my sleep. I shuddered.

Rummaging through the small amount of storage space in the kitchen cabinets and armoire, then under the sink, I was unable to find any traps.

"Listen, you little rodents, I'm going to win. You are *not* going to live here. *I* am going to live here. At least for awhile. You guys looking for a fight? You got it." I was ready for battle.

I grabbed my purse, and marched toward my car. The grass was so long I had to lift my feet with each step to get through it. It had to be mowed. Maybe I could kill two birds with one stone, and some mice, too. Since Mo's car wasn't there, I stopped at Toombses' and used the brass knocker. Martha came to the door, the television tuned to a soap opera behind her. She was wearing what I had seen described in catalogues as a "patio dress," a sort of muumuu, in yellow, green, and orange, with large sagging pockets. The usual pink rollers in her hair completed the ensemble.

"Could you please tell me if I can get someone to mow my grass?" I asked. "Your husband said I was responsible for it, but I don't have a mower. Does Sheila mow yards?"

"Oh, dear, no! It's all she can do to get the shared property done. I suppose you'll have to get someone." Her face assumed its usual worried pucker. "You can always use Freddie, you know. He did it for Ida and he does ours. Have you met him?"

She made no move to invite me in this time, so we talked through the screen door. Maybe she thought she wasn't dressed. Maybe it wasn't a patio dress, but, instead, a bathrobe. Or maybe a nightgown?

"No I haven't met him."

"Freddie lives in the trailer at the far end of the campground. You might have seen his children? Curly-headed little tykes?"

I nodded. The kids at Eve's.

"Those are Freddie and Pat's kids. Do you want to ask him?"

"Sure, that'd be fine."

"I can't get over what happened to Grace. Such a nice lady. And right after your grandmother like that. Goodness gracious." Those eyebrows twitched higher yet.

I nodded again.

"Are you enjoying the cabin?"

"I like it." *Except Gram isn't there.* "It's a cute place." *But how weird this is, talking through the screen.* "I do have a problem, though. Mice. Could you tell me if I can get mousetraps in Alpha?"

"Oh, dear! I remember Ida did have them sometimes," Martha said. "Aren't there any traps in the cabin?"

"I can't find any. Maybe Gram used them all."

"I don't have any right now or I'd give you a few. But there's a drugstore right on the main highway in Alpha. It'll have mousetraps. Do you have very many mice?"

"I have no idea." Was she saying I might have dozens? Hundreds? I envisioned them creeping around inside the walls, waiting for me to fall asleep so they could come out and play. "Haven't noticed any in the day, but I hear them at night. And I found droppings on top of the big wardrobe. I didn't know mice could climb so high."

"Oh my, yes." Martha smiled. It gave her a wistful expression. "They can get anywhere."

Anywhere? The vision of the horrid creatures crawling all over me in my bed was even more vivid. My still-sore stomach gave an extra lurch.

Martha continued. "If there's a hole, they'll find it. We have to keep fighting them."

"Thanks so much, Martha." I turned to go, then whipped back. "I was thinking of taking a walk around the lake sometime. Is there still a footpath that goes around the lake?"

"Sure. You walk across the dam and you'll find the start of the trail over there."

"How easy a walk is it?" *Easy enough for Mo to get over there to murder two women?*

"Well, not too bad. I've done it a couple of times. Not for a long time, though. It's buggy. You get bit by mosquitoes something fierce."

She hesitated one more moment, made a decision, and swung the door open for me. As I stepped in she gave me a smile tinged with sadness.

"You're a nice girl, like your grandmother. She was a sweet person." Martha focused beyond my shoulder, swallowed, and lowered her voice. "I'd like to talk to you about her sometime, but not today. I'm expecting my husband back any minute."

"Okay. I appreciate your help with the mice. And I'll be sure and put on bug spray before I go walking. Thanks."

As I turned, I found myself face to face with Toombs, who had soundlessly come through the front door.

"What were you saying?" he squinted hard at his wife.

"I was… I was telling her about the path around the lake." Her voice was faint. "I just said it was buggy."

"Well, sure it's buggy. It's outside, ain't it?" he snapped, his nasal voice menacing.

"No, I mean, it's just that there are so many mosquitoes."

"No more there than anyplace else. I thought I told you to get more beer this morning." He pushed past me and went toward the kitchen, trailing beer fumes.

"I'm going into town as soon as I get dressed." Her voice was faint and discouraged. "I had to do laundry this morning. I ran out of clothes."

Martha gave me her sad half-smile and shut the door after me softly.

Hadn't he bought beer yesterday? I wondered if he was drinking a case at a time.

I drove down the road and entered Alpha again.

-18-

Accelerando: "Accelerating," growing faster (Ital.)

The small town of Alpha bordered Illinois State Highway 150 for about a mile. It consisted of a large school building, several businesses, and a few one- and two-story wood frame houses. None of the homes had been built recently, and several of the larger ones had wrap-around porches with gingerbread trim up under the eaves. A shiny metallic diner, made to look like a railroad car, stood on the highway. On second thought, maybe it actually was a dining car from a train.

Hoping to find Gram's old house, I decided to explore a bit. My memories of Alpha were hazy, but I did have a few fond ones of visiting here. Gram had grown up in Alpha and she and Gramps had lived here for many years before they moved into Moline.

Several narrow roads led off to either side of the highway, but they only went two or three blocks. All but one were residential. The exception was the downtown street of the village, edged by a post office, fire station, and a few more business establishments.

I did manage to find my grandparents' old house, but it looked tiny compared to my early childhood memories. Even the yard, where we'd played croquet and tag, looked small.

It hadn't been Gram's house in a long time, but it evoked happy times. We spent Thanksgiving and Christmas here, and the kitchen was always filled with the delicate aroma of Gram's Swedish spritz cookies for the holidays. Gramps used to hold back some of the outdoor lights and let me help string them up on Christmas Eve. The present owners were letting it go. The paint on the south side was peeling and the back porch sagged. Gram's porch swing was gone, too. The house not only looked small, it looked diminished. And sad.

I headed back to the highway and drove past the bowling alley where I'd had that burger with Mo and Daryl. My car was making strange sputters, but it kept going, so I ignored them.

I still wanted to somehow try and pump Mo about Gram and Grace. He hadn't struck me as a fast thinker. Maybe, if I could word it right, he would slip up and admit he was nearby when they died.

Two doors past the bowling alley was a square brick structure whose storefront window lay flush with the sidewalk. Pain relievers and cold remedies were displayed in a matter-of-fact manner with no attempt at artistry or appeal.

My car jerked into a shady parking place at the side of the drugstore and I walked around to the front. A bell tinkled as I pushed open the heavy, wooden door, then stepped onto a wide-board oak floor. An ancient wrinkled man, perched on a stool behind the counter, came to life as the bell rang. He didn't say anything, but raised his bald head and kept his dark eyes on me. I was sure his hand was the one that oversaw the no-nonsense window display. The warm, closed-in smell was comforting.

I nodded at him, smiling, and he nodded back soberly.

That's the small-town attitude. I'm a stranger and not to be trusted.

Wanting him to think of me as something other than an outsider, I told him I was Ida Miller's granddaughter.

He nodded, pursing his lips tightly in what may have been a smile. That opened the way to conversation.

"I knew Ida since she was a pup. Too bad about her drowning like that. I guess you're out seeing about her lake house."

I murmured assent. I was relieved he didn't seem aware I had found her body. But then he put it together.

"Wait a minute. Criminy! You're the granddaughter who …" This grimace was definitely not a smile. He must have regretted his outburst of emotion, and his wooden expression came back. "Funny things go on out there, you know."

"Funny things?"

"Forget I said that." He shook his head.

"Funny how?" I persisted.

"Nothing lately. Not for years." I wasn't happy with his answer, but it was all I was going to get. "It's nice," he continued, "especially this time of year. I never had a place at Crescent Lake. Never had time to spend away. My name's Anders, by the way. I've run this store since I was a young lad."

A person who was still a young lad staggered up the aisle laden with a huge carton of baby food. He thumped it onto the worn floor and straightened up, staring at it before he started to rip it open and shelve it. His movements were on the slow side and his employer saw no need to hurry him.

"This here young man, now, his father used to work for me when he was his age. I've employed half of those lake club people when they were teenagers. Yep, I've had Wayne Weldon, Martha Toombs, Al, Norah's daughter Sheila, Smiley, Grace Harmon. All those lake club people. Even Mo for a short spell. It's sure too bad what happened to Grace, too, isn't it? What are you needing today?" He rubbed a hand over his shiny scalp.

"A couple of things. I'm afraid I have mice I need to get rid of."

He surprised me when he jumped off his stool and darted out from behind the counter to show me where the mousetraps were. He also pointed out the antacids when I asked and I grabbed a box of those.

"Oh, and I need a flashlight."

He steered me to the next aisle where the flashlights and batteries were.

He must be as old as he looks to have employed people like the Harmons and the Toombses. They aren't young, themselves. He sure moves quickly, though.

The pace of the little town was much slower than what I was used to in Chicago. A certain amount of chat seemed to be called for while business was conducted. We discussed the weather while I picked up shampoo and sunscreen, feeling comfortable with the old man. The chat and the business taken care of, I thanked him as I paid for my purchases, and he told me I could get cheese for bait at the supermarket right across the road.

I stashed my purchases, taking a minute to pop one of the antacid tablets into my mouth, and left my car where it was to dash across the highway. I had to wait for a chance between the smelly, roaring semi trucks, but I soon got a break and crossed to the parking lot of the big, bright, prefab aluminum building on the other side.

It must have been one of the newest businesses in town—and one of the ugliest—but it was well stocked and clean. However, I immediately missed the ambience of the charming old brick pharmacy across the street with its wide-planked floors and wizened pharmacist who served gossip with his wares.

I quickly found the cheddar cheese and paid for it without the preliminaries called for at the drugstore, then ran back across the highway, anxious to get the traps baited and set. I threw my purse onto the passenger seat and slid into the car.

When I turned the key in the ignition, the motor started, but immediately died. I tried a couple more times. It sputtered until I gave up and climbed back out. The tablet had soothed my tummy, but now it started jumping around again.

Fighting back tears of frustration, I ducked back into the car to retrieve my purse, thinking to go ask Mr. Anders for advice.

A heavy hand clutched my arm as I bent over, and I straightened up in alarm, hitting my head on the top of the door opening. It was Mo.

"You scared me!" I yelled.

"Sorry." He patted my head where I had bumped it and tried to dazzle me with his grin. "I wanted to catch you before you got away. I saw you in the grocery store, but I couldn't get your attention. You were in the express lane."

I swatted his hand away. "There are only two lanes," I answered, still annoyed, rubbing my head.

"Is something the matter with your car?"

"I guess so, but I don't know what. It won't start."

"There's a service station over in New Windsor. I don't have to work until four. Want me to drive you? You have anything in there that will spoil?"

I started to answer, "No, I don't think …" Then I spotted him across the highway, back at the grocery store parking lot.

Len! What in the hell is he doing here?

-19-

*Stringendo: Hastening, accelerating the movement, usually
suddenly and rapidly, with a crescendo (Ital.)*

Since my car was parked at the side of the drugstore, I thought Len might not see me, but as I began to turn away to hide my face, our eyes connected. *Oh shit! Did he follow me here? That must have been him behind me when I drove out here two days ago. Damn.*

Len threw his cigarette onto the pavement. He motioned for me to stay put, and started my way, his steps angry and deliberate. Luckily, there was a long line of diesel trucks between us.

"Where's your car?" I asked Mo. Anything would be better than confronting Len.

"Right here." He gestured two cars down.

"Let's go."

Am I crazy, getting into a car with Mo? My mind went into high gear. We were in a public place. Nothing could happen here. I would be safe. Besides, Len was across the street. This was the chance I was waiting for to talk to Mo about Gram and see how he reacted.

I sucked in a deep breath, not at all sure I was doing the right thing. I experienced a minor tremor of fear from Mo's nearness, but a major earthquake at the sight of an angry Len, still looking for an opening to cross the highway. Behind him, his little blue convertible was parked in the lot. Had he really followed me here days ago? Had he stood outside my window smoking, spying on me? I couldn't picture him not barging in if he knew where I was.

"Straight to the gas station, right?"

Mo pulled out his keys. "Right."

My cell phone had three bars. I would be able to call for help if anything awful happened. I hustled him to his jalopy and crawled in, willing him to hurry. Len gave an astonished look as we peeled past him out of the lot. When I looked back he was shaking a fist at me, as irate as I'd ever seen him.

Mo wielded his big old car down a narrow blacktop road and out of town by a back way, along several dusty lanes that intersected at corners which all looked alike, bordered on all four sides by fields of towering cornstalks.

I groaned almost audibly. *What are you doing, Cressa? This might be the person who drowned Gram and Grace.*

Not necessarily, I answered. *Two little girls think they might have seen him there, that's all. We mustn't panic here.*

You're right, I agreed. *I have to find out if he was there or not. And he's not going to drown me in the car, is he? No, he's not.*

I pulled my shoulders down and tried to roll the tension out of them. There was nothing to be nervous about. A nice Brandenburg Concerto, specifically the last movement of the first *Concerto in F major,* a relaxed piece of music, mentally soothed my jangled nerves. I hummed it lightly, tonguing the *dum, dadadum, dadadum, dadadum* against the roof of my mouth.

One thing was good. We weren't on the main highway. That made it less likely Len could follow us. It would be fun to see what all the stirred-up road dust would do to his upholstery if he did, though. He never put the top up on his convertible unless he had to.

Mo turned at one corner and continued down a road that looked identical to the one we had just left. I was glad the windows were open when he lit his cigarette.

"How on earth do you know where you are?" I asked.

He shrugged. "It's not hard. I've always lived here."

The corn put a clean tang into the air. I leaned toward the window to avoid Mo's smoke and inhaled the outside air, closing my eyes for a second. Some of the fields had neatly spaced rows and others were packed tight. I asked Mo what the difference was.

"Some of the farmers have started growing organic corn and they plant the rows farther apart, the old-fashioned way, like they did years ago."

We soon emerged from the fields into the next town, New Windsor. A black and white sign announced, "New Windsor, Pop. 650." It didn't look much larger than Alpha, Pop. 550.

There were two service stations on the main road, but Mo drove right past both of them.

"Wait," I shouted. "Where are you going?"

"I wanna show you something first. We're going for a ride. It's not far."

I reluctantly agreed, wondering what there was to see except more cornfields. I tried to ignore the alarm bells, sounding like Chinese gongs, clanging in my head. After all, this wasn't Chicago; this was the heartland of America. Good old wholesome, small-town Midwest America.

"I need to get back soon so my cheese doesn't spoil," I said.

"Where's the cheese?"

"In my car. I just bought it for the mice."

"Cheese for mice? You're feeding them?"

"No, no. It's for trapping them in my cabin."

"I was gonna say, we don't feed mice around here, we try to get rid of 'em." He would be so cute if he had more brains. And if he chewed with his mouth closed. And if I didn't halfway suspect him of murder.

I put my finger on the fast-dial number for Neek and hoped she would answer if I called.

I glanced at Mo and noticed that, curiously, he looked exactly like his father in profile.

They have the same features. Mo's are arranged differently. And a lot better. His face isn't so narrow and fox-like.

"Mo," I started. *It's now or never.* "Do you remember the night my grandmother drowned?"

He looked straight ahead as if I hadn't said anything.

"And the night Grace drowned? Were you around?"

Still no comment. He looked away and flipped his butt out the window.

"Do you think it's peculiar they died so similarly?"

He gave me an odd look, roared down a maze of intersecting dirt roads at his usual high rate of speed, throwing plumes of dust high into the air behind us, then swung into a driveway that led to a tumble-down shed behind an abandoned farmhouse. I choked a couple of times on the dust settling over us.

What had once been an orderly hedge across the front lawn had gone wild and effectively shielded the place from view unless one were looking straight down the driveway.

It was shady where we parked. With a growing sense of unease I stared at the way the chain around Mo's neck gleamed in the shadow.

"This is creepy," I said. Goosebumps sprang up on my arms. Traveled up my spine. "Why are you stopping here?"

"Because it's private," he purred, reaching over to put his hand on my neck. He then drew my head to his, and mashed his lips against mine. At the same time he also tucked his other hand down the front of my shirt. His clammy hand.

Startled, I pushed back. Straightened in my seat. Plucked his hand out of my shirt. My cell had fallen into my purse somewhere.

"Mo," I said as sternly as I could, "Please take me back to a service station."

My insides quivered like a vibrating string. All my senses twanged onto high alert.

"What's wrong?" His eyes glittered in the shade of the overgrown hedge.

"Nothing's wrong, but I don't like this place and I don't want to be here." The pitch of my voice rose with each word.

"So, you're too good for me?"

"Mo, please. I don't even know you. You don't know me. And I'm uncomfortable here." Tremors entered my voice. Damn! In another minute I would cry. "This place is in the middle of nowhere. Please take me back to New Windsor."

"I don't think we're quite ready to leave yet." His handsome face grew mean with an ugly sneer that pulled the skin tight over his cheekbones. "I think you owe me something."

"What? Owe you for what?"

"For dinner."

"You call hamburgers in a bowling alley 'dinner'?" I sneered back at him, anger bubbling up inside, overtaking my fear. "Dinners are eaten in restaurants," I spat. "And women do not 'owe' gentlemen for dinners. Not that there are any gentlemen right here."

"You're a snob." His eyes narrowed. The chain around his neck shone just like his eyes. He looked dangerous. And there was something about that chain.

"Never mind, I'll pay you for 'dinner' and then you'll take me home." I started rummaging in my purse as I spoke.

"I don't like your attitude," he said between the clenched teeth of his wolfish smile. He grabbed my shirt, tore it open in the front. Just then I put my trembling fingers on the tube I had been scrabbling for in my purse.

With one fluid motion, guided by pure adrenaline, I whipped out a small leather case, swiveled the lever around with a flick of my thumb, aimed at Mo's handsome face, and pressed.

I threw open the car door and ran out toward the road. I didn't want to hang around for the effects of the pepper spray.

His screams echoed behind me as I sped into the cornfield to hide. I tore blindly down the rows, zigzagging to elude Mo, if he were following. His cries became fainter in the distance, until all I could hear were my own footfalls thudding into the soft dirt, accompanied by the ragged pounding of my heart.

When I stopped for breath, I realized I had no idea which direction I had come from. I didn't want to return to Mo, just back to the road. Shaking with adrenaline and exertion, I collapsed onto the warm earth and gulped in the fresh, tangy scent of the growing corn plants, mingled with the smell of the moist dirt underneath me.

As soon as my heart quit beating in my stomach, I caught a couple of deep, jagged breaths and stood up, trying to decide which way to head.

I was relieved that this was, apparently, one of those organic fields. Otherwise I wouldn't have been able to fit between the rows. But the rows went on forever.

It was definitely time to call Neek. Amazingly, my purse had remained draped over my shoulder. For once, Ivan the Terrible was where I wanted it, fully charged. I slung my purse in front of me. Indecision and terror paralyzed me. Call Neek? Call nine-one-one? Do something!

I put my hand on the phone, then listened.

The cornstalks rustled off to my right. Good, I thought, wind. Turning my head to catch the breeze on my sweaty face, I realized it wasn't the wind. Someone was coming toward me. Could Mo have recovered from the spray that quickly? Would he hear me if I beeped the buttons on the phone? Even setting it to mute would make noise. As usual, the cell phone was useless.

I ducked down to try and avoid detection. The theme from *Jaws* kept rhythm with my wildly thumping heart. A shadow loomed before the approaching figure.

My phone rang.

-20-

Pas de Deux: Dance for two (Fr.)

ot knowing what to do, I threw the still-ringing phone to my right. I cowered closer to the ground, trying to blend into the soft dirt. A faint voice called my name.

"Cressa?"

It doesn't sound like Mo.

"Cressa, it's me, Daryl."

Daryl? It's Daryl? Not Mo? Hallelujah! My breath whooshed out loud enough for him to hear several rows away and he came crashing through the corn stalks between us. His coppery hair shone in the shadows.

"Are you okay?"

I sprang to my feet and, to my complete embarrassment, burst into tears.

"Are you hurt?"

"No," I blubbered. "But Mo might be. At least I hope he is."

"What happened?"

"What happened to me, is Mo!" I snapped. As if it were his fault his roommate attacked me.

"I saw Mo back there, heard him shouting your name, and figured he must have gotten out of line again."

"What do you mean 'again'?"

"Are you all right?"

"Better than he is." I found a smug smile somewhere.

While I was looking for my now-silent cell phone, I pulled out the lethal leather canister. I held it up and said, "Pepper spray."

"No kidding! You big city girls play rough." He laughed. "So Mo finally got what he deserves."

He stuck his hand out to shake mine in mock congratulations. I held the spray with one hand, and my torn shirt with the other; we musicians are more ambidextrous than the general population, but I could have used an extra hand right then. I quickly turned the lever to the locked position and put the spray canister back into my purse, then took his calm, cool hand. I found mine was still sweaty and trembling.

After I retrieved Ivan the Terrible, we started off through the rustling rows and I hoped he knew which way was out of this dark maze. He did. We quickly reached the road where Daryl had left his green Ford two-door. The car was fairly new, but covered with dust from the dirt road. He opened the passenger door for me and we drove off, leaving Mo moaning and stumbling around in circles nearby. Daryl wasn't too concerned about him.

"Should I drop you back at the lake? Or can I stop by my place and get you a T-shirt or something first?" Daryl asked as we headed toward Alpha. "You're not exactly presentable."

"Well, I kind of hate to put myself at the mercy of any more males today." No, not kind of—I *really* hated to. "But my car is over by the drugstore and won't start. Could you take me there?" He nodded, his eyes still on the road, and I couldn't resist asking: "How do you stand living with that idiot, anyway?"

"We usually go our separate ways. I don't see much of him. It's an awful lot cheaper to share rent. And he's not exactly my roommate; he lives in the other half of the duplex."

We returned to Alpha by a more direct route than Mo had taken, bypassing New Windsor. As we turned onto the main highway I rolled the window down and let the rushing air cool my damp face and neck.

"I've been trying to decide whether he's harmless or not ever since I met him." My voice was returning to normal, but parts of me were still shaking. "I guess now I know for sure. What were you doing out there, by the way? It doesn't look like anyone lives around there."

"I had just picked up my car from the shop and was coming out of the hardware store in New Windsor when I saw you two drive through town. When Mo headed for the back roads, I, I don't know, I thought he might be up to no good." He gave me a long glance that held concern. "After I followed you, and saw you were parking, I felt pretty stupid. I was turning my car around to get out of there when I heard Mo yelling. He couldn't tell me what had happened, he just kept yelling and cussing and pointing into the corn field. You left a pretty clear path."

I huddled in Daryl's car, thinking dismal thoughts about my judgment in men. First Len, then Mo. Next Daryl? I couldn't make myself think he was like them.

We reached the duplex Daryl and Mo shared. I was glad to know where Mo lived so I could avoid it in the future. The entrance to Mo's half was around the corner. If he came back, he wouldn't see me going in or coming out.

The house was small, old, and painted white, located about a block off the high-way, with a porch that went all the way across the front. I got out of the car, clutching the remains of my top, then hesitated before going up the steps.

I thought I could trust Daryl. But Mo did live here, too, after all.

"Do you think Mo will be coming back soon?" I asked.

"Don't worry, I'll take care of him if he shows up. He'll probably be a long time recovering from your spray. Technically, he should be back at work at the bowling alley, but I doubt he'll show up there."

Daryl pushed the front door open.

"Don't you people ever lock anything around here?" I asked. *It must be nice—weird, but nice—to live in a place where people don't lock doors.* This sleepy town was blissfully cozy after the terror of Mo's car and the cornfield.

Daryl's smile was open and sweet. It made something inside me curl up and wag its tail. "It's considered unfriendly to lock your door. Anyway, there are at least two or three neighbors looking out their windows at all times to see who goes where. I'll be asked about you tomorrow. Count on it."

He pointed me to a couch in the small living room and ran upstairs. "I'll be right back."

It was not hard to tell a single guy lived here. It wasn't terribly messy, but the furniture was all second-hand, or donated from a relative's attic. Nothing matched and only the elaborate stereo system and the big-screen TV looked new.

I flinched when I heard a noise, afraid it was Mo, but immediately realized it was the sound of Daryl's footsteps on the wooden floor above.

It was beginning to grow dark outside, but I could see into the next room, which was probably supposed to be the dining room. It wasn't furnished like one, though.

In fact, it didn't even have furniture, but, instead, twisted metal figures either reposed or stood around the room, according to their shapes and degrees of completion. An easel in the corner held a canvas that was painted completely blue. Several other canvases leaned against one wall, hiding their surfaces. I crept into the room and sneaked a look at several of the paintings, but scurried back to the living room as Daryl came down the creaking stairs with a white shirt.

"Who's the artist?" I asked.

"I'm the art teacher in the high school," he answered.

I said I liked the sculpture of the birds and Daryl looked pleased.

After I used the bathroom to change my shirt, we drove back to my car. There was no sign of Len or Mo. Daryl looked at my gas gauge and determined I had run out. He didn't say anything smart-alecky, which I had been bracing myself for. I was relieved.

We quickly ran back to New Windsor to fill the gallon container he kept in his trunk. He poured the gas into my tank and, feeling utterly foolish, I got into the driver's seat. I stammered my thanks to Daryl many, many times for coming to my rescue. *I don't know what I would have done if he hadn't been there.* Despite my embarrassment, it was relaxing being with him.

Leaning into the window with a big, warm smile on his face he said, again, that it was nothing, that I could return the shirt any time.

It was hard to get my car keys out of my purse. After my agility in spraying Mo, I was now all thumbs. I tried three times to get the key into the ignition, until Daryl finally offered to drive me home and help me pick up my car in the morning. We both agreed I was in no shape to drive, but I would need my car tomorrow to get to Gram's funeral in the afternoon.

He put my purchases in his back seat. I compared getting into Daryl's car to getting into Mo's. Much better. And even easier the second time. As we passed the edge of the small town, Daryl slowed and leaned toward me, directing my gaze out the window. Darkness had fallen.

"Look out at the cornfields," he said softly. "When we get to this rise, look across the tops of the tassels."

I turned to him, wondering why on earth I should look at a cornfield in the dark. His face was closer than I had calculated and I almost touched his cheek with mine. I could feel warmth spreading from the place our cheeks would have met.

He drew back, but only slightly.

"Look—right there." He pointed out my window.

He slowed even more as we came to the top of a small rise. I held my breath in amazement.

Millions of fireflies danced like tiny Tinkerbells over the tops of the corn plants. The field was alive with them, bright with their twinkling lights.

Above them, the country sky was a black velvet setting for the diamond stars that pulsed with the sound of the crickets. The fertile smell of cooling earth and green plants drifted into the car as I rolled the window down to see better. I was speechless. The glory of the stars paled beside the phantasmagoria of the cornfield and I gazed, mesmerized, at the spectacle. Daryl stopped the car.

"It looks like Christmas lights," I whispered, not wanting to break the spell. "What makes the fireflies do that? Are they always there?"

"This time of year they are," answered Daryl. "I don't know what exactly they're after. Something in the corn tassels."

I looked at him and saw he was smiling, amused at my fascination. I grinned back. I could feel his breath on my cheek. He smiled wider, his head still close to mine as we both looked out the passenger window.

I stole a glance at Daryl, trying to figure him out. Crashing the "date" with Mo was a cloddish thing to do, but I was glad he had, and that I had met him. I was glad there was someone here to serve as a buffer for Mo.

Daryl put the car in gear and continued.

We drove up the gravel hill to my cabin. I remembered Mo's father complaining about teenagers scattering the gravel. And Al complaining about Mo's driving. I was thankful for Al's sake that Daryl's speed was more moderate.

"Thanks for saving me," I said once more.

"I think you had already saved yourself," he said.

"I would never have gotten out of that cornfield. I had no idea where to go."

He carried my bags to my door and made sure I was safely inside. I watched him drive away out my front window. I was still numb from being assaulted by Mo, but Daryl had thawed the ice somewhat.

I shook myself out of my reverie. I needed to check on Al. By the light from one of his windows, I could see him perched on a large flat stump in front of his cabin, his long legs tucked into the stump. The steel of his huge shiny knife blurred as he flicked the scales off a fish he'd caught earlier, threw it aside and reached for another. I stepped outside, he waved the blade, and I walked over.

"Any news?" I asked.

"Sure is. I brought Grace's glasses to Cambridge and turned them in to Dobson."

"Dobson?"

"He's the county sheriff. At first he didn't think they were important. But I asked him why the hell she would have buried them. She always wore them, even when she swam."

A little of his old temper flared, then subsided as quickly. "And way over there on the west shore, when all she was doing was swimming back and forth. But I sure didn't get a good answer."

"Is he at least going to test them for fingerprints? Didn't Chief Bailey say he would?"

"He has to now. He's sending them to the crime lab. Didn't know how long that will take. It depends on how backed up they are."

"What do you mean, he has to?"

"A call came while I was in Dobson's office." Al put his knife down and rubbed his hands on a rough towel draped over his knee, making a faint harsh sound in the still night. "After he hung up, Dobson said the autopsies are done. Grace and Ida both had their lungs packed solid with mud."

"Mud? What does that mean?"

"He said it means they were most likely held down with their faces in the mud till they sucked in enough to kill them." He attacked the fish scales, cutting deep into the flesh with his powerful strokes.

My mouth dropped open. A startlingly clear picture of Gram, struggling face-down in the lake with Mo's strong hands on her, leapt up before me.

"So they *were* killed. It's official." A hot pain seared my heart.

"Yep. But they have no idea who killed them. Why would anyone …" His voice choked. He swallowed and went on. "Dobson told me to go ahead and bury my wife. I suppose I'll have to pick out a casket."

"Is your family going to be here soon?"

"Neither of my sons can make it today or tomorrow." The knife blade stopped and Al's shoulders slumped. "Our oldest has to pick the kids up from summer camp and the other is out of the country on business. I told them to just come the morning of the funeral, and I'd let them know when. I thought I'd set it up for a couple of days after Ida's. There's no hurry."

How, I thought, could he stay so calm? And why didn't he want his children to be here? Was there more to this seemingly open, friendly man than I could fathom? I wanted to meet his sons to see what they were like.

His sigh was deep, heavy. "I wish you could have tasted Grace's brownies."

"But I have. She brought a plate over when I got here."

"Good aren't they?" He voice was barely audible.

I don't know if he saw my nod. "I'll go with you to pick out the casket if you want. You were such a big help to me when I had to make Gram's arrangements."

He gave me a gentle look. "That's nice of you, Cressa. I'd appreciate it, since my boys won't be here till the last minute. I pretty much know what Grace wanted in the way of a service. We talked about it some. We always figured one of us would have to bury the other. But not like this."

His voice grew harsh. "I think I know what happened to her, even if the police don't. She said something to Mo about him stealing her diamond earrings a few days ago, so he went over there and drowned her."

The veins in his neck stuck out like the bones of the fish he was cleaning. He grabbed his knife, took a couple more swipes at a sunfish, set it down, and hacked off the head of a good-sized catfish. What could I say? I knew one thing. He had enough troubles without me telling him about Mo attacking me.

"Maybe they'll find something."

"Oh, they did." His frown deepened the furrows above his nose. "After the autopsy call came in, Dobson sent a couple of cops back over here to do more searching. They found their beach towels and sandals in the water, weighted down with a rock."

"Where?"

"Near the swimming area. About ten feet from the beach. I was there while they searched. Quite a few of us were. The cops said that's another sign they were killed."

"I guess it is." My words were grossly inadequate. A cold spasm ran up my spine.

"Ida's cabin key was tied up in the bundle, too. They gave it to Toombs."

"I'm not swimming at night again." Or probably during the day, either. I patted his gnarled hand and turned back toward my place.

-21-

Niente: Nothing (Ital.)

The cabin felt snug and secure after I went in and locked the door. I stripped down and stood under a hot spray of water for a long time, letting the shower take all traces of Mo off me and down the drain. *I don't care if it is unfriendly, I don't want to see the junior Mr. Toombs anytime soon. Or anyone else, really.*

I hadn't eaten much, but didn't feel hungry. The capricious cell phone was working, so I called Neek as I toweled my hair on the back porch, enjoying the air flowing in through the louvers, past the shades I'd drawn.

"Are you all right?" was the first thing she said.

"Well… "

"I knew it. I should have called the minute I found it. I didn't know if it was for you or for someone else. I found a dollar bill today."

"That's nice," I said.

"No, that's a terrible thing! I knew something would happen. What was it?"

As I paced back and forth on the porch, I recounted my sighting of Len, Mo's attack, and my rescue by Daryl. I had since decided the near-drowning was deliberate, not mere "fooling around."

"Oh, man! I'm glad you weren't hurt. It could have been awful. And there was another note from Len."

He must have left it before he drove out here, I thought.

"I threw it away. But just think—a dollar bill."

"I guess. That's bad, huh?"

"That's almost the worst money omen you can find."

"Where do you get this stuff, Neek?"

"I don't get it anywhere. I just know. You know, whole civilizations have based their decisions on oracles. Look at Delphi, and the Roman sibyls."

I told her I still hadn't arranged for a post office box for forwarding my bills, but would try and remember it the next time I went into Alpha. When I hung up, I was much cheered by our talk. Maybe she was nuts, but at least she was entertaining. The strange thing was, whatever she used for predictions, Neek was usually right.

Would I ever be free of Len? After Gramps died, I had given in to the persistence of my music theory teacher, Len, who had been trying to get my attention for two years.

He was the first older man I'd ever had a relationship with, and I had hoped he would treat me better than my previous string of undergraduate losers.

Len was married. Gram had given me the most normal homelife she could to counteract my unconventional early childhood. In spite of my strong moral upbringing, or maybe because of it, I plunged myself defiantly into the role of the "other woman." At first it was exciting—the forbiddenness of it—and I was able to push Gramps's death to the back of my mind. Maybe the affair was my way of avoiding the grieving process and my guilt over how he'd died. The thought of him dying alone in the darkness haunted me. All because I hadn't changed a light bulb.

I quivered when Len would give me a private look in the hallway between classes; his eyes were piercing. A married man, a drinker, a smoker. I couldn't believe such a worldly man would be interested in a plain little music student like me. His hair was thin, but that just meant he was mature. In retrospect, I probably looked like a naive, gullible little girl: easy pickings.

Our fling was brief, but intense. Well, brief for me; I ended it after about two months. For Len, it never really stopped. When we first started seeing each other, I was the more enamored partner, while he found my infatuation cute. The tide soon shifted, though, and he grew obsessed with me, and I quickly grew bored with our relationship.

Some relationship. I would sneak over to his campus apartment, the one he used during the week, where his wife never came. He would order in dinner or fix steak and salad, the one meal he could make, and we would go to bed. That was it. It didn't take me long to grow tired of this routine. One morning, when it was still dark out, I got dressed to go home and said I wouldn't be coming over anymore.

"Till when?" he asked, his voice groggy with sex and sleep.

"No, Len." I repeated my statement. "I mean, I'm not coming over any more. At all. I'm not seeing you again."

"What's the matter? What did I do? What didn't I do?"

I didn't catch the menace in his tone. "Nothing's the matter, I'm tired of this whole deal, as I keep saying and you keep ignoring. It's the same thing every night and it's boring. I want to be out dating other people and I don't have time for it when I'm always coming over here. I want to do other things and go other places."

Now he was awake. He lit his first cancer stick of the day and sucked while he thought. "Other people—what do you mean? Where would you like to go? Should we take a trip to Vegas? Or Mexico?"

"I don't want to go anywhere."

"But, Cressa darling, you just said you did."

"I'm not coming over anymore!" I shouted and stomped toward the door.

A frightening change came over him. His speed shocked me. I heard him coming, but, before I could turn around, he had yanked me by the hair and thrown me to the floor face down. The skin on my forehead split. Hot blood poured out. I scrambled up. I had to squint through the thickening flow from my head wound. His bare foot caught me in the solar plexus, knocking the wind out of me.

I still wasn't reacting quickly enough. Never in my life had I ever been physically attacked. But when he grabbed my little finger and twisted it until it snapped, I summoned up a rage-fueled strength and kicked him where men hate to be kicked.

While he writhed on the floor I screamed, "Get it through your incredibly stupid thick damn skull, Len, I'm leaving!" and stormed out. The cut on my forehead required two stitches and left a slight scar above my right eye. I wore bangs to cover it for awhile, until the scar faded. My finger healed, slightly crooked. Luckily, after getting used to it, it didn't hinder my playing.

Len obviously didn't understand what I said, though. He kept calling, texting, emailing, and threatening. Then, when I changed my phone number and email address, he started mailing letters and slipping notes under my apartment door. His threats escalated and I finally went through the hassle of getting a restraining order. The mail stopped but the personal notes didn't. It was unfortunate I couldn't afford an apartment with a doorman.

That's when I started carrying pepper spray full-time. That vial gave me enough confidence to leave the apartment and carry out my daily living. I was nevertheless in a state of constant anxiety that didn't really let up until I left Chicago three days ago for this calm, peaceful countryside. Populated with wife-beaters, molesters... and murderers.

-22-

Ritournelle: 1. The burden of a song. 2. A repeat. 3. In accompanied vocal works, an instrumental prelude, interlude, or postlude (refrain) (Fr.)

I had never felt the absence of Gram so acutely. I fetched the afghan from the porch and wrapped it around me. It smelled like lilacs. I was thrown back to the day Gram had called to tell me about this cabin. And the day of our big blow-up. Actually, *my* big blow-up. My *stupid* big blow-up.

She had called on a Tuesday. "Cress, I've finally gone crazy."

"What do you mean, Gram?"

"I just did the craziest thing I've ever done. I bought a cabin out at Crescent Lake and sold my house."

I couldn't process what I'd heard. "Crescent Lake? Is that the lake we used to go to in the summer? Outside Alpha?" I fidgeted with my locket. *Sold your house? Our house? No!*

"That's the one. Remember, you used to think you were named after the lake? This cabin is the cutest little thing. You have to come see it. It looks like Hansel and Gretel should live there, or maybe Little Red Riding Hood's grandmother."

"You *sold* our *house*?" Her words were sinking in and I realized she had sold the only home I'd ever known. It was gone. "Do you have the piano where you are?"

She didn't. She had sold my piano, too. I was so angry, I refused to go see her and the new cabin. By the time I gave in and went to see her, she was dead.

Now, I wondered, though this was my connection to Gram, how I ever thought this cabin on the lake would be the ideal place to finish my symphony.

"The Chicken Dance" was back, wearing grooves in my brain. I finally remembered how it had come to be there; the bowling alley had been playing it when I had a burger with Mo and Daryl.

Utterly drained, I collapsed in front of the TV and lay like a log until it turned dark. Then, with my cell phone, my pepper spray, and my new flashlight tucked into my pockets, I ventured out to the front of the cabin for a short stroll, unwilling to get too far from the light splashing from my own windows. Way in the back of my mind, I was afraid Len would find me here. The chasm caused by Gram's death, my disorientation, the feeling I was losing my balance, were all letting up somewhat, beginning to recede. Perhaps due to the more immediate concerns: Mo's attack and the suspect circumstances of Gram and Grace's deaths.

I couldn't believe I had been stupid enough to let Mo trick me like that. I should have known something was very wrong when he drove past the service station. He said he wanted to show me something. What on earth had I been thinking?

The lilacs bled their fragrance into the heavy air as I passed them, brushing their heart-shaped leaves with a hand that was, finally, steady.

I mustn't let Gram's special place be ruined. I have to find out the truth about her death and if Mo was responsible. I'll have to question him, regardless of how dangerous he is. But how?

What if the police never found out who murdered the poor women? After all, what did they have to go on? All I had was the word of two little girls, and no one ever believed children. It seemed so logical that Mo had done it. He had clearly demonstrated his propensity for violence. And there was the matter of the missing jewelry. If one or both of the women accused him and threatened to take legal action, would that be enough of a motive for him to murder them?

Maybe Martha would want to protect her darling son. Could she have killed them? I thought again of their lungs filled with mud. It would take someone stronger than Martha to hold down my Gram.

And if not Mo, not Martha, then who? Everyone liked both of the women. Well, obviously not everyone. I kicked at the gravel with all the viciousness that had been building up inside of me.

I had to face the fact that the killer might never be exposed. Could I stay here then? Even if the police did find out who was responsible, it wouldn't bring Gram back. It wouldn't change our last angry, strained months. It probably wouldn't heal my conscience. Maybe it was time to read the letter I had found in the cabin.

"Hi there," a voice called. I looked in every direction, seeing no one. Then she called again and I realized Eve, the next-door baking dervish, was kneeling astride the ridge of her roof.

Alarmed she should be up there in the dark at her age, I asked what she was doing.

"Mending the roof. There's a hole up here and the squirrels are coming in and living in my attic. I've got to plug it up."

"Do you need help?" She didn't look any too steady, teetering on the ridge. She stapled screen over the hole with quick, jerky movements. The staples *thunked* into the shingles.

"I have a flashlight," I said. "Do you want me to come up and give you some light?"

"Oh no, dearie, I can do it myself. Nothing to it. I'll be done in a few minutes. I have to try and catch 'em when they're all out. Hope there aren't any inside. I'm coming down in a minute."

Should I stay and make sure she gets down safely? I would, but this wind is getting chilly. I don't have a jacket on, and my hair is still damp from my shower.

I shrugged and left her there. An independent woman, that's for sure.

Walking back to the cabin, I saw a piece of paper fluttering underneath a rock beside my front door. I knocked the rock aside with my toe, snatched up the paper and unfolded it. It was crudely lettered:

Ida Miller drowned. Period.

I almost dropped the paper. I reread it three times, getting angrier each time, trying to picture who would write such a thing and put it by my door. Ida Miller drowned? Period? Like hell she did!

The note wasn't proof, but it convinced *me* someone at this lake killed her. Anyone could have placed the note there, but who knew I was here and which cabin I was in? It also told me someone knew I wanted to find the killer. I shivered in the evening air and decided to stay inside.

The warm cabin welcomed me back. I crumpled the note. An irrational impulse to find Gram and tell her about the note flashed through my mind.

Cressa, you're hysterical. Gram is dead.

And someone had killed her.

I had to find out who had left the note. I owed it to my dear Gram.

Gram, can you forgive me for my stupid, petty anger? If I find your killer, if I write you a masterpiece—would that do it?

A tear fell on the wrinkled paper in my hand. I opened the door of the pot-bellied stove to burn the paper, then thought better of that, since it might have fingerprints. Instead, I stuck the paper on the counter, then lit the stove. The flames hypnotized me. They leapt in blurred beauty through my tears. The fire seared my soul with its first fierce blast. The warmth relaxed my stiff shoulders.

I blinked and my vision cleared. I knew Gram couldn't forgive me; she wasn't here to do it. I had to forgive myself. Easier said than done, like playing a seven-piece drum set. It also wasn't easy baiting the new traps with the cheese I had bought. The mousetraps came with instructions, but the instructions assumed you already knew how to do it before you started reading them. I mangled several pieces of cheese before I managed to get the delicate balance just right. My hands were shaky again. I snapped my finger twice. That's not a good thing for a keyboard player to do.

That night, I piled on the blankets, made sure the shades were drawn, and slept on the porch again. This time I had my flashlight handy in case of midnight excursions. My pepper spray was also handy.

The mystery surrounding my Gram's death was running through my head, keeping me awake, but I must have dozed off because I was awakened by a sharp *thwick*. I bolted upright in the bed, then realized it had been a trap going off. I smiled.

Ah, it's working. Soon I'll be rid of mice.

I had just fallen asleep again when the second one sprang. All was quiet for a few moments, then there was a scuffling sound. It stopped and started several times. I guessed the second mouse had not been killed and was struggling in the trap, dragging it around the floor.

I silently gagged, picturing the torture of the critter's gradual loss of life. I couldn't return to sleep with the chorus of death throes, and it went on for ages.

An owl sat hooting next to the porch, an eerie, haunting cry, like a hoarse ghost, saying *oo-oo-a-OOO* over and over. I was fascinated by the sound, and lay listening to it as the noises from the trap became weaker and weaker.

Then a startling scream brought me upright again. It came from the woods just outside the porch. A ferocious battle ensued on the ground of the forest with screams and snarls and grappling.

A light rain began to fall and I heard the huge wings of the owl flap past the porch screens after the battle had raged and quieted, but the victim had not been taken or killed. It continued to scream at intervals, then to whimper piteously, fainter and fainter, until it, too, was quiet. It took the poor creature about an hour to die.

Loss hung about me, a cold, unwelcome, smothering shroud.

-23-

Marche Macabre: Death march (Fr.)

The droning of the tractor motor awakened me: a comforting, prosaic sound after the torturous drama in the night. I lay snug in drowsy contentment for a few moments, sniffing the freshly mown grass. Then the snapping of the traps in the night sprang to mind.

Reluctant to face the inevitable, I lolled awhile, but eventually struggled out of bed and tiptoed over to inspect the carnage. One mouse, presumably the first one, had been pinned by the neck. The other, the one that had struggled for so long, had been caught across his little tummy.

Oh my god. They look so cute with their tiny pink paws and precious little faces. They seemed peaceful despite the agony they'd been through.

I picked up the traps, swallowed the bile rising in my throat, and carried them outside. I managed to empty the sad contents into the dense growth on the hillside.

The woods drew me to them through the haunting thoughts of the clash I had heard in the night. It was a different world by sunlight. I poked around in the damp underbrush for a trace of the fierce life-and-death struggle I had heard in the wee hours, but could find no signs of it.

Nothing in the cabin looked good for breakfast, so I took a couple of Eve's cookies out of the baggie and looked at them. They smelled okay. A few bites went down well, but I left it at that, not wanting a recurrence of yesterday's sour stomach. For now, my tummy was behaving. I was getting to be overly paranoid, suspecting the worst of everyone. Even suspecting that gentle Eve would give me poisoned cookies. Still, I quit eating the one I'd started.

Daryl, true to his promise, came by early and drove me into Alpha to fetch my car. He came to my door and put his warm hand on the small of my back, guiding me to his car. His hand felt strong and safe. We chatted about his job and my classes on the way to my car. After professing myself still in his debt, I drove back to the lake. On the way, I was surprised at how Daryl lingered in my thoughts.

Bright, brittle sunlight flooded into the cabin when I returned.

Chief Bailey's Alpha police cruiser was parked on the road in front of my cabin, but I didn't see him anywhere. I went inside and tried to decide what to do with my day. Was my stomach upset again because I knew Gram's funeral was this afternoon?

Chief Bailey decided what I'd do with my next half hour when he knocked on the door, showed me a warrant, and said he needed to search my cabin.

"What are you looking for?" I asked, completely bewildered by this development.

He didn't answer my question. "Step outside, please, Cressa. It won't take long. And I'll have to ask you to stay in the area for a few days."

"Wait," I said. "There's something I want you to see."

He ducked to get through the door and I showed him the note I'd found.

The chief scowled at it, then slid it into a paper bag and told me to wait outside.

I hadn't decided what I'd do after both the funerals, but now I would be forced to stay here until the chief said I could leave.

Al was outside his place and we joined each other on the road.

"He just searched my place, too," he said, stooping down to speak softly to me.

"Why? What's he looking for?"

"Evidence, I suppose, that either you or I killed Grace or Ida. I think it's just something they have to do."

"I've read," I said, "that the close relatives become the first suspects, but I never thought it would apply to me."

When Chief Bailey came out he gave me a grim wave, folded himself into his car, and drove off. I assumed he hadn't found anything to prove I had murdered anyone. I still had to fill the hours between now and Gram's service.

I needed to think about Gram and Grace and Mo and decide which course I should take, and what I could do about the murders, if anything. The Alpha chief had searched our houses, but no one was going back across the lake to where I'd found them—and Grace's glasses. If I went over there on foot, instead of rowing across the lake, maybe I could find something additional. Maybe something of Gram's would be there, too.

The sun had burned the dew off of the grass, the air was still humid, and the ground with its puddles reminded me we'd had a night rain.

As I leaned down to put bug repellent on my legs—remembering Mrs. Toombs's comment about the mosquitoes—my head started to pound and my stomach became even queasier. I popped two aspirins for my head, an antacid mint for my gut, grabbed my pepper spray, in case, and started out.

I was met by a tall, beefy, worried-looking man on the road in front of my cabin. He strode along, concentrating on the ground before him.

"Good morning," I called. He looked like a man who needed help.

He looked up with a deeper frown. I drew back at his fierce expression, then he stepped closer and gave me a sheepish grin.

"Sorry to give you a scare. I don't look too friendly today, do I? Don't feel too friendly, to tell you the truth. My kids are all sick, all five of them. I don't know when they've all been sick on the same day. I'm Freddie Fiori, by the way. We live in the trailer at the end of the campground. Over by the fence."

He stuck out his large, meaty hand and I shook it.

"Hi, I'm Cressa Carraway. Ida Miller's granddaughter."

"What a tragedy to lose her. And then Grace, too." He shook his head. "She thought the world of you. I haven't known her long—we moved here recently—but she was a super person. We all miss her."

"Thank you," I gulped. *Someday it won't hurt to talk about her.* As far as I knew, the autopsy results hadn't been released yet. He didn't seem to know, and I didn't think I should spread the news about them being murdered.

"What's the matter with your children?" I knew, from his abundance of black glossy curls that, as Martha had told me, the noisy kids playing at Eve's yesterday were his.

"Stomach flu or something. They're not too sick, it's just that they're *all* sick." He smiled at his predicament. "My wife is at work today so I get to nurse them all by myself. I walked part way down to Toombses' to use the phone to call the doctor—ours is disconnected—then I decided not to. They're really not that bad. I'll tend to them myself today and see how they are tomorrow. Pat'll take over when she gets home tonight. My wife's a nurse."

"They were at Eve's yesterday, weren't they?"

"Were they? I know they like to visit her. She usually gives them cookies."

"So they eat her cookies often?"

"Just every time they go there."

I bit my tongue. If they'd had her cookies before, that probably wasn't what was making them—and me—sick. Al Harmon did say Eve shouldn't be around children, though. And her chopping those rhubarb leaves... I wondered if some of those leaves could have ended up in the cookies.

"They've never gotten sick from her baking before? I wonder if her cookies ..."

He gave an uneasy glance back toward his trailer. "They don't get a lot of goodies at home lately. I'm unemployed and today, with the kids sick, that cuts into my job-hunting time. I'm doing a few errands and odd jobs for Toombs and he's supposed to be taking some of the fees off for staying here. Plus he's supposed to be paying me. Have you met him?"

"Yes, I have."

"Hard man to deal with. Don't get along with him too well. The less I see of him the better. I'm hoping to find a real job pretty soon, get out from under him."

"Good luck," I offered as he walked on. This wasn't the right time to talk to him about mowing the grass at my cabin. "Let me know if there's anything I can do."

"Thanks," he called back to me and continued back to his home.

Songbirds serenaded me as I descended the crude steps that led down to Gram's boat dock. At the bottom of the hill the heat was stronger, the air close and hard to breathe.

Maybe there will be a breeze out on the dam, and surely it'll be cooler in that dense growth on the other side of the lake.

In the middle of the flat grassy space, I spied a rabbit, grazing in the sun. I paused, but he soon saw me and whisked away. A rhythmic sound from the other side of the clearing, over by the dam, caught my attention. Hoping to spot a woodpecker, I tiptoed toward the tapping. On the far side of the meadow, a path led through the bushes to a set of four wooden steps that would take me onto the dam, which sat a few feet higher than the meadow. A small man in denim overalls and a plaid shirt knelt in front of the stairs, nailing a new board onto one of the steps. Not a woodpecker after all.

He stopped working and looked up at my approach. He didn't smile, but didn't look unfriendly either, just curious. I told him who I was.

"Oh, yes, the missus said she saw you. I'm Wayne Weldon. Sheila met you yesterday, she said. How do you do?"

He attempted to rise, but lurched sideways on his way up. He was more successful on the second try, and stuck out a dirty hand, his breath coming hard out of his open mouth.

When I approached within handshaking distance, the smell of whiskey on his labored breath was evident. His lack of sobriety accounted for the rather glazed, dropped-chin, expressionless look.

"Sheila said you was asking if she was down by the lake when Ida died." Wayne was a Jack Sprat counterpart to his wife, dry and lean.

"Well, I'm trying to find out more about her death."

"She drowned." His nod of emphasis almost destroyed his precarious balance.

"Yes, I know." Time to change the subject before he fell over. I was reminded again that the fact of murder hadn't been announced yet. "I told your wife I think this is a beautiful place. Everything is so well tended."

"Well, you know, I used to come here every once in a while when I was a boy. When Sheila's family had their cabin here, of course, nice big one. They'd invite me over sometimes in the summer."

He gripped the rail as he looked past me, his vacant eyes focusing on the unseen past. "That was when it was really nice here. Old Man Grey took real pride in this place. He didn't let a day go by he didn't look the whole place over." Then he came back to the present and bored into me with his bloodshot eyes. "Toombs, now, he don't even get outdoors some days. It's okay, I guess, but there's a lot of things that don't get done. Makes Sheila upset when she thinks about it." He shook his head sadly, contemplating the ground.

"Well, it looks fine to me." I decided to end this conversation. I had things to do. Besides, it sounded much like the one I had already had with his wife. Except she was sober. "It was nice to meet you," I lied with a slight smile, then edged past him up the steps onto the dam.

The lake lay about three feet below the dam, but the shallow creek running through the trough on the other side was about ten feet down. At the edge of the lake, the water was swampy. I wondered if this was where the bullfrogs I heard at night would gather. On a partially submerged log, one end poking out of the shadows into the sunshine, was a bump I thought might be a sunning turtle. I waited a few seconds, willing it to move and prove me right—I wanted something nice to happen today—but it refused to budge. Maybe it was just a knot. I needed to get across to the place I'd found Gram. I turned to move on.

Splash! I whirled around. The bump was gone and ripples spread from the log into the lake. Another loss.

When I got to the middle of the dam, I could see pudgy Sheila still mowing the steep hillside below from my cabin. That must be the chore she was arguing about with Toombs the day before. I didn't think she had done any mowing after that, in spite of the orders I had heard him giving her, but I wasn't sure. The sound of the tractor was becoming so familiar I hardly noticed it any more. Sort of like background music. I waved to Sheila and she waved back.

I was grateful to feel a slight breeze out on the dam. The wind carried the sweet scent of the white and yellow wildflowers that grew there, as well as a faint smell of grass from the distant hillside.

Even the grass that grows here on the dam is trimmed. It would have to be done by hand, maybe with a weed-whacker. Wayne and Sheila have a great deal to do.

I made my way across the earthen dam, the sunlight and sweet-smelling air beginning to dissolve my headache and ease my roiling stomach.

As I walked, one of the themes from my composition wound through my head, but lay lifeless in my mind.

Why doesn't it sing? Why does it just plod along? Is there something I'm missing that prevents my music from coming alive?

If no one ever found out who killed her, this would have to be my memorial to Gram. But for my memorial to make up for failing to find justice, it would have to be magnificent. And this was far from magnificent. I wondered again: was I even capable of it?

First, I had to have something of myself to put into it. I lacked inner focus. My musical thoughts were all over the place; there was no coherence. One idea would come, then another would spring up, but there was nothing to bind them together. Were any of them any good?

I reached the other side of the dam, almost without realizing it, lost in my thoughts.

That's good. It's nice to have a few minutes' break from the trouble in paradise. Although there's a new woe, Freddie Fiori with five sick children.

I put that thought down as best I could, shoved it into the back of my mind, behind Gram and Grace, and started humming one of the themes from my composition again.

The area at the end of the dam was a smooth grassy bank for a short distance. The grass here had been recently mown, also. There was a road beyond the dam that the tractor would use to get here. I even spied distinctive, large-ribbed tire tracks in the soft dirt where the grass was thin at my feet. They led to an obscure dirt trail, behind a screening wall of vegetation that wound off through the woods. This, I thought, must be the trail.

Bursting through the greenery, I set off down the track. The flowers made a nice distraction. Tiny purple blossoms peeped through the shadows beneath the shielding foliage. More of the yellow and white daisy-like blooms smiled in the sunny spots. Small, shy, green plants hid under the cover of the larger growth. Damp spots made me detour onto the high edge of the path in places.

My mood was lifting. What a beautiful spot.

But, as I progressed deeper into the woods, I started noticing the mosquitoes, hovering over the small puddles in the path left from the recent rain, darting out of the growth to buzz beside my head. Small black gnats joined the attack. I pulled the bottle of bug repellent out of my pocket and patted a few more drops into my hair, which the dive-bombing gnats were using for target practice. The sharp menthol smell made my head ache anew.

The path veered near the water in several spots. I came to a place that was clear of large growth down to the water's edge and I could see the lake clearly at that point. I instantly regretted not having my camera with me, but it was back in Chicago. The lagoon was perfectly framed by large trees on either side of the clear space and edged by high-growing sunflowers that nodded happily at the sparkling, rippling waters.

I was cheered again and my head began to throb less intensely. I was short of breath from the exertion of puddle jumping and slogging through mud, so I sat on a stump and watched the lake for a minute or two. I was beginning to be afraid of what I might find, my resolve weakening. Water striders, their legs thin as spider web filaments, did their mysterious stroll over the tops of the ripples. For once, the tranquility was not shattered by loud children, shouting property managers, or noisy machinery.

All I could hear were the gentle lapping of the water on the mud shore, the breath of the wind through the towering trees, and the lazy humming of insects, with an occasional harsh buzz from a mosquito. If I listened intently, I could hear the distant drone of the tractor, sounding far, far away. The forest behind me exuded the odor of damp, verdant growth.

There was a purpose for this walk, I reminded myself. With a sigh I got up and started on, but my eye was caught by something small and bright blue sticking out of the dirt beside the path. I knelt down and dug it out. A Barbie shoe. It had probably come off Rachel's doll. What a marvelous place these woods would be for kids to play. If only murdered women's glasses weren't also buried here.

The path was rather overgrown in places, I thought, but far from impassable. It would be easy to fall into the water if you slipped at one of the sloping places where the path bordered the lake. *I'd better be careful.*

Someone had used the path recently. I could see footprints here and there where the ground was still soft. Two peculiar furrows ran along the middle of the trail, parallel to each other. I left a few of my own prints, too, my shoes repeatedly sinking into the mud.

I walked on past the shy forest flowers that hid deep in the lush foliage. I spotted a few pale pink petals and bright yellows, even colorful orange and red mushrooms.

A few feet off the path, was a large yellow... *something*. It was too large for a flower. I stepped off the path, into the weeds. Waded toward it. But I was halted abruptly by vicious thorn bushes, and had to turn back to the trail.

A peculiar odor drifted by. I wondered if there was an outhouse nearby. The odor intensified as I went on, as did the insects. A couple of large hawks, or maybe vultures, traced graceful arcs above the trees. Clawing at the scratches on my legs and arms, I continued my trek, determined to get to my goal. Annoyed at my clumsiness with the thorns, I batted at the angry insects hovering around my face. The ache in the back of my head was returning with twice its original vigor. "The Song of the Volga Boatmen," the version I had played in grade school, the one we always sang "Yo Ho Heave Ho" to, thrummed with the waves of pain in my head.

"I can't believe there are this many bugs in the world." I realized I had said it out loud. There were dozens of mosquitoes, gnats, and—what was this?—a huge swarm of flies swirling around my feet. The flies were much louder than the other insects.

They whined, louder now, around something buried in the brush by the side of the path. The furrows I had noticed earlier led into a large shrub that crowded the path.

Being careful not to prick myself this time, I stooped and peered under the branches of another thorn bush. I didn't need any more scratches. I pulled up the tip of a leaf and bent further to see into the bush better. One furrow led to a shoe. A very muddy shoe. Another shoe was close beside it, and both of them contained feet.

"My god!" I whimpered to myself and the flies. "It's... It's... I've found another dead body!"

-24-

Netto: In a neat, clear, distinct style (Ital.)

The body was crumpled so that the face wasn't visible to me. The clothes were so muddy, and the light so dim, I couldn't tell who it was, but it looked like a medium-sized man. The shoes were men's loafers, not the kind to wear hiking this trail. Part of me wanted to push into the brambles and see who it was, but most of me was repulsed by the fetid, unhuman, fly-covered thing, and I wanted to stay far away from it. I knew I shouldn't move it this time, like I had Gram and Grace.

No more bodies. Please.

Then my repulsion was overtaken by fear. My skin prickled at the thought that this body had obviously been well hidden, the way it was shoved up under that thorn bush. A hidden body meant someone had hidden it. And that meant someone didn't want it to be found.

Another murder!

I sat back on my heels and took a deep, cleansing breath. That was a mistake. The air wasn't too good right there. I managed to get a few feet down the trail before I vomited. Feeling slightly better, I sagged against a tree, turning away from the vile puddle I had created.

Who is it? Who put him there? Who should I tell about this? For that matter, who can I trust in this place? And how could I have stumbled upon three bodies in five days?

The flies whined on, the sun struck the tree trunk I leaned on, and my mind quit working. My whole body numbed. I didn't know if I could move, but I very much wanted to run away and scream. Instead, I knew I had to think. To think *clearly.* I opened my cell phone. No signal.

It would be best to go directly to the police in Alpha and bypass telling anyone here at the lake, or using anyone's phone to call nine-one-one. I would have to tell the Alpha police where the body was, so I counted my steps back to the clearing where I'd picked up the path.

I tried to walk normally, but my limbs felt stiff on my way back out of the woods, across the dam, and up to my cabin to get my car keys. My legs wouldn't move naturally. I had to concentrate on every step, so I kept counting them. I became paranoid and felt like crowds of people were watching me.

Inside my cabin, my hands still shook as I picked up my purse and dug out my keys. Once again, I stopped and took two deep breaths. It didn't help. I had to run to the bathroom and throw up again.

After I rinsed out my mouth, I got into my car and started for the police station, glad I had located it on my last trip into town.

A fleeting thought registered, that my headache was gone, and my stomach felt better. Small consolation.

I drove straight to the pre-fab metal building with a sign that said Police Department and asked for Chief Bailey.

He came out of the back and stood over me where I sat on a hard plastic chair. Kyle Bailey was so tall, he diminished me. I hadn't noticed before how thin he was. Today, his dark look was stern, piercing.

My voice shook as I managed to tell him I had found another body at the lake. He was silent for a moment, then gave a soft whistle. His look didn't turn any more sympathetic, though.

"You've found three… three bodies at Crescent Lake?"

Did he think I killed them all?

I didn't trust myself to speak and dipped my head to avoid his gaze. Never having had dealings with the police before this lake trip, I was intimidated by all the lore I'd always heard, in addition to the fact that they had the power to arrest me.

He asked me exactly where the body was. I was glad I could tell him how many steps into the woods I'd gone. If he asked me what I was doing there, I wasn't sure what I'd say, but he didn't.

"We ought to be able to find it," he said. "Dobson will want to take your report. I'll take you over to Henry County to his office."

After he dispatched an officer to secure the site, we drove, in the official Alpha police car, to the county sheriff's office in Cambridge. Several times he asked me whose body it was and how it got there. I told him, every time, that I had been out for a stroll around the lake (almost true, if you omit the fact that I wanted to examine further the place the women were found), that I had no idea who it was, but that I was pretty sure it was a male from the clothing. I asked him what had become of the note he took from my cabin. He grunted, then said there weren't any useable prints on it. I wondered if he thought I'd written the note myself.

The sheriff's office was in the Henry County building, a fabulous structure, part new and part old. The inside of the old section was lined with green marble, the doorways framed in lovely, thick old woodwork that soared high enough to admit giants. Since we needed to go to the new wing, Bailey led me out of the old section into the modern, which had a more airy feeling, but retained a grace of its own.

We clattered up the staircase, Chief Bailey taking them two at a time. My shorter stride meant I had to run up the steps. After he'd asked at the window for Sheriff Dobson, a large, thick-boned man with an impressive thatch of shocking, white-blond hair came and invited me back to his office. Chief Bailey said he had business in another department and, after he had a few quiet words with the sheriff, descended the stairs from the waiting area.

Sheriff Dobson's office was a pleasant, cluttered place, where I imagined quite a few unpleasant things happened.

He started up a tape recorder and told me to begin, so I plunged in and explained again that I had found the body of someone on the far side of the lake. He was also suspicious, asking me why I was over there, and acting incredulous when I said I didn't know who it was.

He bounced his pencil on his desk in an irregular rhythm as we talked. My head throbbed with each bounce, resounding inside my tortured skull like a roomful of snare drums played by beginner band students. It was all I could do to keep from clutching my temples.

"Al Harmon told me the ruling came back and my grandmother was murdered," I said. "And his wife, too. This is the third body."

"Yes." He didn't congratulate me on being able to count, but he looked like he wanted to. His stern eyebrows were as blond as his hair. And as bushy.

"Does anyone have any idea at all what's happening?" *Why is he sitting here in his office? Shouldn't he be out investigating? Tracking down leads? Something?* "Are there any suspects?"

"I'm not at liberty to say, Miss Carraway. As soon as there's any progress we'll let you and Mr. Harmon know."

This was pretty exasperating. He acted like it was business as usual to have dead people all over. I wanted to scream, or shake him, or both.

At last he dismissed me and I rode back to the Alpha police station with the chief. When I reached my car I got a call from Neek. She hurriedly told me she wouldn't be able to make it to Alpha for Gram's funeral. She had thrown her back out falling off her Pilates ball.

"I'm a terrible friend," she wailed. "I had my outfit all picked out and everything." She groaned in pain. "I really can't even sit up."

"Neek, it's okay. Go see a doctor. I'll pretend you're beside me. Look I gotta go. I don't want to be late. The funeral is in less than an hour. Call me later. I'm …" Were these words really about to come out of my mouth? "I think I'm a suspect in multiple murders."

-25-

Freddo: Cold, indifferent (Ital.)

Gram's church funeral service went by in a blur, but the burial at the Alpha Cemetery was more vivid. Her casket, the one Al and Grace had helped me choose, was lowered into the dark earth while the same sudden, sharp wind that whipped the green canvas of the tent standing over the grave dried my tears as fast as they fell. Her name and birth date had been cut into the headstone when Gramps was buried. It occurred to me I would have to see someone about getting the final date added. My California cousins, Gram's only other grandchildren, hadn't made it, even though I had let them know the arrangements. I couldn't remember if they'd been at Gramps's service or not. I disliked them intensely, but I still resented them for not being there. It only added to my foul mood.

Daryl wasn't at the cemetery, but, as far as I could tell, the rest of Alpha was. I found myself waiting for him, looking for him in the face of each new arrival. It took me by surprise, but I was downright disappointed he didn't show up. He was different than the guys I dated before, and I had to admit, I was eager to see him again.

I hadn't arranged for a reception after the funeral. I didn't know where or how to do it. Frankly, I knew I wouldn't be up to it. What I most wanted after Gram's poor body was gone from me forever, was to crawl away and seclude myself.

As soon as I had heard all the condolences, I returned to the cabin. My blue sundress and sandals, the most staid clothes I had with me, remained on the floor where I let them slip off. Even though it made the porch stuffy, I closed the louvers and drew the shades so I could crawl into the daybed on the porch almost naked.

My solitary pity party was disrupted by a knock on my door. I pulled on a robe and opened the door to Martha Toombs's worried expression.

"Here you are, dear," she said, thrusting a casserole dish into my hands. "I'm so sorry I had to miss the funeral. I would've come if I could have." Maybe she hadn't been able to get the rollers out of her hair.

I stared at her offering. *Omigod, I'm the recipient of a funeral casserole.* It didn't feel right. I didn't ask her in and she didn't seem to expect it. I thanked her, stuck it in the fridge, and went back to bed.

I cried until vignettes of Gram skittered through my dreams: Gram teaching me piano, teaching me swimming, teaching me to crochet. I awoke up with my stomach lurching, my headache returning like an enthusiastically played tam-tam.

Was this my grief, I wondered, or could it be something else? Something I'd eaten? What on earth had Eve put into those cookies?

After kneeling in the bathroom for a half-hour or so, I knew I had to get something to settle my stomach, no matter what was causing it. So I put on a pair of jeans and a T-shirt to drive into town.

I eyed Eve's cookies and decided to pitch the rest of them first. They were about the only thing I'd eaten lately, besides Grace's brownies, which were all gone. I stuffed the cookies into a plastic trash bag, along with the rest of the contents of my wastebasket—mostly musical staff paper with bad, half-baked themes and melodies—trekked down the hill again to the dumpster where Toombs had told me to take my garbage, and threw it in.

I clanged the lid shut and made my way up the hill, meeting Eve halfway, on her way to the trash bin.

"Hello, dearie," she called. "Trash day tomorrow, you know." She clutched a small bag and darted down the hill to pitch it into the bin.

I was relieved I made it to the drugstore without throwing up again.

Mr. Anders apologized for not attending Gram's funeral. His bald head was, for some reason, a comforting sight.

"Couldn't get anyone to fill in. It's not easy nowadays to find good management help, you know." He surveyed his drugstore from his perch behind the counter.

I couldn't put my heart into small talk when my stomach was threatening to rebel. I nodded. I was doing a lot of that lately. I was waiting for signs that he'd heard about my discovery that morning.

"What do they say about your grandmother's death?"

"Um, that she drowned." No announcement had been made about it being murder.

He snorted. "That place has gone to ruin with those stupid Toombses in charge. I wouldn't give you five cents for the old man."

Maybe I could stand a little gossip. "What about Mo?"

"His son? He's not as bad as his father, from what I can see. I only kept him working here two weeks before I fired him, though. The best worker I ever had was the gal that got burned up at the lake. And I have never thought young Daryl had anything to do with it. Don't pay attention to people who say he did."

He saw my puzzled expression and continued on about Daryl. "He's a good lad, the high school art teacher, you know. And a good artist, from what I hear. He's had some showings already."

I would have asked more about Daryl, but I was desperate to get medicine into my tummy. It was closing time after he rung up my sale and he locked the door as we left.

By the time I returned, I was so woozy it was difficult to walk from my car to the cabin. Al Harmon hailed me before I reached the door, however. I gave him a weak wave and said I'd be right over. I couldn't refuse him if he wanted company, as kind and caring as he'd been to me.

It only took a second to swallow a couple of my new anti-nausea tablets. I knew it would be a few minutes before they worked, but I did want to go talk to Al. A can of pop helped almost more than the pills, or maybe it was the combination. At any rate, I was soon human enough to make my way over to where Al sat in the gathering dusk, near the stump where I'd talked with him last night while he cleaned his fish. He'd been to Gram's funeral, but not the graveside.

He waved his long arm for me to follow him and we went around to the patio, to the fire pit, and talked a bit about Grace. He said he was going to pick out her coffin the next day. When I reminded him of my offer to accompany him, he accepted.

"It's the least I can do." I remained dry-eyed, but I noticed a tremolo in my voice. "I thought of you and Grace when I saw Gram lying in hers today."

Al gave me a long look. "Are you all right?"

"What do you mean?" *Is he referring to my nausea or losing Gram?*

"I heard the news on TV. They say you found another dead body here this morning."

"It's on the news? Yes. Yes, I found him on the other side of the lake." *Can I talk about this now?*

"And the Alpha police car was leaving right when I got back from the funeral," he said. "Chief Bailey said they'd be back tomorrow. The news report didn't say who it was you found and Bailey didn't either. He didn't even say why he was here, but he told me to stay around tomorrow. Who was it?"

"I don't know. I couldn't tell." My voice quavered and my chin quivered. I was afraid I would burst into tears again. Or throw up. *I thought those tablets had started working at least.*

Al sensed my distress and changed the subject. "I'm almost thinking of building a fire," he said. "It's late, though. I think my wood is too damp, and I can't find my knife to cut the twine on a new dry batch. What a bum deal getting old is. I can't remember where I put anything. Even in this tiny place. What will I do if I move from here?" He chafed his hands together, the sound rough in the darkness.

"You're thinking of moving?" I remembered he mentioned it that first night, but Grace had changed the subject.

"Grace and I talked about it. About doing a lot of travel, too. It was never the right moment, we never got around to it. And now she's gone."

"But Al, don't make any drastic changes right away. You need to let things settle a bit first."

"I know—that's the prudent course. I might have to leave, though."

"I thought you liked it here." I remembered the two of them chatting happily, telling me of the hobbies they'd taken up since retiring. My stomach was calming. That was a good thing, because Al felt like talking.

"I was born and raised here," he said. "I know this town and its people like the back of my hand. I know them, all right, just don't like all of them. Don't know if I'll go or stay. Or get driven out.

"Grace and I used to think this place was paradise on earth," he continued as we watched fireflies, flitting above the grass, while we sat in the lawn chairs next to the cold fire pit. "We couldn't wait to retire back here. I spent all my summers at this lake club when I was a kid. Our mothers always told us we couldn't swim before the Fourth of July, even in the years it was sweltering hot in June. We had to wait an hour after eating, too, before we could go into the water." He gave a slight smile. "We were disobedient enough to know nothing bad happened when we went swimming on a full stomach, though. No dreaded cramps, no doubling over and drowning, as threatened."

It was almost too dark to see each other's faces and Al's slow, disembodied voice floated to me. A cricket near Grace's herb garden started *teek-teek-teeking*, steady as a metronome.

"On the Fourth," said Al, "the first swimming day of the year, heaven really came to earth. All my relatives would come to the lake and my aunts each brought something delicious to eat: sweet potatoes with marshmallows on top, fruit with something pink mixed in, homemade bread." His description almost made me hungry, even with the way my stomach was. "Our huge potluck started at noon and, after we finished eating that meal, the grownups nibbled and snacked the rest of the day. An hour after we ate, the kids hit the water. We would sneak food the rest of the day, going in and out of the lake." He chuckled at this memory. "Then, when it got to be dusk, we spread blankets on the hillside by the playground and the men started fiddling around with rockets, bombs, pinwheels, and flares. When darkness fell, they shot them off over the water while everyone *oohed* and *aahed*."

His dark form rose, stirred the dead ashes in the grate with a stick. Those ashes were probably from the night I had dinner with them. He would never again sit here building a fire while Grace did her knitting. Maybe he was thinking the same thing.

"When the mosquitoes started bothering the grownups, they'd pile into the cabins. The men would start card games on folding tables and the women would clean up and chat. We children, though, would run wild through the night, catching lightning bugs, and playing tag and hide-and-go-seek."

He quit playing with the ashes and threw the stick down, then sat, and went on. "We'd run and scream and no one would yell at us for making too much noise or for being up too late, because it was a holiday."

We both, for a moment, pictured the glorious Fourth of Al's childhood.

"Let me walk you back," he said after a moment of silence. As I left, we walked past Grace's herb garden. Al paused there.

"I wasn't really interested in plants until Grace started studying them. I couldn't help but catch her enthusiasm," he said, smiling to himself.

He bent down to point out thyme, oregano, and parsley in the bed beside the back door. Light spilled out onto the garden, but I couldn't see the individual plants well.

"Did Grace raise any rhubarb?" I asked, admiring the neat clumps of green.

"No, we don't like it. Sour old stuff."

"Do you know anything about it? Like, are the leaves used for anything?" The vision of the rhubarb leaves on Eve's cutting board was clear. The leaves had looked as if they were being cut up for a purpose. She had said she was getting rid of them, or something like that.

"They'd better not be," he said. "At least not to eat. They're poison. Grace taught me that. There're so many things in a regular garden that are poison, you'd be amazed. A daffodil bulb will kill you if you eat it."

Almost the exact phrase Grace had used. I pictured her bending over this herb bed, lecturing Al on plants.

"Yes, Grace told me that," I said.

Al squatted and pointed to the edge of the bed.

"Did she tell you about these mushrooms?" He pointed to the ones Grace had shown me. The clump was disturbed, as if someone had started digging them up.

"She said those are called Death Angel," I said. He seemed pleased I remembered that, and insisted on walking me part way back to my cabin to make sure I made it back safely. Before we parted, I looked around in the inky stillness. The scene was prosaic, innocent. A light shone from one of the little front windows in my cabin. Eve's place looked dark, but every window in Hayley's cottage was lit. I pictured the empty site I knew was just down the hill from Hayley's place.

"Do you know anything about the empty place down there?" I pointed past Hayley's.

"You mean where the cabin burned?" asked Al.

"It does look like that."

"It was terrible," said Al. "Norah Grey died in that fire."

"That sounds horrible." *Another death here?* I swatted at the three mosquitoes that had attacked my arm. "Who was Norah Grey?"

"A woman who lived here. It was a long time ago. You'd better go in, Cressa. Me, too. It's been a long day. Thanks for coming over and keeping an old man company."

"Give a holler any time, Al. And take care."

I returned to my cabin at last, mulling over everything, my mind spinning slowly.

This fire Al mentioned. Was it the same one Mr. Anders talked about? Who was Norah Grey and how did her cabin burn?

I wondered if Al would be okay. At least there had been no flashes of that alarming anger tonight.

My phone trilled and I grabbed it, surprised it was working.

Neek said, "Cressa, how did it go?"

"I got through the funeral. But so much has happened here today, Neek. Oops, just a minute." I put the phone down and rushed into the bathroom, but it was a false alarm. When I picked the phone back up she asked what on earth I was doing.

"I was sick for a minute, but it passed. I don't know what it is, but I've felt bad all day. Ever since, well, ever since I ate that cookie."

"What cookie?"

"The woman next door gave me some cookies and I think there's something in them."

"Like what?"

"Well, I'm sort of sick and there's a family with a bunch of little kids and all the kids are sick."

"All of you from cookies?"

"Maybe."

"I really am going to have to bring you some herbs."

"Mr. Anders gave me some good tablets. I'm not actually throwing up anymore."

"Who's Mr. Anders?"

"The druggist in Alpha. He's a good guy."

"What do you think is in the cookies?"

"Eve, the neighbor who baked them, was chopping up rhubarb leaves in her kitchen. Some of them might have gotten into the cookies, and the leaves are poison."

"Cressa, you should leave! Is someone trying to kill you?"

"No, she's just a crazy old lady, I think. Anyway, I have to stay here, police orders."

"Maybe you should give some of Mr. Anders's medicine to those children."

"Good idea." I glanced at the clock. "They're probably in bed now, but I'll go over there tomorrow morning."

"But that's bizarre, Cressa. If the leaves are poison, surely she'd be careful not to get them into anything."

I was silent.

"You mean you think she did it on purpose?"

"She's very strange, Neek."

"Could it be anything else? What else have you eaten?"

I thought back. "The only other thing that I didn't buy at the grocery store was a brownie that Grace made."

"She's the other woman who drowned, right?"

"Yes, and I don't believe for a minute she gave me poison brownies. Hey, how's your back?"

"I'm still nearly paralyzed. I'll have to get out and buy some muscle relaxants tomorrow. Maybe some valerian."

I glanced at the clock again. It was almost news time. "Neek, I didn't tell you what else happened today." I took up the remote control and clicked on the TV.

"… at Crescent Lake near Alpha today. Our lead news story at ten. Stay tuned for 'News of the Day,' as it happens."

Shoot, I bet I had just missed a news teaser about "my" latest body. I glanced at my watch. It was after nine-thirty.

"What else happened, Cressa?"

I choked up; didn't want to, couldn't talk about it. "Turn on the news at ten and you'll see. And take care of yourself." We said our good-nights and I baited the traps again. It was somewhat easier this time. As I returned from putting one of the traps on the back porch, I heard the TV swinging into the news.

"… found today by Cressa Carraway at Crescent Lake, in a secluded area of the club complex." I ran and snatched up the remote to raise the volume. I wanted to know who I had found.

-26-

Counterpoint: 1. The art of polyphonic composition. 2. The art of adding one or more parts (melodies) to a given part (melody) (Eng.)

With the dialogue, a brief picture flashed on the TV screen. It was a body bag being loaded into a coroner's van. The picture was followed by incongruous footage of the lake from the swimming area, taken on a different day.

"Cause of death has not been released, although reliable sources say the victim appears to have suffered stab wounds. Toombs's body was found in a remote, heavily wooded area, but it is not known whether or not he was killed there."

Ohmygod. Toombs. It was his corpse that I'd uncovered.

The news continued. "Another source has told 'News of the Day' that a weapon has been found, although it is not known whether it is in fact the murder weapon.

"The victim's wife declined to comment for our report this evening. No suspect is being held at this time. If anyone has any knowledge of events surrounding this crime, they are urged to contact the Henry County Sheriff's Office. We'll be bringing you more on this story as it develops."

It was eerie hearing my name on the news. Did this make me a celebrity? Was this my fifteen minutes of fame? For a reason I'll never be able to understand, a couple of ideas for my composition popped into my head. My good old subconscious had been working behind the scenes for me.

I got out my keyboard and tried my ideas on it. They still sounded good. One sounded better than the others, so I worked on that one for awhile. I went back and forth, perfecting and rounding, filling out, becoming absorbed in my task. This is the most wonderful thing about music; it can make you forget everything and let you get lost in it.

The traps sprang, one after the other, heard only dimly beyond the keyboarding and occasional pencil scratchings.

I sat back, at last, after several hours, quite satisfied with my night's work. I was finally making progress. There was a chance this piece would become something I could be proud of. It wasn't there yet, but maybe…

Then I remembered Toombs had just died. And Grace, two days before that. And, of course, Gram. My face flushed with shame to think I had completely forgotten about the tragedies so fresh and so close at hand.

I saw the traps with their pitiful victims. Not wanting to empty them and spoil my glowing mood, I merely grabbed my spray for safety, dashed outside for one minute, and dumped them under the bottom branches of the blue spruce next to the door.

As I was pouring a glass of 7-Up to cool off, wishing I had gin to pour into it, a rap sounded on the door. I glanced at the clock.

One o'clock in the morning—who can it be?

Through the peephole I saw Daryl under the front porch light, travail twisting his freckled face. I cracked the door open on the chain latch.

"Cressa," he said. "Forgive me for stopping by so late. I saw your light on. Can I come in?"

I unhooked the chain and opened the door. His copper-colored hair looked dark brown in the dim porch light. As he swept past me into the room, I second-guessed my decision. After all, someone connected with this lake was a murderer.

"Would you like some pop?"

"Sure." He was distracted. "How are you holding up?"

"After finding three dead people, you mean?"

He nodded.

"I could be better, but I'm fine, really. I think I might be getting an ulcer or something from all this commotion. Are you all right?"

"I feel guilty as hell. The fact is, I'm glad Toombs is dead. I could never stand the guy."

"You, too, huh? Join the extremely crowded club."

"Well, I have my reasons."

"I haven't washed your shirt yet."

"What? Oh, my shirt. Fine. Keep it if you want."

I stepped over to my tiny fridge, cautiously keeping a path clear to the front door, got another can out, and poured him a drink. As I handed him the fizzing glass I noticed his hand was shaking. There were a few light freckles on his knuckles to match the ones on his face.

"Why do you think you're getting an ulcer?" he asked.

"Oh, my stomach's been sour for a couple of days. I feel a lot better, though." And, to my surprise, I really did. I'd have to remember to take those pills to the Fioris.

"Doc McPherson in Rock Island's pretty good. Maybe you should see him."

"Maybe I will. What are you doing out here?"

"I've been with Mo and his mother. Hayley was over there, too. They're all really upset."

Once again, shame flooded over me for having forgotten their whole tragedy in my enthusiasm for my work. Daryl sank onto the daybed. I perched on a wooden stool near the door.

"Does anyone have any idea what happened?" I asked.

"Not yet. Toombs left the house after dark last night. He and Martha had had another fight. She has a bruise on her cheek."

"What sort of man do you think he was? How bad a person was he?" I had my own ideas, but wanted to hear Daryl's perspective.

"He wasn't good to Martha, or to Hayley. Hayley thinks he's been molesting her girls for awhile. Pat Fiori brought it up not too long ago. No one could get Hayley to do anything about it, though, except tangle with him every once in a while. Hayley was intimidated by Toombs."

"Those poor little things."

"The whole family makes me sick," Daryl spat. "They're a pathetic bunch. Why they've put up with the old bastard all these years is beyond me."

"You said Mo is there, too?"

"He's as bad as the old man, in my opinion. You know I don't usually see much of Mo, even though we're in the same duplex, but after what happened to you I've decided I'm moving out as soon as I can. The less I see of the Toombses, the better."

"The old man who runs the Alpha drugstore said he didn't much care for Toombs, but that Mo was, I think, not too bad, or something like that."

"Mr. Anders? He's a character, isn't he? I liked working for him. Almost everyone in town has worked summer jobs there."

I scraped my shoes on the rung of the stool and my mind ran back to Len. When it was good, at the beginning, everything was intense and exciting. But even then we never sat around talking at one in the morning.

It's comfortable being with Daryl. Even under these strange circumstances, sharing our low opinions of the Toombses.

Daryl glanced at my keyboard and the papers that covered the breakfast bar in their disarray. "Are you writing music?"

"I'm working on a composition for my master's thesis."

"So you're a musician. A music major?"

"Yep."

"That's almost as bad as being an art major." He smiled an easy smile. "I remember a quote I learned in one of my fine arts classes in college: 'All art constantly aspires towards the condition of music.'"

"That's Walter Pater," I chortled in glee that he knew the passage. "We had to learn that quote, too. What do you mean, art is 'almost as bad'?"

"Well, there's not a whole lot you can do with it, is there? If you want to do serious work you have to figure out another way to support yourself."

"That's true. There's always teaching." I didn't feel ready to admit to him what I really wanted to do.

"I know. And that's how I pay the bills. Could I hear your stuff sometime? When it's ready, I mean?"

"Sure," I beamed. *Imagine, he wants to hear my music.* My heart instantly warmed to him. Even though Len had been my theory instructor, he had never asked to hear my pieces. He said he had to work with students' compositions all day long and he didn't want to do it in his spare time, too.

It'll be fun playing my music for someone who is interested in it, not just grading it. Since Daryl is sensitive enough to understand it shouldn't be heard until it's ready, he'll probably be able to appreciate it.

I got up and set my empty glass in the sink. "Mr. Anders said you've had showings."

"Nothing big so far. But a gallery in Chicago sounds interested in giving me a show this fall. I'm pinning a lot of hopes on that. Could be a big break.

"Oh yeah, that's the reason I came over here and I haven't even mentioned it. I want to apologize for not being at your grandmother's funeral today. I got a call from that Chicago gallery as I was about to leave. The guy took forever. Did you notice I wasn't there?"

"I did, actually."

"What sort of piece are you working on?"

"It started as a concerto, but I think now it's a symphony. I know it's an old art form, but one I love. A major composition is required for my degree, which is required for the job I'm hoping for." Maybe I could trust him with this part of myself. "I've been having a lot of trouble getting it going, but—I know this sounds really strange, sort of ghoulish even—but I got sort of inspired tonight by all the horrible things that have happened here."

I couldn't help pacing as I spoke.

"I've been trying to write a piece commemorating my grandmother's life, but I've had a lot of trouble getting it to pull together. I've made progress tonight, but not enough yet. I want it to have fire. I want it to blaze, to burn up the page."

Daryl shuddered.

"Are you cold?"

"No, I'm sorry. I have a personal thing about fire. Had a bad experience when I was younger." He stood up abruptly.

"Gotta go. Thanks for the pop." He thrust the glass into my hands—his were shaking again—and fled out the door.

I stood there, dazed. *What in the heck was that? We were getting along so well. I was about to tell him… We were having such a good conversation. Weren't we? Was I doing all the talking? What came over him? The fire. The fire?!*

Mr. Anders mentioned fire in connection with Daryl. He didn't think "young Daryl had anything to do with it. Don't pay attention to people who say he did." Anything to do with it? With *what*?

❦

-27-

Lento: Slow (Ital.)

The next day dawned bright and clean, the air crisp compared to the soggy stuff we had been breathing since the rain.

When I awoke, I felt more groggy than crisp. Something lodged in the back of my brain, but I couldn't quite dredge it up. What was it? The joyful birdsong washed over me, attempting to lull me into distraction.

Sitting on the edge of the daybed on the porch, gazing out at the tangle of branches and boughs between me and the smooth water, it all came crashing back.

Gram. Gram was still gone. Gone forever. Grace, too. She left the same hole in Al's heart. I hoped the two good friends were together somewhere.

Toombs—the only death I couldn't completely regret.

The sickening confirmation that they were all murdered, the horrible knowledge that an unknown killer lurked somewhere near, that everything had happened was almost too much. It had to be someone at the lake. Something swelled in my head, threatening to shut my mind down if I didn't stop thinking about that.

Then there were my guilty–good feelings over how well things were going with my symphony.

And Daryl. Oh yes, Daryl. *Oof!*

Something was haunting him last night when he left. He fled as if trying to escape something. What on earth could be wrong with him? It was the mention of fire that set him off. I had to see what that was about, and if I could help him.

I wanted to like the guy, to at least be friends with him. *But last night, when I thought we were getting closer, bam. He blew up.*

Okay, Cressa. You have to get through another day. You have to stay for Grace's funeral. And help Al at the funeral home this afternoon. That leaves this morning.

I got out of bed and shuffled my way into the kitchen area. Shoving my manuscript sheets aside to eat breakfast, I hummed softly to myself, pleased at what I had accomplished the night before. *If only I can make the same progress today, I'll start to relax and feel good about my piece.* I had perched on this same stool, sitting and writing, and, oh yes, hearing with half an ear those traps springing in the background. A pang of conscience struck me at the way I had thrown them out under the tree with the mice still pinned under their bars.

With my stomach still behaving, I managed to eat some toast before going out the front door in my robe and slippers to clean the traps.

A metal glint caught my eye. Two Henry County patrol cars were parked at the bottom of the hill. Before I picked up the traps, two uniformed men came out of Hayley's place and headed toward Eve's.

They must be questioning everyone. Finally, officials are getting involved here.

I willed them to find the killer this morning. More cars, some with county markings, some with Illinois State Police logos on their doors, drove in. Two came up the hill, parked in front of the public showers across from my place, and disgorged more uniformed men.

I ducked back inside without the traps when they headed for me. True, I had a robe on, but I didn't think that was ideal attire for talking with police officers. I started to throw some clothes on, then out my side window I saw them head down the steps between my cabin and Eve's. I guessed they were going to take another look at where Toombs's body had been.

Curious, I kept watching. A few moments passed, and I saw two men come out of Eve's and walk back down the hill.

They're skipping me. Maybe, since Chief Kyle already searched my cabin, I'll be left alone. At least for now. That's a relief.

I waited inside for a couple more minutes. Then, when I saw the last cruiser head down the hill, I tiptoed outside. Kneeling to retrieve the mouse traps, I spotted them deep in the shade under the spruce branches. I gingerly pulled one into the sunshine and steeled myself for the sight of the pitiful mangled bodies.

But they weren't there. Could this be the same trap I had thrown out here last night? It looked brand new. Never been used. I pulled the other out. It, too, was clean. Not a hair. Not a whisker.

I set them back on the ground gently, impressed by the symmetry of Mother Nature. Their deaths hadn't been futile, like Gram's and Grace's had been. A creature must have made his evening meal from the mice I provided. Not a bit of their tiny bodies had been wasted.

A noisy engine and clanking metal got my attention. The garbage truck had a hard time maneuvering around all the extra cars, but it eventually made it through. Its huge metal arms grabbed the dumpster. I watched trash bags tumble into its craw.

I returned inside, showered, and decided to put on a denim skirt, for a change from my usual shorts and jeans, with a cotton shirt and a pair of loafers. It almost felt like a private celebration day. I knew I should be sad Toombs was dead, but the fact was, his death might push the authorities to find the killer running loose at this resort.

I brushed my hair and searched once again for my locket.

Darn! I should have asked Daryl last night when he was here about the chain around Mo's neck.

It had looked suspiciously like the one to my missing locket. Next time I saw Daryl I'd ask him if Mo had recently acquired a new chain.

-28-

Lullaby: A song to quiet children or lull them to sleep (Eng.)

Sitting at the counter to work, my mind strayed to the clean, empty traps. I couldn't concentrate on my music. Those mice posed a dilemma. I hated catching them, despised cleaning out the traps even more. It was obvious to me I didn't want to deal with traps anymore. But I certainly didn't want to share the cabin with any mice, either.

I went back outside to collect the empty traps, not sure what I was going to do with them.

"Cressa! Miss Carraway!" Freddie Fiori ran up, breathless and frantic, his wide face a map of worry.

"What's the matter? Are your children worse?" I stooped to picked up the traps.

"Much worse. It happened all of a sudden. Just this morning." Freddie shook his head like he couldn't believe it, sending his dark curls tumbling. "I have to call a doctor. The kids have been throwing up for a couple of hours. Quaid and Blain, the twins, don't have the energy to even get out of bed today. On top of all that, we're running out of diapers."

"I have super medicine from the drugstore, but it sounds like they're a lot sicker than I was. Can I do anything to help?"

He hesitated. "Do you have a phone I could use? Ours is still disconnected. Haven't had the money for the hookup fee. I could use the Toombses' land line, but I hate like the devil to have to bother them. Or to get that far away from the kids."

"No problem." I saw the relief in his face at the offer of tangible help. "I'll get it right now."

I dropped the traps and ran in to get my phone. He snatched it from me as soon as I returned.

"I'd like to call Pat first. See where she wants me to take them." He started pushing numbers.

"Your wife's at work?"

"Yeah, she works in the Cities. And she has the car. We only have one."

However, Ivan the Terrible was unresponsive again. No signal.

I cringed to remember my phone bill, no doubt in the batch of bills Neek was saving to forward to me, would soon be overdue. I still hadn't rented a post office box.

Freddie's shoulders slumped. I reached my hand out and held his.

"It's okay," I said. "I'm sure you can use Al Harmon's phone."

"I should have thought of that." He handed me the phone and looked back toward his trailer. "Maybe you could call a doctor and see what he says? I'm worried about being away from them for too long."

"Do you know the number?"

"We haven't seen one since we moved here. Al must have a doctor. Can you call his?"

"Sure, I'll do that."

"I appreciate it, Cressa. Tell him they're throwing up nonstop and hurt all over. And I'll go ahead and get back to them. Thanks again. You're a lifesaver."

I flew to Al's and banged on the door.

"Cressa, what's the matter?" he said from across the room as I scrambled in.

"There's an emergency."

"Are you all right?"

"It's not me, it's Freddie Fiori's kids. I need to use your phone."

He motioned me in, unfolding his length from the chair.

"My cell isn't working again. I just saw Freddie Fiori and he said they're all sick. Really sick. He doesn't have a doctor in Alpha. Do you think yours would see them?"

"There isn't one in Alpha. Mine's in Rock Island. Doc McPherson. He's a great guy. I'm sure he'll help. Let me call."

He dialed the phone, asked for the nurse, then handed me the receiver. I described their condition, thinking to ask if it was a life-threatening situation or not. The nurse put me on hold and the doctor came on the line.

"I can't say for sure what the treatment should be until I see them," he said after I repeated their symptoms. "And it sounds like I'd better see them at the hospital."

"Okay. I'll tell their father they need to go in." I thought about the lack of a vehicle, but maybe they'd all fit into mine somehow.

"What did you say the name was?" Dr. McPherson asked.

I told him it was Fiori.

"Are they related to the nurse who works in emergency?"

"That's their mother."

"I'll have her paged to let her know what's going on. And I'll leave right now to see them when they get to Moline."

I tore along the road to the Fiori's trailer. He opened the screen door and the smell of vomit hit me.

"I phoned Al's doctor," I said, "and he wants to see them at the hospital. He's going to meet you in Moline."

Freddie bowed his head and swore softly. "The van's not here."

"Maybe we can all squeeze into my car. Or use Al's, too."

He agreed.

"I'll go get my car and bring it over here."

I first dashed to Al's again and he brought his car, too. We didn't have any child car seats, but we would at least have enough seatbelts.

Freddie led us into a small bedroom, close with the rank odor of sickness. The children were huddled under their covers in two sets of bunk beds. I looked closer, and one bottom bunk held two of them. Al and I helped Freddie wipe their sweaty faces and we trooped out, the three oldest dizzy on their feet, and Freddie and I each carrying a toddler.

We strapped the three oldest into my Civic, then installed the two youngest with Freddie in the back seat of Al's Chevy Impala.

"I think I might have an idea what's wrong with your kids," I called to Freddie as we climbed into the cars. "Do you mind if I ask them a couple of questions?"

"Ask away. But let's get going."

As we raced through Alpha and headed north on 150, I turned to the oldest one, sitting beside me. "What's your name, honey?"

"Kisha," answered the girl, leaning her head on the window, her face pale and sweating.

"When you were at Mrs. Evans's cabin the other day—"

"Day before yesterday," she interrupted. Her voice croaked, but she was alert.

"Yes, that's right." *At least she's still with-it enough to know what day it is.*

"Did you eat anything she made, Kisha?"

"Yes, she gave us cookies. We all ate them."

I glanced in the rearview mirror. Al was close behind me. "Did you eat a lot of them?"

"No, I didn't eat *too* many."

"Did, too! You pigged out, Kisha," squealed a voice from the back seat.

"Well, you did, too, James! You just gobbled 'em up," she retorted, turning around and showing some spark.

"They were funny cookies, though," said James from deep in a blanket, his voice muffled by his cocoon. "They looked like they had dirt in 'em."

Or rhubarb leaves.

"I thought it looked like they had pepper in 'em. But they tasted okay," piped up the other small one in the back.

"They were probably good cookies," I said. I didn't want them to worry about anything besides getting well. "It's all right if you ate a lot. You didn't do anything wrong. I just wanted to know if all of you ate them."

Kisha looked at me sheepishly, her dark curls falling forward when she bowed her head. "We all pigged out. 'Specially Quaid and Esta. I knew if Mom or Dad found out they wouldn't like it. We're not supposed to pig out at other people's houses. It's not polite."

I heard a horn behind me and saw Al swerve to the shoulder. A minivan heading southbound did a quick, skidding U-turn and pulled up behind him while I braked, then backed up on the shoulder.

A short, trim woman in a white uniform jumped out of the van and ran to Al's car. By the time I reached them, she had snatched up one of the little ones, her competent hands soothing, her low voice crooning a soft melody.

"Pat," said Freddie. "This is Cressa Carraway, the one I was telling you about. Ida Miller's granddaughter."

She turned and a weary smile softened her drawn face. She was slim and efficient-looking. "Thank you for making the phone call for us. Dr. McPherson told me they were coming in, but I knew Freddie didn't have a car or a phone."

"But we can drive them on in, Pat."

"No, I want to take them. I want to be with them. Besides, they need to be in their car seats. It'll only take a minute to get them into the van."

I didn't want to argue; debating the matter would take more time than switching them. I helped Kisha out of my car. She had become more unsteady, so I supported her along the way back to the van.

"Did I do good?" she asked me.

"When, sweetheart?"

"When you asked that test."

"You did a wonderful job, Kisha." I kissed the top of her damp head and swung her up into the van.

"What was that all about?" asked Freddie as he and Pat buckled in the two little ones. I realized they were twins.

"I think they may have been poisoned."

"Poisoned?" Pat looked horrified.

Al and Freddie stared at me.

"At Eve's?" asked Al, his voice soft.

"You think it was the cookies they ate at Eve's?" said Freddie.

"I'm not sure."

Freddie and Pat glanced at each other and ran to my car and brought back the other two.

"What do you know about Eve's family history?" I asked as they whisked them into the van.

"Nothing. Why?"

"Are you from around here?"

"No," answered Pat. "We've only been in this area a few months."

"I got laid off at Deere and we thought the country air would be good for the kids," said Freddie. "What a time for this to happen."

"I know," said Pat. "My insurance kicks in next week. Freddie, do you think Martha would loan us—"

"Forget it," Freddie said. "After what we—"

"Hush, Freddie." She shot me a sideways look.

"Mommy!" wailed one of the kids from the van.

"Let's go!" said Freddie. They both jumped into the van.

I stuck my head in the passenger window and quietly told Pat, "Tell the doctor the kids might have eaten rhubarb leaves."

Al and I watched them disappear around a bend.

"Godspeed," he murmured.

"Amen," I answered.

I went home and decompressed after all the excitement. It was early for lunch, but my appetite was returning and I was hungry for the first time in a couple of days.

I pulled Martha's casserole out of the fridge and sniffed it. It had a strong smell; too many onions for me. I scraped the contents into my trash and set the dish to soak. I would return it to Martha and tell her I'd eaten it.

I found I wasn't that hungry, after all. After nibbling cheese and crackers I stopped by Al's on the way to Martha's. He was outside on his picnic bench fastening hooks onto a shiny silver lure, his long fingers working expertly.

"I hope those kids aren't as bad as they look," I said, sitting on the other bench.

"Kids usually look a lot sicker than they are. They bounce back."

"It's not right their dad should be here with them, without a car."

"They're trying to get back on their feet after Freddie's layoff. They'll be okay. Freddie's not lazy, you know. He'll get work pretty soon. He's out hustling for odd jobs whenever his wife is home to baby-sit. Guess they can't really afford a sitter very often to job hunt."

Al set his lure down and looked at me intently. "Strange how they're all sick at once, isn't it? You really think Eve poisoned them?"

"I don't know," I answered vaguely. *Should I confide in Al? Should I confide in anybody? Better not spread further rumors about Eve until I know more. And how will I know more? The garbage truck probably just took away the evidence.*

"I'm not sure," I said. "It was just a hunch. They probably have some sort of stomach upset." The back of my mind was concocting a plan to try and confirm my suspicions about Eve.

"You still going with me to get Grace's casket?" Al asked.

"Is one o'clock all right? I'd like to return this dish to Martha first," I said. "I haven't seen her since… since her husband… died."

"That's fine. I can't understand that Martha," he said, picking up his lure again. "I understood his first wife, though. She left him right after they got married. That makes complete sense to me. But to stay with such an idiot all these years?"

"I don't think it's very easy to leave an abuser, Al. I've come close to a situation like that. It's like you're being brainwashed and you lose your will."

"I still say it's a wonder Martha didn't kill him long ago. Her life has been miserable ever since she married him."

He shook a metal rattle and snapped it onto his lure. "Of course, Martha didn't have it all that great with the guy before him, either. She was never good at picking men. Poor Martha."

I rose and turned to go.

"Watch what you do when you're around those Toombses," he warned as I left his cozy cottage and headed toward the cheerful-looking yellow house, both places of mourning. I glanced at Grace's sunbathed herbs and flowerbeds on my way past, and noticed that the Death Angel mushrooms had all been pulled up.

-29-

Suivez: Continue, go on (Fr.)

I lifted my hand toward Martha's brass knocker, but a tap on my shoulder stopped me from reaching it. A short, young man in a police uniform gave me a stern look.

"Are you Cressa Carraway?"

I thought of answering "Guilty," but thought again. Not a good word to use while I'm still a suspect. "Yes."

"Captain Palmer. Need to ask you a few questions."

I nodded.

"First of all, where have you been just now?" His eyes were narrowed to such small slits I couldn't tell what color they were.

"Nowhere… Well, I was driving to Moline, but I'm back," I stammered. "I'm, um, returning this dish to Martha."

He flipped his wallet open to his ID card, which told me he was Captain Palmer of the Cambridge County Sheriff's Office. "I understand you found the body."

The word "body" gave me a chill and brought back the pitiful faces of both Gram and Grace. "Which one?" I asked. His pained squint was not friendly. *Are his eyes always scrunched up like that?* "I found all of them."

"Sheriff Dobson only assigned me to the latest one."

That would be, I assumed, Toombs. "Well, they're probably all tied together." His piggy eyes scrunched even smaller. Did he think I was telling him how to do his job? "Don't you think they're connected?"

He changed the subject. "When did you last see the victim?"

"Uh… when did I last see Toombs? Alive?"

He didn't answer. I struggled to remember.

"I saw him coming out of Hayley's. I had just met him earlier that day."

"What day was that?" He fished a small spiral-bound tablet from his jacket and made a big show of printing my name and the date at the top of a page.

"It was, let me see, two days ago, no… three days ago, I think."

He scribbled in his notebook. *Aren't cops supposed to have tape recorders?*

"No, wait." Now I remembered. "I saw him day before yesterday."

"The day he was killed?"

"I guess so."

"Where was he and what was he doing?"

"He was by the road on top of the hill, talking with Sheila."

"And where were you?"

"I was on the water, in Gram's boat." *Do I sound like a suspect?* "I wasn't eaves-dropping, but I could hear them talking." I didn't want to say they were arguing. That might cast suspicion on Sheila. "It was probably around midmorning, say, ten o'clock."

"What was their conversation about?" He tapped his pencil on the paper.

"I couldn't really hear." Just one side, not both.

"And the last time you spoke with him?"

"That was when I saw him in front of Hayley's."

"What did you talk about?" This man did not like me. He gritted his teeth and his eyes got still narrower. I wouldn't have thought it possible.

"Well, he talked about Hayley, his stepdaughter, and the two granddaughters." Had Toombs been yelling at someone every time I'd encountered him?

"Let's move on to the crime scene."

I remained contrite and polite for the rest of his questions, which were exactly the same ones Sheriff Dobson had asked me in his office. Except I did say I'd already answered all those questions. And I added the fact that I had thrown up near Toombs's body, in case they found the evidence and wondered what it was. I now knew I threw up when I encountered dead bodies.

He continued taking notes. Kept me waiting and fidgeting for a minute or so after we quit talking.

"Okay," he said. He slapped his notebook shut and gave me another sharp, narrow look. "We won't bother you anymore for the time being. Stick around, though."

"How far can I go?" The thought of being confined to the cabin, or even the resort, panicked me. "Into Alpha? What if I need groceries? And I need to go to the funeral home this afternoon."

"Alpha is fine. But don't leave the area. You need to be available in case we have more questions."

Different ones next time? I wondered.

Captain Palmer drove away in one of the Henry County cars.

"Thanks for returning my casserole dish, Cressa. I'll have to apologize again for missing your grandmother's funeral. I don't know what's wrong with me."

Martha Toombs, in a housedress again today, took the dish from me and set it on a nearby end table. Her eyes were moist, troubled, underneath her knit eyebrows. "I'm having a hard time feeling sorry my husband is dead," she said, her voice low and timid-sounding. She patted her pink foam rollers, then leaned down and scratched some nasty looking bites on her legs.

"It hasn't been an easy life I've had with him. But what I feel so bad about mostly, is what he's done to my sweet granddaughters, Rachel and Rebecca." She stopped talking and pulled a very used tissue out of her pocket. "Have you met them?"

I nodded. We took seats in her shag-rugged early-American sitting room after Martha turned down the volume on *Days of Our Lives*.

I waited for her to continue. I couldn't think of a single thing to say. The whole business of incest, or child molesting, or whatever it was in this case, was completely out of the scope of my experience. Despite what I'd told Al, I didn't really, and never truly would, understand why Martha stayed married to such a man. Maybe she had never been able to afford leaving him. But she had spent many years with him, and was feeling nothing at his death. I could easily imagine her guilt.

She started talking again. Her husband's death had opened the floodgates of her emotions and as her anguish poured out, her voice grew stronger.

"He was my knight in shining armor a long, long time ago. Hayley's father left us, ran off with a farmer's wife. I wasn't sorry to see him go—he drank, you know—but we didn't have any support." She dabbed at her red-rimmed eyes.

"Albert was older than me. He was so masterful and he didn't drink hard liquor the way my father and my first husband did. All he ever had was beer. I never thought it was so bad to drink beer. But he drank an awful lot of it, I guess."

She stared at the silent television for a moment, then shook her head and plowed on as a wildly inappropriate ad for a sexual enhancement drug came on.

"Hayley tried to tell me a couple of months ago about him bothering her girls, that Pat Fiori told her she knew he was, but I didn't believe it. He was a hard man and had a bad temper—that's the only time he would ever hit me, when he lost his temper, or when he'd been drinking. But to abuse those beautiful children. I couldn't believe it. I thought having granddaughters was going to be easy after all we went through with Mo and his problems."

Mo and his problems? What was that about? Other sexual attacks? Murder? Or just the jewelry-filching problem? Instead, I asked, "How did Rebecca get the bruises on her face I saw the other day?"

Mrs. Toombs touched the bruise on her own cheek. "He gave it to her." Her voice was soft, breathy. "And he gave me this one." She bowed her head. Was she ashamed? "You can't see the ones where he punched me in the stomach." She scraped her finger-nails at more mosquito bites on her arms.

"And you're feeling guilty not to be mourning him. Does anyone expect you to?" I ventured, trying to give her comfort. Her anguish tugged at my heart.

"Well, I don't suppose so. I'm afraid to show it, but I'm very glad to be rid of him, even though I'm not sure what I'll do without him."

She raised her head and looked me in the eye. "I don't dare tell that to the police." Her frightened eyes pleaded. "Please don't tell them I said that."

"Of course not, Martha."

She straightened and patted my arm. "You're a nice girl." Her voice strengthened. "And there are things you should know about your grandmother. A couple things I need to tell you. Unless… What bothers me the most is Mo. He's in a terrible state. I'm afraid he might …"

For this remarkable soliloquy she had begun to come out of her shell. She had even sounded the slightest bit belligerent. But the last statement was spoken *sotto voce*, in her habitual half-whisper. She even looked around as if her husband might be coming in from the kitchen any minute.

I jumped to my feet when he did. Then he turned, and I realized it was Mo.

"I, I didn't know you were here," I stammered, a hot flush spreading up my face.

"Hello, Cressa," he said, his voice low and even. I shivered with its menace, sound-ing as dark as his hair. "Mom, don't you think you ought to get some rest?" He turned to me. "She really shouldn't do too much for a few days. Doctor's orders."

Martha gave him a strange expression. He returned her enigmatic look with a stony one.

I knew when I wasn't wanted, and I certainly didn't need to be in the same room with Mo. "Sorry to bother you. I came to return your mother's dish and report on the Fiori kids. They've been taken to the Moline hospital."

I could tell Martha wanted to ask me about that, but Mo's deep frown followed me as I hustled off, glad to be leaving that house.

"I have to go into town with Al now. Bye," I called over my shoulder on my way out, pausing momentarily as I wondered if I might be leaving Martha in danger.

-30-

Ponderoso: Ponderous; in a vigorous, impressive style (Ital.)

gain we made the sad trip to the funeral home to pick out a casket, this time Grace's. Al was in an ominous mood. It wasn't that he turned red and threatened to explode, like he'd done the time we roasted marshmallows, but he smoldered the whole way into town. He sighed heavily beside me as I drove the dirt road toward Alpha and moved his long legs restlessly on the floor mat.

I wasn't sure if I should bring up what was gnawing at me, given his frame of mind, but I did anyway. "Do you think all three of them—my grandmother, your wife, and Toombs—were killed by the same person?"

He turned his head my way, slowly, but didn't answer. His direct gaze disconcerted me.

"I know the news said Toombs was stabbed," I said, "and they weren't stabbed, of course, they were pushed into the mud—"

He shot me such a black look I stopped short.

Okay. I won't talk about it.

But another thought suddenly occurred to me. It chilled me to the core. Toombs was stabbed, yes. And Al's knife was missing. And Al hated the man.

I stole a look at him. He stared out the passenger window, his thin shoulders sagging with the weight of Grace's death. I inched further toward the driver-side window.

That night of the marshmallow roast, and again last night, Al had hinted he might be leaving the area. Was Toombs the reason he and Grace had thought of leaving? Or, was a plan to kill Toombs and then vanish his reason?

"What do you think, Cressa?" Al whispered, overwhelmed by the selection.

"Do you know what her favorite flower was?" I ventured.

He looked across the rows of burial boxes.

"There," he pointed, then walked over two rows. He rested his hand lightly on a metal casket lined in soft pink. "Grace loves daffodils. I mean, she loved them." He swallowed hard and deflated, his anger smothered in the cloying atmosphere of the room.

A border of pale yellow daffodils ran around the outside rim of the coffin, and the handles were shaped like leaves. Even the interior had shiny flowers embossed on the satin lining. It was similar to the one I'd picked for Gram. Grace had been the one to point it out to me. I'd settled on a plain brass-colored one when she spotted, in the corner, a casket rimmed in violets.

"They both loved early spring flowers, didn't they, Al?" I said. "Yes, this one would be lovely."

He didn't ask the price, just told the funeral director he'd chosen the one with daffodils.

"Yellow is a good color for her," he told the director while he signed papers for the purchase. "The color of sunshine. She was my …" He couldn't finish the sentence.

⌒∞⌒

After Al chose Grace's coffin, he suggested we stop for coffee in the diner on the highway. He was in a much better mood.

We ordered at the old-fashioned Formica counter and carried our cups to a booth with a window that overlooked the road.

"Glad that's over with," he said. "Is there any sugar over there?"

I handed him the dish of paper packets. "I'm glad, too," I said. "And I hope I don't have to do that again any time soon."

"Hope I *never* have to do it again. Next one should be mine. Someone else will have to pick out *that* coffin." He ripped open four packets and stirred them into his coffee, one by one. I watched his strong, veined hands holding his cup, clanking the spoon against it.

Are they the hands that killed Toombs? That stabbed him with his fishing knife? He could not kill Gram or Grace. I do so want to believe that. Toombs? That's another matter.

He and Daryl were the only two people in this area I trusted. But *should* I trust them? Mr. Anders, the drugstore owner, was the only person whose opinion of Daryl I'd heard.

"Do you know Daryl?" I asked, picturing his open freckled face when he'd rescued me from the cornfield.

"Daryl Johannson? Sure. He grew up in Alpha. Why?"

"Mr. Anders said something about a connection between him and a fire."

"That cabin at the lake we talked about last night. He's the one who set the fire." He knocked his spoon on the rim of the mug and gulped down the hot coffee.

"What?! Why would he do that?" I should have been ready for Al's statement, in light of what the druggist had told me, but I was still stunned. Al thought Daryl set a fire that killed a woman? "That was long ago. How old was Daryl then?"

"Daryl was a child, maybe ten or eleven, when his mother died of cancer. He was deeply troubled afterwards and got caught setting a few little blazes. They didn't do any harm, and he was taken to therapy. Must not've worked, though. Next thing we knew, Norah was dead."

"But how could you possibly know it was him?" Daryl was the nicest person I'd met here, after Grace and, I supposed, Al.

"The fire chief said so. Told everyone who would listen, too. And the fire was deliberately set, he said. But Daryl wasn't convicted."

No, not in a court. But he was convicted just the same—in everyone's minds.

"Probably because he was so young," Al said.

"Mr. Anders says he didn't have anything to do with the fire." Loyalty to Daryl flared up in me. Daryl didn't kill anyone, I told myself, because I like him.

"Some folks think that way. Not most."

Our coffees were finished in silence.

We didn't talk much on the drive back. This placid lake had a long history of violence. Maybe every place did, if only you delved deep enough.

Two trips in one week to pick out caskets had worn me down. Caskets for two murdered women. It was way too much.

I sat on the daybed-couch to think, but popped right up again. Uneasy, I wandered to the doorway out to the porch and stood there for a moment.

A thin cloud darkened the sunlight and a wind shook the leaves outside. I shivered. The cloud moved on.

I couldn't decide whether or not I was secure here. The locks worked, but...

The sun shone brilliantly through the louver windows onto the wicker furniture. The warmth beckoned me, and I decided to sit on the beach and try to think things through. It would be safer.

The killer can't get me in plain sight in the middle of the day, even if he—or she— wants to.

I donned my bathing suit, grabbed my beach bag, and slammed the door on my way out. Maybe the sun would relax and calm me. I wouldn't get into the water today, perhaps never again.

After I spread my towel on the sand and settled myself, Wayne's red plaid shirt and overalls caught my eye. He was trimming bushes at the edge of the beach area, and looked about as steady on his feet as the last time I'd seen him. I wasn't close enough for a whiff, but I knew he was exhaling whiskey fumes just the same.

I put down my bottle of coconut-scented sunscreen and waved to him in greeting. He raised his shears and waggled them at me in response, then dived deeper into the brush. I lay down, closed my eyes, and tried yoga breathing.

In less than ten minutes a shadow fell across my face and I found myself peering up at Martha Toombs's pinched face. At first I didn't recognize her without her pink foam rollers. Her hair looked nice, if a bit tightly wound. I remembered she hadn't been able to finish telling me something last time I saw her because Mo had shown up.

I sat up. "Hi, Martha. Are you doing okay?" *I didn't see how she had kept from murdering her husband all these years—but maybe she hadn't.*

"There's a couple of things I need to tell you." Her fingers played with the skirt of her housedress for a second, then she sank onto the ground beside me and ran sand through her fingers. This was the most decisiveness I'd seen from her. "You need to know. And I need to tell you. I tried before, but… It's about your grandmother."

"I want you to know," she went on, "Mo probably stole jewelry from her."

"Do you know where it is? I would love to get Gram's wedding and engagement rings back."

"I might… I need to… I'll let you know if I can get it." She plucked at the material of her dress again and didn't continue.

"Do you have any idea who could have killed them? Or your husband? Do you think the same person killed all three?"

A dense cloud shrouded the sunlight and the temperature of the air dropped a few degrees. She shivered and looked away. "How could… ? I have no idea." I didn't know if she was evading my questions or being her usual wishy-washy self.

"Your granddaughters told me they thought Mo was present when my grandmother died."

The animation of a moment ago returned. "They did? What a thing for them to say. They shouldn't go around telling lies like that. Mo does have his faults. He has that… that weakness for jewelry."

Weakness? Is that what you call it?

"He's always stolen jewelry, even when he was a little boy. I could never talk about it with my husband. He wouldn't hear a word against his son. Not ever. Not his Mo. But, Mo wasn't there when your grandmother died." She looked away again. "I think, that is, I'm pretty sure, that the truth is… I mean, I can't prove anything, but …"

Martha sprang up and turned her back to me, staring out over the rippling water, to the place of Gram's death. The sun burst forth again, its rays picking up shards on the water and flinging them skyward.

"The night your grandmother drowned, my husband acted strangely." Her voice fell flat. "You have to understand, he always had such great hopes for that boy, and never could stand for anybody to criticize him." Silence again.

I couldn't sit still any longer. I rose and took a step toward her and balled my fists to keep my itching fingers from shaking her. "And that's what you wanted to tell me? That Mo stole her rings? Does this have anything to do with her death?"

She turned and faced me. Her eyes pleaded for something from me, but I didn't know what, and couldn't give it to her.

"Grace told everyone Mo stole earrings from her, too," she said.

"And both those women are dead. But you don't think Mo did anything beyond stealing?"

"No." She was adamant. "I don't."

"So, I'll ask you again, do you have any idea who killed all these people?"

She reached down and scratched her leg. More silence.

"If you do, Martha, you should tell the police."

"I know," she said, surprising me. So she knew who killed them? Is that what she meant?

She took a deep breath. "I've thought and thought about it, and maybe, maybe I'll go to the station this afternoon. But maybe not… I only have an idea who killed Ida and Grace, but I do know who killed my husband."

-31-

Stridente: Strident; rough, harsh (Ital.)

U p on the hill, Mo came out of Martha's house and opened his car door in the driveway, a scant fifty feet away. She rushed away from me. I started after her, then saw Mo turn toward us, minus his movie-star grin. He wore the same dark frown as the last time I'd seen him.

"Martha, wait!"

Martha threw me a frightened look over her shoulder and I shrank back. Mo slammed his door shut, whirled, and went back into the house. I squinted into the afternoon sunshine, watching Martha trudge back up to her house and her pathological son, then fell back onto my towel, my head spinning from all the weird goings-on.

Did Martha tell me the truth? Or does she know Mo killed them, and she's trying to shield him?

I needed to call Neek. Luckily, the capricious Ivan decided to work.

"Cress, what's up?" she asked. For once she didn't sound breathless.

"I didn't interrupt your work?"

"Oh no. I'm on break, meditating. You haven't seen Len out there, have you?"

"No, why? Isn't he back in Chicago?"

"I've seen him a couple of times, so, yes, I think he's staying here. Maybe he's done harassing you. I hope so."

"There's something I need to talk out with you. I had the most awful conversation with Martha Toombs."

"Wife of the guy you found dead, right?"

"Right. She's not very broken up about his murder, but I wouldn't be either if I were her."

"How come?"

"She's the one I told you about, the one that was scared of her husband. And the mother of Mo, the guy who attacked me."

"Ah, makes complete sense. Who would miss a jerk like that?"

"Anyway, she just told me, at least it sounded like, she knows who Gram's killer was. In fact, she makes it sound like she knows there are two different killers. Obviously, Toombs couldn't have killed himself, but I keep wondering if he killed the two women in defense of his darling boy. She was trying to tell me something that she never finished. I wonder if that's what she was trying to say."

There was no cloud at that moment, but cold air breathed on my skin.

And then something clicked into place, like perfect, terrible harmony.

"Oh Neek, I can just see it." My voice caught with my vision. "It all fits. I can just see Gram confronting the Toombses about her rings with her hands on her hips and her chin up, ready for a fight." I squeezed my eyes shut and gritted my teeth. I was so mad at Gram for confronting them. But then, she never let anyone walk over her.

Dammit all to hell, Gram! You didn't have to confront them. You could have told the police—you could have sued them—you could have done a lot of things that wouldn't have gotten you killed. Oh Gram! Did you know how much I loved you? Do you know how much I miss you?

Forlorn tears welled up, quenching my anger.

"Maybe if I'd come sooner …"

"Cressa, don't do this to yourself. It's unlikely you could have prevented her death even if you'd been there. Even if you'd never gotten angry about her buying the cabin and selling the piano, even if you'd been to visit her before this, that doesn't mean you would have been present at the very moment to prevent her death. Right?"

I knew she was right. I also knew, in spite of what Martha said, the Toombs family was involved. Somehow. She was blind to Mo's shortcomings; his kleptomania was a "weakness" to her.

A cold, hard fact hit me. "But listen, this is the worst part. If Toombs killed them, there will never be real justice for either of them. Ever. He can't be held accountable. He can never be punished. And if Gram was killed by Toombs, who cares who killed him? Not me. I don't care if his killer is never caught."

Neek's words, accompanied by the sitar music in the background from her interrupted meditation session, began to soothe me.

I said good-bye and turned the cell off. The fact that I was now truly an orphan swept over me. Of course, I had been an orphan since my parents' early death, but I'd never felt like one, surrounded by so much love from Gram and Gramps. But now, who could I turn to? Who that had loved me my whole life? No one. I swallowed and held my tears back.

Out of the corner of my eye I saw Wayne's slight, gaunt form coming out of the brush with a tied bundle of trimmings. He flung the branches into the dumpster and they landed in the empty bin with a hollow clang.

Could I assuage my guilt by finding Gram's murderer? And Grace's, of course. Was this all connected to Mo's stolen jewelry? I had to make Martha tell me who she suspected.

But I rewound the tape a notch. How could Martha know who killed her husband? Maybe it was her. Could she have killed them all? She doted on Mo at least as much as his father had. That was one of the first things I noticed about her.

My thoughts chased themselves round and round, like the squirrels skittering after each other up and down the nearby tree trunks, until I had to get up and move. I stuck my towel and lotion into my bag and trudged up the hill. Maybe I should tell the police what Martha had confided to me.

Sheila was lumbering out of the concrete-block shower building across the road from my cabin as I passed, a towel wrapped around her wet hair and the usual slim cigar hanging out of the corner of her large lips.

"Hello, Sheila," I called. "Isn't this all a horrible mess?"

"Sure is," she answered, waddling toward me. Her breath smelled of beer. "What a day! I hate it about Grace. Me and Wayne was pestered by that detective forever. Did they talk to you long?" She squinted in the smoke from her cigar.

I walked over to her, beside her mowing tractor. "Quite awhile. I went to the Alpha police station yesterday to report that I found him, then Chief Bailey drove me to talk to Sheriff Dobson."

"You found the body? Those cops never said nothing about that. I'll be damned. I wondered who found it. Me and Wayne wondered. It's good to know we ain't the only ones being questioned." She took the cigar from her mouth and tapped ashes onto the ground with a chubby finger.

"Oh no, they've been questioning everybody, as far as I can tell. It looked like they went door to door."

"Well, I'll be goin' in now. Gotta dry my hair." As she turned she lurched against the tractor and dislodged the red seat cushion, then staggered up the steps into her decrepit trailer, leaving the cushion to lie on the ground.

-32-

Interlude: A musical composition inserted between the parts of a longer composition; an intervening or interruptive period (Eng.)

Rubato: Literally "robbed"; meaning to dwell on and prolong prominent melody-tones or chords. This requires an equivalent acceleration of less prominent tones, which are thus "robbed" of a portion of their time-value (Ital.)

It seemed like lunch had been days ago. I was out of cheese, and the sandwiches from Grace were too bedraggled to eat, so I made a peanut butter sandwich in my kitchenette and ate it on the back porch, a soft breeze sifting in. I could see the side of Eve's place from the wicker rocker.

I was formulating a plan.

After only a few bites, I looked around to see what was making the floor vibrate so violently. It was my knee, jiggling up and down like a snare drummer's stick from thoughts of my "plan." The realization killed my appetite. I hoped this reconnaissance mission wouldn't get me killed.

Okay, it's not a big deal. I've been there already. Eve will think I'm visiting, just a normal visit. I'll say I want to chat about, um, about what's been happening, about the Toombses. She likes to trash them.

I knew I could get her going on that subject pretty easily. But what if she had killed Toombs? If anything, however, she was a poisoner, and he was stabbed, right? I told myself I was doing this for the Fiori kids. I had to go through with it.

Eve had put something into the trash bin last night. I would have a problem if she had already thrown out her cookies. Shoving my misgivings to the back of my mind—with a great deal of difficulty, I must confess—and pushing myself out of the rocker, I headed for Eve's, leaving it swaying behind me.

Eve threw her front door open and clasped my hand in her bony one, dragging me inside. "Hello there, dearie. Come on in, come on in for awhile. Good to see you, Cressa."

No problem getting in. She guided me to a dark green stuffed chair and invited me to sit, sit. Now, would she offer me something to eat?

"Wait a sec," she said, grabbing the small plastic garbage bag beside the door. "I'll be right back. Gotta take this bit of trash out. I forgot it last night."

She looked at the bag and shook it, wiggling the loose flesh on her upper arms. Then she rushed out and scurried down the hill. I stood at the screen door and watched her thin, wiry form scurry down to the big canister at the fork in the road. At first I was afraid she had read my mind and dashed out to destroy the evidence. Maybe it hadn't gone out with this morning's trash. But I should be able to retrieve it if there wasn't too much garbage in the bin.

She stood still for a minute after the metal lid banged shut, the first time I had ever seen her not moving. Then she shook her head several times and rushed back up the hill.

"Sit down and relax," she said, panting from her hurried trip. "You've had such a terrible time. I heard all about it on TV, how you found that old Toombs's body and all. What an awful thing! All this on top of Grace and Ida."

Her eyes unfocused and she gazed past me, into an unfathomable distance, and intoned, "I have found bodies, too."

A hush descended as she sat silent for a moment. I shivered, spellbound, waiting for her to reveal her deep, dark thoughts. Maybe she was seeing her murdered children? She soon went on, talking as if she were in a trance.

"No one ever comes over now." Her voice was oddly flat. "No one but the children. And their parents tell them not to come. You see all my antiques?" She gestured around the crowded room, gave me a vacant stare, and went on.

"I always had a passion for antiques. Henry had a pickup truck. He let me use it weekdays. To go scouting for furniture. I used to find wonderful old pieces. Solid oak." She stroked the low round table beside her seat. "Covered with layers of paint. Years worth of grime. I'd buy them for next to nothing, haul them home, wrestle them down into the basement. Strip, sand, and finish them. Henry never minded giving me money for my antiques.

"The house looked so lovely." She sat perfectly motionless, staring straight ahead, her hand lingering on the table, but I could picture her bustling about, acquiring and refinishing furniture at a mile a minute. It was eerie. Goosebumps rose on my arms. "All those old oak and maple pieces, satin finishes. Hardly anyone ever saw them, though. Henry got real upset if I had people over. Antiquing was fine with Henry, socializing was not. I had no idea it would be that bad before I got married.

"It was wonderful to have the babies." Her voice turned soft and gentle, her eyes warm, for just a moment. She clasped her hands in front of her, looking like she was in prayer. "They loved me so much. And I loved them. Maybe Henry was jealous." She cleared her throat and continued with a bit more volume. Her knuckles tightened.

"He did try to bring them up right, from the time they were tiny. He was very strict. Well, sometimes he was and sometimes he wasn't. He had spells where he didn't notice anything they did, and other times, he would be on their backs about every tiny little thing.

"I wonder if it was my fault." A fleeting grimace may have been remorse. Or sorrow? "Maybe I should have kept them in line more. Henry always said I let them get away with murder."

I shuddered at her phrasing.

"You know," she said, turning her glassy look my way, "after they were gone I had to leave that house. I woke up screaming every night. My beautiful children."

Eve's face puckered, but her gaze remained fixed on something unseeable.

"Hayley's girls. They're not happy. Someone is beating them. And Freddie and Pat's kids. They're so poor. It's nice when the children come. The beautiful children. All my beautiful children."

Eve was so still, I was afraid to move, worried I'd break the spell. And I was terrified of Eve.

Then she shook herself and came back from wherever she had been. She started talking in her usual warm and chatty manner. A drop of chilled sweat ran down my spine.

"I was up on the roof two nights ago, you know, trying to get those darn squirrel holes plugged up. And you know what I saw?" She jumped up. "Would you like something to eat? I have fresh-baked cookies."

She jumped up and grabbed a tin sitting on the counter. She brought it over to the ornate inlaid coffee table in front of me and opened it.

"Oh no, that's the wrong one. Those are from an old batch." She frowned. "I thought I dumped those. Hang on a sec. There's a full one somewhere."

She went back to the kitchen area and, while her back was turned, I recovered myself enough to remember my mission. I reached over. Looked at her again. Her back was still turned. I put my hand into the tin. Kept my eye on her as my hand searched for a cookie.

Eve turned halfway toward me. "You want milk with this?"

I froze. "Sure."

She turned back and got a carton of milk out. As she stretched up for a glass from her cupboard, I snatched two cookies from the tin. They looked delicious, but they had dark flecks in them.

"Here! Here's a batch I just made this morning." Eve thrust another tin at me and picked up the first one. I had barely managed to stuff the cookies into my pocket. I waited for Eve to notice they were missing. There had only been five to begin with. What would she do if she saw some were missing? She merely snapped the lid on, however, and asked if I'd like a napkin.

I swallowed with difficulty. A squeak came out when I tried to speak. I licked my lips with a dry tongue and tried, desperately, to look normal.

"I'm terribly sorry," I muttered when I found my voice. "I thought I was hungry, but I think my appetite is still gone. Losing Gram was such a blow. But thanks very much for the offer." I didn't know where that thought had come from, but I was glad I figured out how to avoid eating another cookie, and there was truth behind it. Besides the fact that my hands would shake if I tried to hold a glass, there was also the worry of what might be in the milk.

"Don't you want to hear about that night? On the roof?"

"Of course. What were you saying?" *How soon can I leave?*

"It must have been the night Toombs died. You found him the next morning. I heard that tractor going. It was way after dark."

She slipped onto the edge of her chair. "I was up there for ages trying to fix my roof—had a problem getting that screen to stay put."

She sat back with a look that said she had delivered a revelation. I didn't see why it should be so unusual to hear the tractor. It was running half the time.

"The tractor," she repeated, bobbing her head up and down.

"What was it doing?" I was truly puzzled. What was I supposed to make of this?

"That's it, isn't it? It was after dark. Sheila's husband came out of that trailer house they live in, if you want to call it a house—I call it a mess—and he started up that tractor. It was parked right next to their trailer like always. I couldn't see what he was doing too good, but I could see it was him that came out the door. I think Sheila was there, too, but it was too dark to tell. It looked like they hauled something out their door.

"Anyway, he drove that tractor right over to the other side of the lake. Right over to where Toombs's body turned up." She waved her hands in that direction.

"But the body was way into the woods," I protested weakly. "The tractor couldn't get in there."

"Well, I know what I saw. Martha was out there, too."

"Martha Toombs?"

"Yep."

"With Wayne and Sheila?" *What?*

"No, it was later. After Wayne drove that tractor back up here and parked it. They went in, I guess. Then I was climbing down the ladder, couldn't see a blessed thing, it was so dark, and here comes Martha walking up the gravel road. But she wasn't walking on the gravel, she was on the side, on the grass, where it doesn't make any noise."

"Where did she go?" I couldn't fathom what meek Martha would be doing out there.

"I was nosy about that, myself, although I didn't know anything yet, of course. About her husband's murder, I mean. But I climbed back up and watched. It was too dark to see well by then, but I could catch a glimpse of her every once in a while, and it looked like she went to the Weldons' trailer. She didn't go in, though, or knock or anything. She went past it. I don't know how far she went, but I don't think she had time to go all the way to the other side of the lake before I saw her coming back. Do you think they're all in cahoots?"

"Have you told any of this to the police?"

"Nope. What do you think I should do?" She leaned toward me, her eyes wide. "A lot of suspicious doings went on that night. Do you think they would all have something to do with Toombs?"

"I couldn't possibly tell, Eve. And you can't either. Don't you think you should tell the police what you saw?"

"I might," she said slowly, squinting at me and turning it over in her mind. "I don't much like talking to police."

It dawned on me she might not be telling the truth. Could she be making these things up because she didn't like the Weldons, or the Toombses? How could she see Martha in the dark when she couldn't even tell if Sheila was with Wayne just before that?

Or is she trying to use me? This could be a sly way of getting false information to the authorities without implicating herself. She probably thinks I'll report her stories if she doesn't. Then she can either deny or affirm them.

"Wouldn't you like a cup of tea or something?" Eve asked, an anxious look on her wrinkled, yet childlike face.

Sure. Probably laced with arsenic.

"No, really, I'd better be going." I rose from my seat and thrust my hands into my pockets. Bad idea. I hoped she hadn't heard the crunch of the cookies.

"But what did you come over for?" She nailed me.

I didn't know what to say. I had prepared an excuse for my visit, but I had counted on using it when I first came over, and now I forgot what it was. *What I really came for was to steal the cookies that are now in my pocket, and to see if you're as mentally unstable as I suspected. I guess I found the answer to that one.*

"I, I guess I wanted to talk with someone about… about this tragedy." *Yeah, that's it.* "You've been a great comfort. Thanks so much." I smiled insincerely and fled.

-33-

Attacca: "Attack" or begin what follows without pausing,
or with a very short pause (Ital.)

Before I could become faint of heart, or fainter at any rate, I grabbed my purse from inside the cabin, made sure to lock the front door, and roared off into Alpha. I may have thrown gravel with my tires, but Toombs was no longer around to complain.

I drove straight to the police station and asked to talk to Chief Bailey.

When he came out to the waiting area he peered down and gave me such an odd look, I reached a hand to my nose to feel if a blob of coconut oil was there. His expression, and his height, flustered me.

"I have some evidence," I said. Damn, I wished my voice wouldn't squeak like that.

"Evidence of what?" How did he manage to look bored when I had *evidence*?

"Well… it's evidence about the murders."

"The evidence needs to go to Henry County, whatever it is."

"You don't need to … ?"

"Take it to the county sheriff's office. It's in Cambridge. Do you remember how to get there?"

He made sure I had the directions straight and sent me on my way, not even wanting to see it. I could hear a radio broadcast of a baseball game coming from the office behind him as I left.

Reluctantly, and feeling underappreciated, I got back into my car and made the short trip to the county headquarters building.

I walked through the cavernous old part of the building into the addition and up the modern staircase, trailing my hand along the cool green ironwork banister, to ask the woman at the glassed-in window for Sheriff Dobson. As before, he ushered me into his inner office.

After I sat in the plastic chair in front of his desk, I handed him my package over his littered desk. He peered at the contents through the plastic and aimed his pale blue eyes at me, raising those bristling white-blond eyebrows.

"What is this?"

"These cookies were in Eve's house. She baked them. I'm pretty sure I ate one from this batch. And the Fiori children are in the hospital. And they ate some of these, too. And this is evidence that they were poisoned. By Eve."

He drummed his fingers on his desk blotter.

"How did you get them? Did she give these to you?" He shook the bag, then set it on his desk.

"Not those, but some just like them. I went and took them when she wasn't looking today. Just now."

He picked up a pencil and bounced the eraser end on the top folder of a stack to his right. When I'd given my statement about finding Toombs's body, that incessant drumming had almost put me over the edge.

"What you have here," he said, "is stolen property, not evidence. It's only evidence if the officials have gathered it. I told Harmon that when he brought me those glasses."

I was startled. I hadn't seen it that way. "Oh. Um, there are a few more in a tin in her house. If she hasn't thrown them out yet."

He pondered a moment, scratched his temple with the pencil, standing a patch of hair on end, then said, "I'll have these analyzed. They can't be used for legal evidence. You do understand that, don't you?"

Those ice-blue eyes bored into me.

I nodded.

"If they do contain poison, I'll make sure the results are given to the hospital immediately."

I leaned toward him. "I think they contain rhubarb leaves. I always thought they're poison. Isn't that right?"

"Oh yes, indeed. Especially for a child." That was confirmation for me that Eve had put those kids into the hospital.

"What about an adult?"

"Are you thinking this has something to do with Toombs's murder?"

"I don't see how it could. Toombs was stabbed, wasn't he?"

Sheriff Dobson contemplated the corner of the ceiling for a moment before he answered me. The overhead light glinted off his light haystack hair. I initially thought he was calling for patience, but he may have just been deciding whether or not to tell me anything more. "Yes, he was stabbed, but the coroner hasn't released his report yet, and, last I heard, he wasn't sure what the cause of death was. Watch the late news tonight. I really can't say any more to you now."

He thanked me for my misguided help and stood, making it clear it was time for me to leave.

I drove back to my cabin at a crawl, truly puzzled. I followed the turnoff into the complex and passed the yellow house. Mo's car was still parked outside.

Martha Toombs and Mo are in there.

Mrs. Toombs was full of mosquito bites. The woods where Toombs's body was deposited was very buggy. Much more so than anywhere else I'd been around the lake, in spite of what Toombs said about all the outdoors being buggy.

Martha, unhappily married and not sorry her husband was dead. A cringing coward to the bully, Toombs.

And then there's Mo. He was upset his mother was telling me about her personal life. Like father, like son? Would he intimidate her into submission, falling into his father's role?

What was the meaning of Mrs. Toombs's confession about Mo stealing Gram's jewelry? I didn't think that's what she actually wanted to say. Had she been on the verge of confessing she killed her husband? Had she been going to tell me Mo killed him? Or that Mo killed my grandmother and Grace? Maybe she wasn't able to speak her mind. She probably didn't have much experience at it.

I started driving up the hill, past the site of the burnt cabin, a sad derelict place to match my dismal thoughts.

Then past the white house with pastel blue shutters. Hayley's house.

Toombs was shouting at Hayley about "decimation of character" that day when I walked by.

Was Hayley about to expose him as a child molester? Did she kill her stepfather to keep him from her daughters?

Past Eve's cabin.

Crazy Eve. I'm certain she has poisoned the Fiori children. And me, to a lesser extent, since I didn't eat many of the tainted cookies and am an adult, besides. The weird thing is, she seems to be poisoning people she likes, me and the kids.

Why on earth would she poison those kids? Did she poison her own children long ago, as well? Or had the murder of her children, by her husband, unhinged her after so many years? Had she been trying to poison Rebecca and Rachel, too? Sheriff Dobson hinted Toombs may not have died from stab wounds. Was he poisoned?

I stopped in front of my storybook red house, climbed out of the Honda, and unlocked my front door. I turned before going in. The Weldons' trailer was quiet. Neither of them was around.

Could the Weldons have killed Toombs? Since everyone else is suspect, I might as well include them.

Did they dispose of the body using the tractor to transport it part of the way? It wouldn't have gone all the way to where I found him. The vegetation was too thick for a tractor. But he had been dragged. Could I believe any of what Eve told me?

I turned and entered my cozy paneled room. My work was piled on one side of the counter. I spread it out, perched on a stool, and went through the motions of composing. I wasn't really looking at the music, though. Instead, I was seeing a parade of people I suspected in the three deaths.

Lost in my circular thinking, I jumped when a knock sounded at the door.

I slid off the stool, crossed the small room, and cracked the door open.

Mo stood there frowning. It looked like he'd been wearing that shirt for a good long while. And the shirt might have been clean the last time he combed his hair. His black waves were greasy and out of control. Shocked at his condition, I involuntarily backed up a step. Even then the creep was too close to me. I had failed to fasten the door chain, I realized.

"I want to explain about my mother to you, so you won't get any wrong ideas," he snarled, slashing the air with the flat of his hand, nearly hitting my face.

I wasn't about to invite him in, of course. I spread my feet apart and stood blocking the doorway.

"I have to come in for a minute," he insisted. "It won't be long. I've got to get back to her."

"No, you can't—"

But he swept past me with a rough shove and faced me from the middle of the room. I stayed next to the open door, clutching the handle. Sweat sprang up on my palms.

"All right," I said evenly, drawing a huge breath. I hoped I sounded calm. Animosity, pure hostility, radiated from Mo's thunderous visage. I tried to match it.

"What did you want to say?" I spat, as rudely as I could. "Why not just leave a note under a rock?"

"What? What are you talking about? I want you to understand," he whined, his voice rising. "I know my mother talked to you."

Pathetic. You do NOT have my sympathy, no matter what you're going to say.

"My father was not a child molester. Rebecca wouldn't finish her meal and was smarting off to him the other day. That's why he hit her. He never struck anybody without a good reason."

He glared at me. I glared back. My gaze strayed to his neck. He wasn't wearing a chain. *What a thing to notice.*

"The other thing is, I think my mother is going through some kind of adjustment period. She's confused about how she feels. You might even think, from what she said, that she wanted him dead. She's always been afraid of everything, but now, I don't know, she's more afraid. I don't know what her problem is."

"She didn't tell you what we talked about, did she?"

"Whatever it was, I want you to know she's not in her right mind. It's probably the grief or something. You understand?"

"Yes, I do. Perfectly. I'm glad you came over and explained it. Thank you." *Of course, Mo wouldn't recognize sarcasm if it coiled around his throat and bit him.*

"About the other day," he began.

"Please leave, Mo. I still have lots of pepper spray left."

"Bitch," he growled as he stalked across the room.

I held the door wide open for him and he threw me a hateful look as he brushed by me. I slammed the door and collapsed against it, sliding down to the floor as my legs gave way.

-34-

Nervoso: In a forcible, agitated style (Ital.)

L almost screamed when another knock sounded on the door. I was still leaning against it. How long had I been there? I yelped, then jumped up and peeked out the peephole. Relieved, I snatched the door open.

"Daryl! Hi. It's good to—"

"Hello," he glowered, and pushed into the room, much as Mo had done. I had never seen such a dark look on his usually open and friendly face. "I just saw Mo coming out your door on my way here. What the hell was he doing here? How long was he here?"

"Well… I'm not sure that's any of your business." *I shouldn't snap at Daryl like that. But isn't anyone in a good mood today?* "What are you doing here?"

It was good to see him. How could I have ever thought that Mo was better-looking than Daryl? Mo had a brooding handsomeness, but Daryl had that gorgeous, glinting, dark red hair and those darling freckles.

"I came by to talk to you," he said. "I thought maybe… But if you're seeing him, never mind." He vibrated with energy.

"I'm not 'seeing' Mo. Don't be ridiculous. He's a creep. You know that. What's the matter with you?"

"I don't know, Cressa. I'm sorry." He looked away for a moment, then chafed a hand over his face as if he were trying to rub his freckles off.

"You must think I'm crazy. Maybe I am."

He opened the door to leave and started to make his way outside. He looked to the right and stopped, then took a step back.

"There's a cop out there, Cressa."

I came to the doorway and stood beside him, peering out, our heads close, almost touching. Two Henry County deputies had just emerged from Eve's cabin. One of them held her by her left elbow. The other walked ahead and opened the back door of their cruiser. She looked so small, like a shriveled prune next to the deputies.

"Good God," I breathed. "I wonder if this is because I… That was quick."

It was Daryl's turn to ask what was wrong with me.

"I'm afraid maybe... Maybe it's something I did."

He turned and gave me a steady, calm gaze. His eyes were a darker green than I remembered.

"Do you want to tell me about it?" He put a warm hand on my shoulder. I wanted him to put the other hand on my second shoulder.

Under different circumstances I could be attracted to you. Maybe even these circumstances. If only you didn't act so oddly sometimes.

"Come back in," I said. "I have to tell someone."

I leaned on the counter and Daryl stood behind one of the stools, his foot propped on a bottom rung.

"God, you look good in that skirt and top, Cressa."

That made me smile.

"I noticed Eve chopping leaves on her cutting board the other day," I began. "I later realized they were rhubarb leaves. Freddie and Pat's kids were over there eating lots and lots of cookies that same day and they've been extremely sick ever since. They're all at the Moline Hospital now. I ate just one of the cookies and felt horrible afterward. Then today I went over there and pinched a couple of them, the ones with the dark flecks in them—the dark flecks that I think are poisonous rhubarb leaves. I took them to the sheriff's office and told him what I've just told you."

"Because of Eve's children, right?"

"Yes. I heard about what happened."

"That was a long time ago. Her husband is still in prison for it, you know."

"I know." I jiggled my foot and pondered a moment. "But what if he didn't kill them? What if she did? Or even if he did do it, what if she has gone off the deep end because of it, and has started to poison people herself?"

"How do you figure?"

"Think about it. It must have been horrific for her when they died. And ten times worse to know her own husband killed them. Agonizing over that for years and years could eventually affect her mind." I could see that glassy stare in my mind. "She got awfully strange when she mentioned her kids to me."

I started to pace the room as I babbled. Why was I rattling on like this? Because Daryl was there? "But she was chopping up rhubarb leaves that day. And they are poison. And after I gave them to the police to analyze, here they are arresting her."

"You must be right." He turned to face me, then took a step toward me. I backed up. "At least about her poisoning the Fiori kids."

I dropped to the daybed as my knees gave way again.

"I hope I did the right thing. If they've arrested her and she didn't do it, I'll feel awful. She's such a social outcast already."

"The courts will examine the evidence. Nobody's going to be convicted of anything just because you suspect them." He smiled.

I relaxed a notch. "I guess so."

"Everybody's a little crazy lately. It's been hard to keep your sanity around here. Is that six o'clock?" he asked, looking at my wristwatch. "Can I turn on the news?"

"I don't know if I want to see it. Oh, go ahead. Maybe Eve will be on it."

He picked up the remote, perched on a stool, and switched on the set.

An earnest newsman was launching the report.

"This breaking news just in from Crescent Lake at Alpha, Illinois, our top story this hour. A female resident of the Crescent Lake complex was taken into custody just minutes ago on suspicion of allegedly attempting to poison several children who also reside at the complex. They are currently at Trinity Hospital in Moline where their condition is not known. There may be as many as six children involved."

The footage of the lake that I had seen on the last broadcast rolled over the screen.

"A spokesperson for the Henry County Sheriff's Department said the suspect will be questioned, but has not been formally charged with anything. Preliminary lab results show the children were possibly fed tainted cookies baked by the woman, whose name is not being released at this time."

The female news anchor took over from the male. "Viewers will recall the case, sixteen years ago, of the Evans children, who were fatally poisoned by their father on Halloween, in order to collect the insurance money on them. Henry Evans is presently serving a ninety-nine year sentence at the state penitentiary in Joliet. His wife, Evangeline Evans, is a resident at the Crescent Lake resort."

Here they flashed a video labeled "Henry Evans" that must have been taken many years ago. A young man glowered toward the camera as he was marched down a narrow hallway in shackles.

"It is not known whether this incident has any connection to the recent murders at the same complex, where three people have turned up dead, but police are not ruling out the possibility.

"We have been asked to repeat the sheriff's request that anyone with information or knowledge relating to these deaths please report to their office in Cambridge."

"Cute," said Daryl, shooting me a glance. What an interesting color of green his eyes were. "They didn't say it was Eve, but there isn't anyone who lives in Alpha who won't be able to figure it out."

"At least they didn't have cameras here when she was taken away. And they didn't say my name."

"Your name?" asked Daryl.

"Yes, as the person who turned in the cookies for lab analysis. I wonder if Eve knows what happened. My name was given out as the discoverer of the other bodies. I don't think I care to be mentioned on television again. I don't need any more connection being made between me and the weird stuff going on around here."

"I see your point," he agreed.

-35-

Ballet de la Nuit: Dance of the night (Fr.)
Répète: Repeat (Fr.)

I peeked out the side window at Daryl's retreating form. He had a nice build, especially from the back: broad shoulders tapering down to his neat, narrow hips, and a very nice rear. He walked away into the twilight.

I wished I could ask him about the fire stuff. Maybe another time.

Dusk was beginning to fall. I had a lot of questions milling around in my mind about Toombs's murder. If all the murders were connected, more information about his death ought to shed light on the others. And Toombs's was the only one I had any leads on.

If only I had paid more attention to the area where I found the body.

There was something there that struck a discordant note. Something that stuck out like a *forté* brass entrance half a beat too soon.

I really would like to look it over once more. It's not that far from where Grace and Ida were found, either. I need to see both places again.

Eve might have seen the tractor going over there the night before I found him, the night he was killed. A hidden thought of something overlooked was nagging at the back recesses of my mind. I didn't know what it was, I only knew it had something to do with the place where I had found Toombs.

I tugged a sweater over my head for the chill that I knew would descend, grabbed my flashlight, and scurried down the steps and across the dam in the lowering dusk. So far, I hadn't seen anyone. My cell phone still didn't work in this area, but I knew my pepper spray would.

When I reached the other shore I examined the ground, and, as I remembered, tire tracks led through the dirt to the edge of the woods.

Of course, that didn't mean anything. Tire tracks were all over the place from the mowing Sheila did.

Nothing here rang a bell, not even a small triangle. No, what was bothering me was in the woods. I batted at the barrier of greenery and found the path. It was easier this time. A lot of county and state personnel had been here after the discovery of the body, so the trail was trampled.

Something rustled off to my right. I whirled around, then stood still, but I didn't hear the sound again. I checked behind me. No one was around. The water lay calm and I heard only the half-hearted twittering of a few birds thinking about bedding down for the night.

There was no yellow police tape at this point; it must have been farther into the woods. Still, I hesitated, afraid to approach the crime scene.

But I knew there were no officials at the lake. None of their vehicles were here. Who would ever know if I just walked in? I wouldn't disturb anything. Anyway, they'd already examined everything. They wouldn't post a guard, would they? No, I decided they wouldn't.

I plunged into the woods and hurried along the dirt trail. Darkness would fall soon. When I was almost to the spot where I had discovered Toombs's corpse, I faltered, then stopped.

The terror of that morning returned. Gorge rose in my throat again. I swallowed the bitter tasting bile down and forced myself to think.

Just ahead on the path, the fluttering yellow tape that closed off the area where the body had been caught my eye.

Maybe it was seeing the tape that did it; I realized the large yellow object in the thorns was what had been bothering me.

It had been, I remembered, behind me at least twenty feet. I picked up a long stick and backtracked. After poking around in the bushes for a few minutes, collecting nothing more than a few more scratches on my arms, in spite of my sweater, I gave up. It wasn't there. I knew what it was, though. A bright yellow thing had been in these bushes. The yellow cushion from Sheila's tractor.

I shone my flashlight into the undergrowth, but it was definitely not there, the tractor cushion that had fallen off with Sheila's difficult dismount the first time I met her. The one that was now replaced with a red cushion. The old one, the bright yellow one, had caught my eye the day I found Toombs, even though it had been shielded by the shadowed growth.

I took a moment to think the situation through, carefully.

The mental image of the cushion wavered and swam before my eyes. I held my reeling head with both hands to keep it from spinning off my body. An annoyed squirrel ran halfway down a tree trunk and accused me of trespassing with a shrill clatter.

Think, think!

I was dizzy. Deep, slow breaths. Okay. No panic.

The cushion must have come along with the body when it was dragged in here. But how did it get under this bush? Was it hidden here on purpose? If that were the case, the killer must have come back to dispose of it. Could it have fallen unnoticed?

And did this mean, positively, that one of the Weldons killed Toombs? No, it only meant the tractor was used to get him here. It's possible someone else used it to haul the body over here. Maybe Eve did, and invented that story implicating Wayne and Sheila. Her story was fishy. Could she see well enough in the darkness to tell who was on the tractor? She hadn't seen a body on it.

Eve was probably strong enough to drag a dead person along a path for a bit.

As I dabbed at the bright drops of blood where the thorns had punctured my arms, I pictured Eve's wiry arms with the folds of loose skin hanging from them. I could also picture the strength evinced when she viciously whacked at the rhubarb leaves with her sharp kitchen knife.

Toombs's shoes had been muddy on the sides, like they had been dragged along the ground.

Did that leave Wayne Weldon out? Wouldn't he be strong enough to carry the body some other way? Unless it was so bloody he didn't want to soil his clothes with it?

I swatted at the battalion of buzzing mosquitoes attacking my legs and arms, even through my clothing; I hadn't taken time to put on insect spray. I clawed at my arms, remembering Martha Toombs scratching her bites. She had an awful lot of them. Did she get them over here?

Before the bugs ate me alive, I had to move on. I left the spot where the cushion had lain, but took note of the surrounding trees and bushes.

It occurred to me that the police might have taken it. I made a mental note to ask Sheriff Dobson if they had found it.

A shudder went through me. What if the murderer saw me going over here? Would he think I was getting too nosy, finding out something poking around this place? And I'd been back to the place where Gram and Grace died, too.

Maybe I should stay away from this side of the lake.

I made my way back toward the edge of the woods, but a sound halted me before I reached the clearing. I clicked the flashlight off and listened. Someone was close by. My nape prickled. Had the killer followed me here? Had he or she watched me search for the cushion?

The growth was especially dense at the edge of the clearing, but I parted it, slowly, quietly, to see who was there.

A man's voice muttered curses under his breath as he stomped around the grassy area, bent over, inspecting the ground. One end of a boat was pulled onto the land. The small waves made sinister sucking sounds against the sides. I squinted through the gathering gloom, trying to discern his features. As he straightened, I recognized the tall, thin form of Al Harmon, his face an angry red.

What on earth is he doing here?

Frightened, I stood perfectly still, cringing in the brush, afraid he would notice me. I didn't want anyone to know I had been messing around near the police-tape line.

He neared my hiding place. I sucked in a breath.

Did he hear that?

He raised his head and tilted it, listening. After a few agonizing moments he turned away, climbed into his rowboat, and shoved off.

It would be too long before his boat was out of sight of the earthen dam, though, which I had to cross to get back.

What could he have been doing over here? Looking for the yellow cushion? Did Al Harmon kill Toombs in one of his fits of burning rage? He could have used the tractor. Anyone could have. The keys were always left in the ignition.

I watched his slow progress and made up my mind to go the long way around the lake to avoid being seen. Especially by a killer.

Darkness thickened as I stumbled along, reaching the tape again and passing it, treading on an unfamiliar part of the path. It was heavily overgrown here and the mosquito situation didn't improve one bit. They were feasting on my arms and clusters of them clung to my skin beside the blobs of blood trickling from the gouges the brambles had made when I poked the stick in to try and find the cushion.

I came to a depression in the path. It dipped so low the lake flowed over it slightly, just enough to make the dirt turn to thick goo. Boards had been placed over this area in the past, but they were mostly rotted and broken. My loafers were not the right shoes for this hike.

I picked up two pieces of board and tried to place them strategically. I succeeded somewhat in making a bridge, but a little of the ooze squelched up onto my shoes.

Night was falling in earnest as I hurried to get out of the woods before it was so dark I wouldn't be able to find the path. I was afraid to turn on my flashlight again; someone might see me. The insects were fierce in their attacks and I swatted almost continuously, trying to keep them out of my eyes.

A beetle crawled up my neck and I almost screamed. Swallowing the cry I wanted to make, I slapped it off me. Another one crouched on my arm. I looked up. They must be falling from the trees. I shivered, then shook the second one off.

Why had I decided to do this? Was insanity contagious in this place? Why had I ever come here? How could I even think of staying on in Gram's cabin?

I tripped over a tree root and landed on my knee, hard. I cursed, wiped my hands off, and kept on. I had to get out of the woods. More mud sucked at my shoes. Overgrown branches whipped my face and caught my sweater. And the insects didn't stop. My sweat, I was sure, encouraged them.

Night creatures started to stir. I heard small animals skittering along the ground, and a distant owl. I sobbed. But only once. I told myself I had to march on.

At last I reached the end of the forest. Darkness was almost complete.

The path came out of the woods onto the paved road outside the complex. Grateful to be out in the open, I looked back to the one black amorphous mass of branches and leaves against the faint luminescence of the sky. I tried to get my bearings and had a flash of panic when the lake buildings weren't anywhere in sight. A few feet up the lane, however, I could see the turn onto the gravel road of the resort. I breathed a sigh of relief and headed that way.

I hiked around the end of the lake, my stomach complaining about the smell. This end of the lake was shallow and stagnant, the water covered with green scum in the daylight. The brackish water was black at night.

As I walked, the rising moon poked above the treetops and sent shafts of faint light into the water.

And that moonlight would illuminate me, too. I would be visible soon. At least there were no houses at this end of the lake.

I reached the main complex and made my way past the beach area, treading on the grass beside the gravel so I wouldn't make any noise. Where the road forked, the right-hand branch would be a shorter distance to my cabin, but it would also go past the Harmons' place. After Al's suspicious behavior in the clearing, I was reluctant to let him know I had been in the woods and had seen him. I took the left branch, past the Toombses' and on around. Martha and Hayley weren't usually outside, so I felt safe going past their places.

As I neared the Toombses' house, I heard an odd noise. It sounded like metal scraping against something. I stopped, then crept forward until I saw, around the corner of the house, a silhouetted figure with a spade, prying up the stepping stone nearest the front door. The metal of the spade glinted in the light from the newly risen moon, and the figure grunted as it heaved the stone up and turned it over.

The person reached into a pocket and, stooping, deposited something where the stone had been, then rose and replaced the rock, stopping often to scratch arms and legs.

My eyes widened in amazement and I tensed as Martha Toombs—I could see the outline of her rollers—walked straight toward me. Had she seen me? She turned to go to the carport and I relaxed. She hung the spade back on its hook.

Martha returned along the stone pathway, still not aware of my presence, stomped on the last stone a couple of times, and entered the house.

Wow. I guess it's true what stage people say. If you don't move, you aren't seen.

I had taken exactly three steps when a vehicle started up not too far away. I turned to see a state trooper car driving out of the complex from the other fork.

Now what?

I managed to reach the cabin without anyone seeing me. I was filthy from my muddy, buggy walk. Sweat dripped down my back, partly from heat, partly from fear of being caught. I stunk of fear.

A long shower did much to restore my equilibrium. I curled up on the daybed, rubbed my bites and scratches with salve, then, noticing the time, turned on the TV as I sat up to scrape my shoes with a table knife.

The ten o'clock news had relegated the Toombses' story to the third item, but it was still there.

"New developments in the puzzling deaths at Crescent Lake. Autopsy reports confirm the latest victim had poison in his system at the time of death. It is not yet known whether he actually died of the poison or of the knife wounds, either of which would have been sufficient to cause death.

"The weapon found earlier has been identified as a fishing knife belonging to Alvin Harmon, a resident at the Lake. Harmon was taken in for questioning this evening."

No! Not Al Harmon! My knife clattered to the floor. That must have been the departing police car I saw. Picking him up.

"According to police reports, Toombs was last seen alive by his wife when he left their house at dusk to consult with the caretakers, Wayne and Sheila Weldon, who live a short distance away, also in the complex. The Weldons deny seeing him that night.

"Anyone with knowledge of events that evening should report to the Henry County Sheriff's Office."

Good grief! Al Harmon's knife! It could be him! Poison! It could be Eve! It could be anybody!

I didn't want it to be either one of them. There was one more likely candidate now, though. And it might be a piece of the puzzle that would tell me more about Toombs's death. I slipped on a pair of jeans, a sweater, and my sneakers and stole out the door to see what Martha had put under the stone.

-36-

Fantasia: A work in which the author's fancy roves unrestricted; something possessing grotesque, bizarre, or unreal qualities (Ital.)

It was another clear, fair day, the air soft and caressing against my cheek. I climbed out of my car, shouldered my purse, burning with its burden, and, again, walked through the high-ceilinged Victorian portion of the county building, then up the graceful wrought-iron staircase to Sheriff Dobson's office. First, however, I would have to get past the pleasant-looking brunette behind the glass barricade once more.

Pleasant-looking, that is, until she saw it was me on the other side. Before I could state my business she intercommed with a snarl into the sheriff's office that "Miss Carraway is here again." I didn't care for her tone of voice. In answer to a muffled question she replied she was sure she didn't know.

"Be with you in a minute," she said to me, riffling through the papers on her desk instead of looking at me.

I felt, even in the modern part of the building, like I had stepped into another century. Most of the building, indeed much of the town, had been built in the eighteen hundreds. The two-story wooden houses trimmed in gingerbread, so typical of that period, faced the quiet streets with their wrap-around porches, some of them with round corner towers. But the town's slow pace vanished inside the sheriff's portion of this building.

The receptionist, turning pleasant again, soon asked me to have a seat on a bench against the wall. Finally, Sheriff Dobson came to the heavy door, swung it open, and waved me into his cluttered office, an annoyed frown on his face. He sat on the edge of his desk while I took the plastic chair, then raised his bristling white-blond eyebrows in question. "You need to talk to me?" His sky-blue eyes were cold.

I wonder if he thinks I'm going to confess. "Yes, I'm afraid I've found something. Something new."

After a long-suffering type of a sigh, he said, "Let's see it."

I opened my purse with shaky fingers and pulled out the plastic baggie that held a couple of mushrooms, plus an extra surprise from under Martha Toombs's stepping stone. The mushrooms were crushed flat, but still recognizable as such, tan with white spots on the tops and white gills underneath. I held the bag out to him. He reached for it.

"And this is?"

"Well …" I took a breath and began, looking at the floor to avoid those eyes. "I was out last night and walked by Martha Toombs's place. It was after dark. She didn't see me." He drummed his usual pencil on his desk and swung the bag with the other hand. "She was prying up one of the stepping stones in their walkway and I saw her put something under it."

"And this is it?" He waved the bag at me. "How did you get it?"

"I went back later and found those mushrooms squashed under the rock like that. And those earrings."

"They were in this bag?"

"Noooo, I carried them to my place and put them in the bag. I just took a couple of them. The rest are still there." I still didn't look up. If this was grilling, I didn't like it.

"And why do you think we would want these things?" He ducked his head down trying to catch my eye. I knew those blue eyes would be icy. It felt cold in the office.

"Because, because I think the mushrooms are poison—Death Angels."

"More poison? And your theory, I assume, is that Mrs. Toombs poisoned her husband?" He slid off the corner of his desk.

"I don't know. But the news report said they're not positive he died of the stab wounds. He might have died of poisoning. Why would she be hiding these things at night, anyway?" I looked up at him with my question.

"That's a good point. If she did." He stepped closer and loomed over me.

"What do you mean, if she did?" Ah, yes, this was indeed grilling. I had never felt truly threatened by him before. But I did now.

"Once again, I only have your word for it that you saw her bury these and that you retrieved them. Once again, if you had told us they were there, we could have uncovered them ourselves and would know where they came from, wouldn't we? The chain of custody would be maintained and they could actually be used as evidence, if the day ever comes when we need them."

He raised those thick eyebrows again. His look was still cold. My blood ran similarly.

"But there are more under the stone. And why would I lie about it?"

"Maybe to incriminate Mrs. Toombs." His voice was soft. He moved in even closer. "Maybe because you don't like her. Maybe because you fed the mushrooms to Toombs yourself and you want to shift the blame. Maybe you put mushrooms in Mrs. Toombs's yard yourself."

The room wasn't cold any longer. He hunched over me and an unpleasant heat of intimidation emanated from him. A faint tinge of pungent aftershave hung in the stale office air. I sucked in a hot lungful of it. "You… you really think I did it? I killed him?"

"No, not really." He relented. He backed up, lifted his hip onto the corner of his desk again, and tossed the bag onto his blotter with a plop. "I really think you're tampering with evidence, though. This, like the cookies, is stolen property, technically speaking. We'll examine these, but we won't be able to use them as evidence."

I tried to let my breath out slowly, unobtrusively. "Well, there are more mushrooms still there. But what about the earrings? They're in the bag, too."

He re-examined the bag. His raised eyebrows said, *okay, what about them?*

"Did Grace Harmon tell the police her diamond earrings had been stolen?" I asked.

"Not that I know of."

"Well, they were. She thought Mo Toombs took them."

"Are these Mrs. Harmon's earrings?"

"Probably."

"Probably." He threw the bag down, jumped off the desk, and exploded his words in my face. "What in the hell am I supposed to do with a pair of earrings that *might* have belonged to a dead woman?"

I hadn't been willing to ask Al if he recognized them, thinking it might upset him more. This, evidently, had been bad planning on my part.

"I… don't know." I shrank into the hard plastic chair. "It… seemed like evidence."

"Let *us* gather evidence after this. You're *not* helping. Besides—" He sighed. "You might get yourself into a bad spot, Cressa." Was he worried about me?

He gave the baggie another doubtful glance. "We'll look into the earrings and, if they were stolen from Mrs. Harmon, I have a pretty good idea who stole them."

I let out the air I had been holding again.

"Go on home," he continued. "We won't arrest you for murder today. Should you find anything else you consider relevant, though, please, please, please let me handle it."

"Yes, yes I will." I jumped up and headed for the door.

"And Miss Carraway—" I stopped and whirled around. I was Miss Carraway again, not Cressa. That was a bad sign. "You need to keep in mind that three people have been murdered at the place where you're staying. If it looks like you know too much about those murders, your life will be in danger."

That thought had crossed my mind, too. "Uh. Yeah." My voice broke as I hurried, with relief, through the door he held open for me. I turned back a moment.

"Thanks, Sheriff Dobson. Please don't tell anyone I found those things. Could it be confidential?"

"Maybe. We'll see."

When I returned to the lake I couldn't even think about concentrating on the finishing touches for my music. The room spun slightly as I stood in the middle of it. My head hummed with tension.

For once, Ivan cooperated and I called Neek.

"Is your tummy feeling better?"

"Yes, much. How about your back?"

"Could be better."

"Those kids are in the hospital. I hope they'll be okay."

"And are you okay with finding that body? Three, Cressa. My God!"

"I know. Listen, I just went to the county sheriff and took him some things I shouldn't have."

"Huh?"

"He was pretty steamed about it. He says I shouldn't have touched them, and, damn it, I knew that, but …"

"Cressa, some day you'll have to start looking before you leap. How many times have you done this now?! Jeez!"

"Not you, too, UU." I used to be so overly cautious. Maybe I'd started a tendency toward all this premature leaping at the same time—dating inappropriate guys and making rash decisions about other things, too. I was beginning to think the rebellious nature that started in my late teens might do me in."

I heard her sigh. "Gosh, you're having a tough time, kiddo. I'm sorry. I won't yell at you anymore. Well, what did you find? And mess up?"

I told her about the mushrooms and earrings, but then remembered. "Oh crap!" I said. "I forgot to ask him about the cushion."

"What cushion?"

"I saw the tractor cushion at the side of the path when I found Toombs's body, but when I went back to look for it, it wasn't there. Sheriff Dobson got me so rattled I forgot to mention it." I explained to her how I thought that meant the tractor had transported the body.

"At least I didn't touch that cushion. I can imagine the lecture I'd get. Maybe with handcuffs. Should I go back and talk to the Sheriff?"

"Cressa, no. Just sit tight. They'll find the killer. Look, I have a couple customers lined up. Gotta go. Take care."

After the call ended I looked around the cabin. It closed in on me like a death trap. I slipped into a bathing suit, grabbed my beach bag, and slammed the door on my way out. I was becoming accustomed to fleeing to the beach. It was a safe place to be, in plain sight where no one could harm me.

But before I got there, Martha beckoned me from her doorway.

Oh damn—I really didn't feel like facing her right now. Would she detect my guilt? Could she already know I'd taken the mushrooms?

I walked to her door. Had she used the mushrooms to poison Toombs? There might be another explanation for her odd behavior the night before. But what could it possibly be?

"Good morning, Martha. Beautiful day today." *If she's a murderer, the one thing I must not do is let her know I saw her last night.*

"I need to finish," she said. She peered out the door, swiveled her head around, adorned with its ever-present rollers, and pulled me inside. Mo's car was in the driveway again, but I saw no sign of him in the house. I wondered if he ever worked at that bowling alley. The hours must have been pretty liberal.

"Okay," she began. "This time I have to tell you. I don't have much time."

She didn't, though. Her mouth was moving, but she didn't get any more words out.

"Martha, if you have something to say, say it."

Her wounded look told me I had spoken too harshly.

"I do have something you need to know." More silence. She walked away from me and headed toward the kitchen.

This was maddening. I took off after her, grabbed her arms and spun her around, shouting. "Martha, what the hell are you trying to say?"

She stared down at my hands. I was squeezing her arms. Too hard.

"I'm sorry, Martha," I said, letting my hands drop. My fingers left red dents in her soft flesh.

"No, no. I do have to say it. I thought," she went on, rubbing her upper arms. "I mean, I told you my husband acted strangely the night your grandmother died. That's not quite true. What I've been trying to tell you …" Her voice trailed off.

I waited a long moment, resisting the urge to grab and shake her again.

"He killed them. My husband killed them." Her face began to crumple.

My knees weakened. I groped in back of me for a place to sit. Was she delusional? How could she know that?

"Do you want to sit down?" I asked Martha. We were both standing in the middle of the room. "Do you want a drink of water?"

"No, let me finish." She flapped her hands for me to wait and let her go on. I sank onto the couch. "The girls thought they saw Mo, but the night Ida drowned, Mo wasn't even here, he was up in Moline for a couple of days. You know Mo and his father look alike in some lights? Looked, looked alike, I mean. The girls saw their grandfather, not their uncle." She looked away.

"His clothes were all wet when he came in that night, the night your grandmother drowned. He said he'd fallen off the dock."

"What? And why would your husband kill her, and Grace, too? Both of them?"

"They said Mo stole their jewelry."

"You think your husband killed my grandmother and Grace because they accused Mo of stealing?" Would a person actually murder someone because of that?

This was too close to what I had envisioned—Gram confronting the Toombses and them killing her. Not Mo, but his father.

Gram! I don't want this to be true!

"Not just from them. From lots of people. I know Ida had been talking about going to the police because of her stolen jewelry. He was afraid of what would happen to Mo." Martha rubbed both hands on her cheeks and forced out her strangled words. "He didn't just steal from your grandmother and Grace, he's stolen from almost everybody here. He has bad friends up in the Cities, too. I think they've even robbed jewelry stores there. Mo turns up with such nice stuff sometimes. Every once in a while he gets strange calls, then disappears for a couple of days."

She lowered herself into the recliner, but popped up as soon as she touched down.

"The night Grace died, my husband came home soaking wet. The next morning I snooped in Mo's room. I didn't find anything there, but I found Grace's earrings in our bedroom. In my husband's drawer. Then I knew for sure Mo had taken them. And that his father knew."

I guess I knew about those earrings. And what Martha had done with them.

Oh, Grace. I don't want any of this to be true.

"Grace told everybody about those missing earrings," she said. "I knew what they looked like. She wore them a lot. I know they were hers."

"So you think your husband killed Ida and Grace? Are you going to tell the police?"

"I don't just think he did, I *know* he did. He was trying to keep Mo out of prison. I can't really blame him for that. But the police will be here soon anyway. They were here just now and, and they, they dug up something."

-37-

Oder: Or; or else (Ger.)

I t was official: I couldn't hope to punish Gram's murderer—he was already dead. My shoulders sagged at the thought, as I trudged back up the hill, playing Martha's statements over and over in my mind, my desire for the beach evaporated. I would never have the satisfaction of seeing her killer punished. I thought Toombs must have been the person who left that note on my porch.

How could he have killed my grandmother? My incredible Gram? Both she and Grace Harmon, wonderful women, would have had lots of good years left. They were gone just because that moron, that idiot, that bastard, Mo, stole their jewelry.

It was not to my credit that I had hurt Martha. The poor woman had had enough suffering without that. But I would love to hurt Mo further. She said the police had dug up something. I assumed that would be the rest of her mushrooms.

An engine noise behind me made me look back to see two Henry County cars pass the beach and turn onto the concrete apron of the yellow house. When Mrs. Toombs emerged a short while later and was escorted into one of the cars, I tried to fade into the scenery. I was sure I was the reason she was being arrested. This was all because of the mushrooms I'd given Sheriff Dobson.

I hurried back to my cabin and flipped on the television. A soap opera was interrupted within two minutes. A reporter, face set for serious news, was accompanied by a logo that screamed "Breaking News."

"Martha Toombs has just been picked up at her lakeside home and taken to the County Courthouse for questioning in connection with her husband's death, sources say. It is not known if she is a suspect or not. The funeral of Grace Harmon, the second woman murdered at Crescent Lake, will be held tomorrow at the Alpha Lutheran Church at two o'clock. No other details are available at this time."

This was accompanied by a jerky video of Martha looking bewildered and walking from the squad car into the county sheriff's building. At least they'd given her time to take her rollers out.

"Evangeline Evans, of the same lake complex, is still being held in conjunction with the poisoning of the five young children, who remain in stable condition. A charge of attempted murder is expected later in the week, according to the DA's office. And now these messages."

The station swung into a series of ads and eventually the news returned to cover other topics. At least they had the right number of children this time.

It was getting hot out. I changed into my sundress and piled my hair up off my neck, feeling fretful and restless. I had nothing to do. Nothing I *could* do. It was all so unreal. A few days ago, these were all normal people living normal lives, or so I thought. Right now there wasn't a single one I wouldn't suspect of at least some crime.

It sounded like Toombs had died of poisoning. Why else would they pull Martha in? And they were focusing on her because of the deadly mushrooms I had turned in. I didn't want the poor soul to be guilty of killing him. Okay then, if she didn't do it, who else could have poisoned him? For the umpteenth time, I made a list in my head of possible wrongdoers.

Mrs. Toombs—poisoned her husband with the mushrooms. Or did she? Hayley may have done it because he was molesting her children, and Martha was helping her daughter hide the evidence.

Eve—poisoned at least the Fiori children, maybe her own. She had certainly poisoned me. Maybe she did it to others, too.

Al Harmon—certainly knew about poison mushrooms, too, through Grace. What was he looking for in the clearing near the place where Toombs's body was found? I wondered if it was his knife, which police said was the murder weapon. If it was his knife, wasn't it logical that he had killed Toombs? Did he poison *and* stab him? Would he have killed Gram and Grace, too? I'd never believe that.

And the Weldons—if Eve was to be believed, they had driven the tractor to the clearing. I knew the yellow cushion could corroborate that the tractor had been used to transport the body. The cushion that was no longer there. It had to have blood on it. But I couldn't think of a reason for them to have poisoned or stabbed Toombs, other than he was working them too hard.

Mo could even have killed his father to protect his mother. But, I had to admit, that wasn't likely. Certainly not by poisoning.

The Fioris—they'd done something Pat didn't want Freddie talking about in front of me. He didn't think they should ask Martha Toombs to loan them money after "what they had done." Maybe he had scruples about asking for money from the widow of the man they had murdered?

And Daryl? I didn't want to believe Daryl could have anything to do with any of this. He might want to kill Mo, but how about Mo's father? Hmm, he did say he hated Toombs the other night. I recalled the startling similarity of the father and son, especially in silhouette, and presumably also in the darkness. If Rebecca and Rachel could mistake one for the other, Daryl could, too.

Too many "ifs" and "maybes." One more thing puzzled me, on top of all this. Might as well try to clear that thing up. At least it was one mystery I could solve.

-38-

Narrante: Narrating; as if telling a story (Ital.)

I slipped my sandals on, walked to Hayley's, and knocked on her screen door. The inside door was open and a television was blaring in the front room. Her cabin, like her mother's, was more of a house than a cabin, with several separate rooms. I could see through the screen into a living room with a kitchen beyond that. Two doors led to what were most likely bedrooms.

"Yes?" Hayley's greeting was tentative.

"I wonder if I could talk to you for a moment?"

"Do you know they've just arrested my mother?" Hayley's voice was ragged, tears ran down her face. "I don't think I can talk to anyone right now."

"I'm sorry." I put as much sympathy as possible into my voice, considering I had to raise it quite a bit to be heard over the television. "I was trying to get to the bottom of what happened to the Fiori children, and I wondered if your girls could help at all."

"Oh, all right." Hayley sniffed, then reluctantly let me in and pointed me to a stuffed chair. She even turned the TV volume down, much to my relief. Hayley went to call the two girls in from the back porch, which, like mine, overlooked the water.

"This lady wants to ask you something," said Hayley, resignation on her face.

I realized Hayley and I hadn't formally met, but this wasn't the time for formal introductions. We both knew who the other was. She wasn't at her best, her eyes rimmed with red and her light-colored hair flying around her face in tangles.

The two girls stood silent and curious in front of me, waiting.

"Tell her about your grandpa," Hayley said.

Before I could protest I wasn't going to ask them about that, the older one answered. "I don't want to talk about him. He wasn't nice to us. He wasn't nice to Grandma. And he wasn't nice to Mrs. Miller."

Mrs. Miller? He wasn't nice to my grandmother? I guess not. He killed her, huh?

"Never mind that," I said. "What I wanted to ask you about was, I wondered if you ate any cookies at Mrs. Evans's the last time you were over there."

The younger girl looked down at the carpet, swinging her Barbie doll upside down by one foot, but the older one, Rebecca, spoke for both of them.

"I had one bite and I spit it out and Rachel had two cookies."

Rachel raised her head and flashed defiance up at her older sister. "No, I didn't, I didn't eat any."

"You took two," countered her sister and thrust two fingers before her face.

"I know, but I didn't like 'em, so I put 'em in my pocket and threw 'em away." The girl wrinkled her nose and stuck out her lower lip to illustrate her distaste.

"I see," I said. "That's all I wanted to know."

The girls shot each other relieved looks. Then they ran back to their game on the porch.

"Thank you," said Hayley to me.

"For what?"

"I thought you would ask them about their grandfather. Mo says my mother told you that story about them being molested by him."

Not exactly. But that's what Mo thought she told me. She took my silence for assent, though.

"I'll tell you what sort of person my stepfather was." She glanced at the porch and lowered her voice to a harsh whisper. "He was a drunk. Just like my father and my ex-husband. Life can be so damn discouraging, you know. I try to find a guy who's suitable, but there aren't any unattached guys in Alpha or New Windsor, or any of these little towns. I have to go into the Cities to have a drink, even to meet any guys. And, somehow, all the ones I meet are the same. I think they're nice, then …" She looked at the ceiling and pressed her lips together, her eyes growing moist again.

Since no one had ever mentioned the father of the girls, I assumed he was absent and her judgment of men was even worse than mine.

"But my stepfather had more problems than drink. He hated everyone except his precious Mo. Mo has *real* problems. Like he takes after his father, mostly. But at least his father didn't steal things—that I know of."

"Did Mo take anything besides jewelry?"

"That, and money." She shook her head. "I don't know what's going to happen to him without his father there to bail him out of every jam he gets into. He's never been punished, or even caught, for anything he's ever done." She huffed out a breath heavy with disgust. "Mo is the only person in the world that's sorry that old bastard is gone."

Rebecca and Rachel shrieked with laughter in their play. I was glad to hear it; I'd never seen them smile. Hayley scooted closer to me and lowered her voice again. "I'll tell you what was happening to my girls. He molested them all right, but I don't think it was the way Pat Fiori thinks. It's true, he would hit them for the tiniest stupid thing.

He hit my mother, too. He's, I mean, he *was* a bully, hitting women and children whenever he felt like it."

Hayley's eyes sparked, looking like Rachel's a minute ago when she defied her sister.

"For some reason, one day Pat talked to Rebecca and Rachel. I wasn't there, but she later told me she thought he was sexually abusing them. The old coot even belted me when I brought that up with him. I don't know whether he really was or not, but, whenever I ask Rebecca and Rachel what they do with their grandfather, they never say anything about sexual stuff." The soft hair she ran her hand through was the color of corn silk. Maybe it was a preview of how her daughters' wispy hair would look when they were grown.

"Don't get me wrong," she said, "I'm glad he's dead. Real glad. But I think the rumor Pat Fiori started may have been what caused him to be killed, and I'm terrified my mother may have killed him."

"Why are you telling me this?" *I wish she wouldn't.*

"They've already arrested Mom. What can it hurt? She's probably told them everything."

"I don't think they've exactly arrested her. The news said they were questioning her."

"Oh sure. And keeping her in a jail cell in between questions."

"So you think she killed him because of Pat's story?" My curiosity got the better of my common sense, as usual. My common sense told me I was better off not knowing any more than I already did. My curiosity said: "nonsense!"

"Probably not just because of that. But it was the last straw. I had dinner with them that night." Hayley leaned back and spoke in a soft monotone that belied the emotion she was suppressing. An advertising jingle on television for toilet bowl cleaner made for surreal and noisy background music.

"I'm so afraid for Mom. That night she was acting real strange. She made a casserole that was stuffed with mushrooms. She knows I don't like mushrooms, so she had fixed a tuna salad for me to eat. I thought that was kind of funny. She knew I was eating with them that night and she fixed a casserole full of mushrooms, which I hate. She usually doesn't do stuff like that."

Had my casserole contained those mushrooms, too? Good thing I'd thrown it out.

"She didn't eat any of it, either, and she loves mushrooms. My girls don't eat casserole at all, so they had peanut butter sandwiches in front of the TV. Then, after supper, she threw away the leftovers, which was the strangest of all. Mom never throws away leftovers." Hayley shifted in her chair and I shivered. I chose to believe my casserole was a fresh one, and Martha hadn't tried to poison me. Hayley had said she threw the bad one away, right?

Rachel came running in with a decapitated Barbie doll in one hand, a head in the other. Hayley absentmindedly stuck it back on and Rachel ran back into the other room giggling.

"All he talked about at dinner that night was the Weldons, Wayne and Sheila. He was sick and tired of being compared to Sheila's parents. They used to manage this place, did you know that?"

I shook my head.

"He said he was also sick and tired of the way they disobeyed his orders. He had pretty much decided to fire them. He thought maybe Freddie Fiori would do their work, but he hadn't asked Freddie yet.

"Mom didn't think he ought to fire them, but she didn't say too much about it. He was in an ugly mood, he'd been drinking beer all afternoon and evening. She knew she'd better not cross him or he'd hit her. Well, he did anyway, and for nothing at all. She hadn't put enough salt in the casserole, he said, and he hauled off and popped her one."

I shivered at the thought of the blow.

"I tell you, I was ready to kill him, myself. Mom was crying, the girls were sitting there scared to death, and I was screaming at him. He said he was going to the Weldons' and left.

"Mom told me to take the girls home so they wouldn't be there when he got back, but I didn't want to leave her, so we stayed. We waited for hours, but he never came back." She glanced toward the porch that held her two daughters.

"The girls fell asleep on the couch. After I don't know how long, Mom told me she'd put bad mushrooms in the casserole. He ate a lot of it, and she pitched the leftovers, but she had a few extra mushrooms she didn't use. I told her to get rid of them."

Yep. That's what got her arrested. That, and me finding those mushrooms.

"I know she stuck them under a stepping stone—she told me she did that. I thought that was stupid, but she said she didn't want to leave traces of having dug up the yard.

"We didn't know if the poison would kill him or not. We waited and waited and he never came back. We couldn't decide whether or not to call the cops and report him missing. We decided not to. I took the girls home about two in the morning, and the next day you found him over on the other side of the lake."

Hayley's soft droning voice ran down and fantastic images whirled in my mind as I looked at her bowed head, the cloud of soft hair falling into her face.

It's all true! Martha did poison her husband! And he killed my Gram.

The paradise I'd envisioned as I first drove up here a few days ago fell to pieces. *These aren't regular people with normal problems. There is real evil here.*

If I'd thought the police would permit it, I'd leave today.

I stared down at Hayley's carpeting, a pretty two-tone beige and gray, and thanked God my grandmother wasn't here to witness what had become of her Eden.

Then I remembered Grace telling me about the delayed effects of mushroom poisoning. "Hayley, the authorities haven't released the cause of death. There were stab wounds, too."

"Yeah, I've thought about that. How bad were they? You saw the body." She looked at me with hope.

"I couldn't see the wounds." *I couldn't even tell it was him.* "But listen, Grace Harmon was talking to me about gardening one day. She had a clump of poison mushrooms in her flowerbed, the same ones your mother used, and she told me they would take several hours to make a person ill. Maybe your stepfather didn't die of your mother's poison. Maybe he was stabbed to death before the poison took effect."

Please don't ask me how I know what kind of mushrooms your mother used.

Hayley brightened. Then sagged. "It would still be attempted murder, wouldn't it?"

"I have no idea," I said.

I opened the door to leave and there was Martha walking toward me, her head down. She looked up as she neared the door, startled to see me there. About as surprised as I was to see her.

"Martha," I exclaimed. "How wonderful! They've let you go?"

She nodded, but wasn't overjoyed. "Chief Bailey brought me home. He said something about being born under a lucky star. Ha!" Her bitter laugh was tired, she looked deflated. The curlers hadn't seemed to work because her hair hung lank around her ears. "I don't know when that luck is going to kick in."

"Mom!" Hayley ran out and hugged her mother, shedding tears of joy and Martha sobbed with her. Rebecca and Rachel soon followed, squealing with delight to see their grandmother.

I left them to their reunion.

-39-

Caloroso: With warmth, passion; passionately (Ital.)

It was still early when I slipped into jeans and a T-shirt and took my morning tea outside to see what the weather was going to be like for Grace's funeral. From the extra cars at Al Harmon's, I deduced both his sons had arrived for their mother's funeral in the afternoon. I hoped their presence would comfort him.

Al appeared around the side of his house and waved me over to introduce me to his sons and their families. His sons were twins, both tall and slim like their father, and each had a blonde wife and two children, not twins. The four kids, who all looked grade-school age, were relieving the sobriety of the occasion by hollering and cavorting on the nearby playground. There were three boys and a girl.

The mood was subdued at the house, but everyone seemed to be holding up well. I eyed Al, trying to picture him as a murderer, but couldn't make it work. He was too sane to be a killer. Wasn't he? We made small talk for awhile, then I went back to my place to change clothes.

I glanced at the flowers in the window boxes as I opened the door to enter the cabin. They were past their prime. Or maybe they were just dead because I had never watered them. It saddened me that I hadn't tended Gram's blossoms. Another way I had failed someone I loved.

It was horrifying. To get to the church, I had to thread through a throng of cameras and newshounds. The street outside the parking lot was packed with television vans. At least three reporters stood before cameras gripping their microphones and speaking in their appropriately solemn tones. One wore a suit coat and tie with jeans and track shoes. I guessed his cameraman, who was a camerawoman, was good at head shots.

Having reporters shove their microphones in my face and shout belligerent questions was a new experience for me, but, as I had seen felons and the accused do on television, I put my head down, stayed silent, and plowed through them.

The church had probably been built before the turn of the twentieth century. The Victorian architecture gave me a serene, secure feeling, maybe because it reminded of the house I grew up in.

A long wooden stairway led gracefully up to the front double doors and, above, an old-fashioned painted steeple held a heavy bell. A wheelchair entrance had been added at the side.

The interior of the church was bright and airy. Some of the double-hung windows of stained glass had been raised and a soft breeze wafted in. Primary colors shone through the panes and threw bright patches on the people gathering in the pews. The quiet rustlings and murmurings inside contrasted violently with the chaos outside.

Gram had attended church here and occasionally I had gone with her when I was very small. At the thought of her, I reached to my throat for the locket she had given me. Annoyed, I remembered it was still missing. The chain I had seen around Mo's neck leapt into my mind's eye and I knew, I just knew, he had stolen my locket, along with everybody else's precious things. It was clear as a bright *ping* on a percussion triangle. My annoyance turned to hot, hard anger. I wasn't sure what I'd do if he turned up.

It would be easy for the Lutheran minister to eulogize Grace Harmon. She had attended the Alpha Lutheran Church regularly, as had Gram. Almost everybody from town turned out and the church was crowded. By the time I signed the official guest book, a dozen pages were full. Some of the attendees were, no doubt, just curious. After all, the multiple murders were the most sensational thing to happen in Alpha since the fire at the lake years ago. What on earth would Toombs's funeral be like? *There might be international news crews here by then.* I shuddered at that thought.

I could look around and notice things more easily now that it wasn't my grandmother being buried. Her funeral had been such a blur; I wouldn't have recognized this building had I not already known it. Hayley and her daughters were about half-way down the aisle, but I didn't see Mo or Martha. Good thing. I might have socked him. A stripe of yellow from the stained glass window glass caught the wispy, flyaway hair of Hayley and her daughters. Hayley wore a long-sleeved dress that was too warm for the day, but her girls were cute in matching sundresses and sandals.

I looked for Daryl, but didn't see him. I was surprised to see Eve hunched at the end of a pew near the back, her conventional black dress hanging on her skeletal frame, her body humming with nervous energy. She'd obviously not been charged after all. I wondered why not.

Wayne and Sheila came in just before the service began and sat immediately behind me, in the last row. As Wayne sank into his seat I could smell the liquor on his breath. Out of the corner of my eye I caught Sheila's enormous green and yellow dress, a welcome change from her usual muumuu, but didn't turn further to look at them. Her cigar was missing today.

As we rose, Al and his family filed in and sat in the front pew reserved for them. Al looked old, but stoic. His tall sons and their families all wore dark clothes and somber faces. The little boys, hair slicked down and parted, looked like they were trying to play a part.

The minister rose and ascended to the pulpit, but when it came time for him to talk about Grace, he came down the altar steps and walked back and forth, his black robe swirling, and gave his message. He seemed to truly grieve the death of Grace, and gave her a beautiful send-off. Several older people stood up and told stories and anecdotes about her. One was a woman who had attended grade school with Grace and related how she had organized a group to make stuffed animals for hospitalized children. Another was a man who said they'd been on the debate team together in high school, and Grace "beat the socks off" all comers.

Since I'm the type that cries the minute anyone else does, I was soon on my last tissue. Grace had had many friends in this town.

Near the end of the minister's final oration, he spoke the words, "We can all take comfort from the fact that we know Grace Harmon has now met God."

Wayne stumbled into the aisle and shouted, "That Mizz Harmon was a good soul, but I'll tell you who ain't goin' to meet God nowhere, the old devil."

"Wayne," Sheila pleaded softly. "Come on, baby. Sit down." She stretched her chunky arms out to grab his red plaid shirt. She missed, and the fat on her upper arms wobbled as she held them out for a second. The extent of Wayne's funeral attire was a clean plaid shirt and a pair of threadbare slacks instead of his usual overalls.

The congregation, stunned into a sudden silence, swiveled their heads in his direction, as if choreographed. For an instant, everyone froze. Then the whispering started.

Wayne stumbled down the aisle, just out of Sheila's reach, continuing to wave his arms. Every eye followed him. A few people put their heads together. I wondered if they were thinking of getting up and expelling Wayne.

"Sheila's mother is restin' easy in her grave, I'll tell you that," he shouted. "And that old son of a bitch—"

Sheila jumped up, caught his hand, and bustled him out the main door in the back.

Over the faint murmurings of the crowd outside, I could hear them clomping down the hollow wooden steps, Sheila muttering, "Wayne, you gotta stop drinking. You're making me nervous." Wayne shouted incoherently. It sounded like he was saying he'd take care of something, or had taken care of something. Sheila continued her soft pleading as the entire congregation listened to their voices fading into the distance while the door swung shut.

I hoped for their sakes the camera crews were gone, or they'd be getting some dramatic, unexpected shots.

The minister bowed his head and raised his arms, his wide sleeves falling to his elbows, and swung into his final prayer as if nothing had happened. That gave us all a sense of relief and returned us to normality.

My mind wandered as I half-listened, and my gaze drifted across the bowed heads.

Whoa! My heart skidded in my chest. This couldn't be.

I didn't process it at first, denying what my eyes were seeing. That thin, lank hair. Those serious, piercing eyes. I scrunched down as soon as I spied Len, but he turned his head and looked at me.

I refused to look that way again and scrambled to leave as soon as we were dismissed, frantically dropping my purse. I scooped the spilled contents up and stuffed them back into my purse, stumbling out the door.

The reporters were gone, but wads of people were gathered and whispered together outside the building, blocking my way. They were mourners who hadn't been able to fit into the church. I tried in vain to get through them, a lump of panic rising in my throat. The crowd had to have been there earlier, when Wayne and Sheila left. Her heft was probably an advantage plowing through a crowd. I was stuck.

The coffin was carried past me, the delicate daffodils ringing it, but this brought all other movement to a standstill until the attendants loaded it into the hearse with practiced, smooth efficiency.

I tried to push through the crowd watching the casket, but it was no use. Len caught up to me and grabbed my bare arm with a steely grip.

"What are you doing here?" I whispered angrily, trying to jerk my arm away from him. He held fast. His touch made my skin crawl.

"I happened to be at the airport when you drove past on Highway One-Fifty the other day." His nauseating smile looked smug. Had I really liked those stern, remote, judging eyes at one time? "I had an educator's meeting at the Holiday Inn and I had just dropped off a music professor who flew in."

"So that *was* you." I knew it. I had driven out to Alpha past the airport—and right past Len.

"I figured out what town you went to." His feral grin widened. I scowled back at him. "That's why I was at the grocery store, too. I knew you would have to eat sometime."

"You drove all the way back out here from Chicago? Twice?"

"It's not that far. Three hours or so. Also, I saw the story on television, the one where they said Cressa Carraway found two bodies near Alpha." He still gripped my arm. "The notice of the funeral was in the Chicago paper. These murders are receiving a lot of press. I figured I would see you here."

"Leave me alone, Len. I don't want to see you." I tried to shrug him off again. His fingers tightened, pinching me now.

"But Cressa, babe, I have good news."

I jerked my arm away with a strong pull and dashed to my car.

"Wait!" he shouted, but remained standing where we had talked, looking disappointed. I sped off, glancing in my rearview mirror to make sure he hadn't followed me. Bastard.

The rest of the people had already started to head for their cars, many of them on their way to the reception at Al's.

Maybe, I thought, the safest place for me right now would be the reception.

On my way up to the cabin, I passed Pat Fiori driving out and waved to her. Several people were already gathered at Al's, waiting for the family to come back from the graveyard.

Pat slowed and rolled her window down. "Kids are a lot better," she yelled to me. "I'm driving in to see them now."

It looked like the Fiori kids would recover. That was a huge relief.

After the reception at Al's, a backyard affair that started out gloomy but grew warm with memories and the delicious home-cooked dishes of the women of the church, I prowled around the cabin aimlessly. Lamenting the death of Grace all the more for having met her many grieving friends and relatives, I made a decision. What I needed was a new beginning. My old life with Len was over, my life with Gram was over, and I needed to do something to signal a new beginning; I needed to feel in control of something.

I took the road into New Windsor and stopped at a greenhouse I'd seen earlier. Potted geraniums and daisies, sitting on the sidewalk, bobbed their bright heads and nodded to me. I bought six of each and took them back to the lake.

A moment of irrational terror gripped me when a car like Len's, a little blue convertible with its top up, pulled into the lake complex after me. It didn't follow me up the hill, though, so I relaxed.

I pulled over at the top of the hill, waiting to see if the blue car would appear. Feeling like a fool, my heart pounding all the same, I opened my car door, left it open so it wouldn't make a noise, then crept down the road. No blue convertible. *Must not be him.* I puffed a long breath of relief and climbed back to my cabin. Didn't the threat of a jilted lover pale in comparison to death and murder, anyway?

As I yanked up spent flowers and planted new ones in my window boxes, I dug my bare hands into the moist dirt, wallowed in the feel of the warm earth, and inhaled the fresh, sharp smell of the geraniums. I tossed the shriveled discards into the wild vegetation beside the cabin, knowing they would fertilize something in there. I was replacing the ugliness of violent death with the beauty of these blossoms.

I had a solitary supper in my cabin and watched a few mindless TV shows during the evening. I didn't want to think about anything. The night was warm and it grew so stuffy I cracked one of the front windows, but only a half an inch. I had every right to be paranoid.

Pat had stopped by my front yard after she returned from the hospital and we spoke briefly. She said her children were expected to make a full recovery and she and Freddie were discussing whether or not to press charges against Eve.

I mentioned I had eaten one of Eve's cookies and hadn't felt very well the next day, but Hayley's girls hadn't touched them, and hadn't been ill.

"Speaking of Hayley's girls," I began.

"Um," Pat interrupted me, "I know what you're going to say." Pain flitted across her soft face. "That stupid story I started." She reached out and fingered a daisy petal in my newly planted window box. "It was an idiotic thing to do."

"So Toombs didn't really sexually abuse his granddaughters?"

Her shoulders hunched forward as she held her elbows. It was, by bizarre coincidence, the same gesture Hayley made when discomforted. "I don't know if he did or not, Cressa." There was pain in her voice. "I mean, I wasn't sure, but some of the signs were there. I guess I started that horrid story in retaliation for the way he was treating Freddie."

"Which, you know, is the way he treated everybody."

"I know that now, and I've wished a million times I could take back what I said. Freddie was slaving away working for him, doing everything he asked, and Toombs was refusing to pay him more than a few dollars. He kept stalling us and we needed the money. Desperately. I'll never do anything like that again."

Shortly after nine-thirty a knock sounded on my door.

I peeked out and saw Daryl Johannson. My heart gave a little leap. I opened the door wide.

"You missed the funeral today," I said. I wasn't really accusing him. I had genuinely missed him, and wished he'd been there when Len confronted me.

"I know." His hair was a mess and his freckles stood out in his stark, pale face. "Have you heard about Martha?"

"No, what about Martha? She wasn't at the funeral. Come on in. Would you like a Coke?"

He sat mute on one of the couches while I splashed Coke over ice into two glasses and brought them into the front half of the cabin.

"I've been at the county building all afternoon," he said. "Seems I'm a suspect."

"In Toombs's death?" I handed him a glass and took a stool at the counter.

"Martha's."

-40-

Espandendosi: Growing broader and fuller; with growing intensity (Ital.)

Daryl blew at the foam on his drink, then leveled his green eyes at me. They looked dark today. "Martha was murdered sometime this morning." A chill shot through me. *Another murder. Another freakin' murder.* My glass jerked in my hand and a couple drops of pop leapt onto the floor.

"That's why you didn't see her at the funeral," he said. "She called me last night and asked if I'd drive her to Grace's funeral today. Mo is missing. When I stopped by to pick her up, the place was crawling with cops and they hauled me in."

Gulp! Am I entertaining a murderer?

"Don't look at me like that," he groaned.

"Like what?"

"Like I'm Ted Bundy." He swigged his Coke as if he hadn't had anything to drink for hours. Maybe he hadn't.

"I figure, from how they questioned me, she died early today. I worked at home by myself all morning but I also made a couple of phone calls, which the police were finally able to verify. One to my dad and one to an art supplier. After they got confirmation of my phone records they let me go, but I'm still under suspicion."

I breathed out. *I'm not serving Coke to a killer.* I told myself that they would still be holding him if they had anything to go on, but was only seventy percent convinced.

"Is Mo clear? Does he have an alibi?" I asked.

"Why would Mo kill his own mother?"

"Well, because she killed his father. Or tried to."

"Huh? You think Martha killed her old man?"

"I saw her hiding something under one of their stepping stones night before last. I went back later and dug it up, and it was poisonous mushrooms. I took some to Sheriff Dobson because it was such a suspicious thing to do, burying them under a rock at night like that."

I traced the path of a drip trickling down the outside of my sweating glass, glad the chill had left my spine.

It was so good to have someone I could talk to about all this. Someone I could unburden myself to about my feelings of guilt over the mushrooms.

Should I tell him about Hayley's confession?

I continued, "I guess the sheriff agreed, even though he gave me a hard time about 'disturbing evidence' because, right after that, some sheriff's deputies came out, picked up the rest of the mushrooms, and she was pulled in for questioning the same day."

Yes, I would tell him. I decided I trusted Daryl, if no one else. How could Daryl have killed anyone?

"Hayley told me yesterday her mother did serve him poisonous mushrooms the night he died, so I thought maybe Martha killed him. But now someone's killed her?"

"Yep. But I thought Toombs was stabbed."

"One news report said he was both stabbed and poisoned, but they haven't figured out the cause of death yet."

"Jesus! Poisoned and stabbed." He jumped up and slammed his drink onto the counter, then started pacing. "He did have a lot of enemies, didn't he? I never thought his enemies were that violent, though. I didn't think the people here in my own town were like that."

"He was a violent man, from what his wife and his stepdaughter said. Mo says he hits people, too, although—how does he put it?—he never hit anyone unless they deserved it. Something like that."

"Mo said that? Sounds like Mo. He's the same way, as you know. He was always getting into fights all through school. He could never see what the big deal was. If he wanted to punch somebody, he punched them."

"How did Martha die?" My voice sounded weak.

"That's kind of odd. You say she hid the mushrooms under a stepping stone?"

"That's right. The one nearest the door."

Daryl stopped pacing and looked directly at me. "Yep, that's the one. Captain Palmer said her head was bashed in with it."

-41-

Romance: Originally, a ballad, or popular tale in verse, in the Romance dialect; now, a title for epico-lyrical songs, or of short instrumental pieces of sentimental or romantic cast, and without special form (Eng.)

aryl's revelation took a minute to sink in. He took the stool next to mine, picked up his glass, and rattled the ice cubes while I wrapped my thoughts around that. "She was killed right there?" I stammered. "In front of her house?"

"No, Palmer says it happened inside."

"Palmer? Is he that short one with the piggy eyes?"

"I guess you could call them piggy." He shrugged. "Yeah, that's him. He said the county got an anonymous phone call telling them to check on Martha. The door was standing open and the rock was lying beside her when Palmer got there."

"Wow. Poor Martha." Harboring no warm feelings for Mo, it surprised me to find that I felt sad for him; he had lost both his parents to murder.

"Have you talked to Mo?" I asked.

"He hasn't shown up. I've seen Hayley, though. She and the girls are pretty broken up."

"I didn't tell you, but Martha let on to me, before she was taken in for questioning, that she's always known her husband killed my grandmother—and Grace."

Daryl whistled softly. "What a mess! Does Al Harmon know that? You think he did Toombs in, taking revenge for his wife?"

"No, I don't think Al knows about what Martha told me. I got the impression Martha didn't tell anyone else."

"I wonder if Mo knows, though."

"Could be. Speaking of Mo, since you live beside him, you're in a position to do me a big favor."

"Okay." He sounded cautious. "What?"

"It's a small thing, but it means a lot to me. If you get a chance, when Mo's not around, could you go through his things and see if my locket is there? I think I saw him wearing the chain from it the day he attacked me." I rubbed my neck where the chain should be.

"You think he took it from you? And then wore it in front of you? What a jerk!"

A whiff of wood smoke came through my front window, despite only being opened a crack. Al Harmon must be making a fire with his grandchildren, I thought. Good for him.

"Do you smell the fire?" I asked, thinking maybe we could go join Al.

Daryl rose quickly, knocking the stool over. "Fire?" He ran to the door and threw it open.

"What's the matter, Daryl? It's just Al's campfire."

"You're sure?" He hesitated, then closed the door. His eyes were wild, so wide open they showed white all around.

I walked over to him and laid my hand on his arm, trying to calm him. His skin jumped underneath my touch.

"What is it with you and this fire thing?"

He set the stool back up and perched uneasily on it. I sat on the couch, at a distance from him, to give him room.

"It's been bothering me for years, Cressa. I had a bad experience when I was younger." At last he was going to open up to me.

"My folks had a cabin out here, the one next to the Harmons', closest to the playground. The Greys had the one that used to be between Toombs's and Hayley's." *Ah, where the empty, burnt foundation was. I was finally going to learn its story.* "Of course, Hayley didn't have that one then, she wasn't grown up and she lived with her mom and stepdad, but the Toombses have had that yellow one for a long time." He struggled a moment, then went on.

"One night, the Greys' cabin, a really big, nice one, burned to the ground. Norah Grey died in the fire. I was eleven years old."

The same age I was when my parents both died.

"I learned, years later, that she took sleeping pills. She never had a chance, probably didn't even know her house was on fire until the last moment."

Daryl closed his eyes briefly, then went on. "My mother had died the year before and I was going through a hard stretch. I'd been caught a couple of times playing with matches. Lighting piles of leaves and stuff, but nothing really dangerous."

He gave another glance toward the window where the smoky smell was coming in, then gave a smile full of sorrow.

"But Mrs. Grey was like a mother to me after mine was gone. She made sure I had homemade cookies to put in my school lunch and gave me gifts for my birthday and Christmas. I was always welcome in their house."

He scratched at the condensation on his glass. The cabin was too hot. It needed more windows open, but I wasn't about to move an inch.

"Toombs had called the cops on me once already and, when the Greys' cabin burned, a lot of people assumed I set the fire. The police grilled me for hours—an eleven-year-old kid. I was exhausted and somehow admitted I did it. I guess 'cause I thought I'd get to go home? I don't even remember saying it. Like I would ever do anything to hurt Mrs. Grey." He swallowed melted ice water with an audible gulp and continued. "Then I had to have a trial and the whole bit. My lawyer convinced the court my confession wasn't real, and I was set free. Toombs got on the stand and claimed he saw me set the fire, but his testimony was thrown out after he contradicted himself about a dozen times. It was a total lie. I never knew why he did that. Plus my father testified I was at home at the time."

"No wonder you couldn't stand Toombs."

"But most people here still believe I did it. I was teased at school a lot." Daryl wasn't seeing my cabin. His eyes were focused on a memory, his head tilted back, toward the wagon wheel light fixture hanging in the center of the room.

"I'll never forget the night of the fire. Dad and I ran down and stood across the road watching it go up. He had called the fire department on his ham radio. I can still see those brilliant flames, red, white. Those awful flames. I can hear her screaming, too. I woke up at night for years hearing her and seeing those flames in the night."

We were both silent for a few minutes. A cricket chirped somewhere near the window and locusts buzzed in the trees beyond. His sad eyes haunted me, and my heart ached for him. We stared into each other's eyes for a moment. Something else developed in our gaze. My heart quickened.

"And the fire was definitely set deliberately?"

"That's what the fire chief said."

"Then someone else set the fire."

He looked at me gratefully. "But nobody else was ever accused."

"What happened to Mrs. Grey's husband? Did he die, too?"

"He moved into town with his daughter. But he had a heart attack and died a few years later."

"Do you think he could have done it?"

"I don't know, but I don't think so. He was a gentle soul. Everyone liked him." Daryl set his glass on the counter with a firm hand, back in the present. "Do you know the reason I came to see you tonight, Cressa?"

"I guess not."

"I knew being with you would make me feel better after what I went through at the station. I can't get you out of my mind."

I don't think I'll be able to get you out of mine, either.

Our eyes caught again.

"I'm really glad you came by, Daryl. I don't want to be alone this evening. I had a shock at Grace's funeral. My old boyfriend was there."

"That was a shock?"

"Maybe that's too mild a word. He scares me to death lately."

"How come?"

"When I broke up with him, he started calling me a dozen times a day. I stopped answering his calls and he started slipping notes under my apartment door."

"Threatening notes?" The alarm in his voice comforted me. *He's concerned about me.* My toes curled and my heart gave a skip.

"Not at first, but he got more and more angry when I kept avoiding him. The last one scared me the most. In the letters before that, he threatened to kill himself. The last one said he didn't want anyone else to have me. *Have* me, like I'm his possession."

"And he was at Grace's funeral? All the way from Chicago?"

"He saw my name in the paper and knew he would see me there. He's been to Alpha once before, too. In fact, the reason I got into the car with Mo at the drugstore was because Len was across the street. He knows I'm in the vicinity, but not where I'm staying. I'm afraid he might find me here, though. I thought I saw him follow me after the funeral, but I was mistaken."

"It does sound like he's dangerous. How did you ever get involved with someone like that?"

"I don't know. I'm not the best judge of people, I guess. I was mostly raised by my grandmother and, since she was a generation older than the other kids' parents, I grew up feeling out of step with my peers. They always knew something I didn't. I was unhappy for most of junior high and high school. And shy."

I tucked some hair behind my ear. "Most of my boyfriends were losers, but Len was older and, well, I guess Len paid attention to me and made me feel special for awhile."

"It's understandable, though, that a person who pays attention to you is attractive. I've had some loser girlfriends myself. Did he ever hurt you, physically?"

"Just once. I can see, now, the whole thing was unhealthy. I'm glad it's over and I never want to see him again."

Daryl moved to the couch to sit next to me. "Do you want me to stay awhile?"

I did. Yes, I did. My old fear fell away. I felt safer than I had in years.

I nodded, then touched Daryl's hand, and this time he held mine back. So I laid my head on his chest. He stroked my hair and sent shivers up my back. Good shivers.

The television was running softly in the background. The theme music for the ten o'clock news interrupted our tête-à-tête.

"Look," said Daryl. "It's the main story again."

I picked my head up. After the lead-ins and ads, the attractive female talking head, dressed in a vibrant striped top that strobed on the screen, spoke over the same pictures of the lake they had run previously. I wondered if she had shorts on under her desk.

"More developments at Crescent Lake. In the brutal murder reported Tuesday, an autopsy has revealed the victim had a large amount of poison in his body. But, in a startling twist, the coroner has released a report indicating he actually died from the stabbing he received that night. The poison had been recently ingested and wouldn't have had time to take effect before he was stabbed to death. The stab wounds killed him instantly. Time of death has been estimated at between eight-thirty, when he was last seen alive by his wife and family, and approximately midnight that same evening. There are no suspects in his death."

But I knew Al's knife was missing. What could that mean?

"And, in an even more bizarre twist, the victim's wife was found murdered today in her home at the lake. No details are available yet on this latest death."

I shuddered. "Should I be staying here?" I asked.

Daryl put his strong, secure arm tight around me. The hair on his arms was thick and sandy-colored. I nuzzled my cheek against it. He smelled faintly of paint and thinner, a good, clean smell.

"Isn't that strange?" I murmured. "First they arrested Eve Evans for poisoning people. She didn't poison Toombs, but put those rhubarb leaves in the cookies for Freddie and Pat's kids. Then they took Martha in, but she didn't do it either, although she tried. Then she was murdered."

I snapped up upright. "Oh my god! I know why Martha was killed. She said her husband killed Grace and Ida. And she knew who killed her husband. She told me that. Whoever killed him wanted to shut her up. Does that make sense?"

He frowned. "I think so." He looked at me. "Yeah, it makes perfect sense."

"This place is lousy with murderers." I shivered in his arms. A bad shiver.

"I won't go if you don't want me to," said Daryl. His grip tightened and his eyes darkened.

I nodded and tipped my face up.

For a breathless moment, we explored the depths of each other's eyes. His face lowered, his lips slowly approached mine. They parted slightly. I could feel a tingle just before we touched.

-42-

Mit Nachdruck: With emphasis, strongly marked (Ger.)

I awoke to bright daylight and the usual birdsong, trying to think—what was different about this morning? Sunlight streamed into the porch, across the bright green indoor–outdoor carpeting, through the lattice work of the wicker chairs, and up onto the bed where I lay tangled in the bed clothes, alone.

Where's Daryl?

There were a few bright hairs left on my pillow.

I found a note Daryl had left by the coffee maker on the kitchen countertop. The note was soft and tender, like last night. The heat ramped up in my chest and a blush rose to my face. Smiling to myself, I reread it, folded it, and put it into my purse.

We'd spent the night on the porch, crowded into the single brass bed together, the shades drawn, but all the louvers cranked open. The owl was hunting again, but not close by. His hoot had sounded eerily in the distance. It didn't bother me at all that night.

My composing material, my keyboard, laptop, and staff paper still lay on the countertop. Something had solidified in my subconscious during the night. I was ready.

I sat down and creative energy surged through my body, veins, and brain, and I turned to my composition, lying lifeless until now. With startling clarity I knew what the problem was. And the solution. Why hadn't I seen it before?

With fresh vigor, I tore into the music, scribbling notes on the staff paper so quickly my fingers ached, stopping only occasionally to check what I had written by running through it on the piano keyboard. Wholly formed themes were appearing to me, crystal clear—I had only to capture them before they dissolved into the air.

I finally understand that I can't put life into my composition without including death. After all, life is only meaningful when it is linked with death. Life can't go on without death. They are two aspects of the same unnamed thing.

The void that had ached inside me since my grandmother's demise cried out and I heard it. I filled it with music; I put her death, as well as her life, into my piece.

The notes that had been only notes until then, limp ditties that sat and mocked my efforts, sprang to life when paired with the darker rumblings of the menace of death. My piece pulsed with the rhythms of the water, the wind, the woods, and the waves.

The melodies soared, the harmonies sang, the rhythms danced. I caught in my creation the light and the dark, the balance of nature, the awful, awe-full duo of life and death.

I scribbled hotly, desperately racing to capture the ideas tumbling through my brain before they evaporated. My music evoked the frogs, the owls with their haunting calls and their sudden swoops of death, the cries of the hunted and suffering, the terrible dark things of the night; it sang the birds in the morning, the joyful flight of squirrels through the topmost branches of tall and mighty trees, the delight of the sun rising through the mist. Even the new vigorous plants replacing the withered ones that would, in their turn, nourish new growth.

My music took shape; it worked. When I coupled life with death, presented the whole picture, passion entered my music. The concept was so elementary, so basic, and yet I didn't see it until now. Death is not just loss. It *is* loss of life, but not loss of the person; it's also a part of life. I hadn't lost Gram. Not really. Just her body. I still had the essence of her and always would. I would always have my memories of her.

Looking around, I felt I was returning from a long journey. At last, after several hours of feverish pursuit, I was drained of ideas. I scanned what I had done, and it was so fine I felt like leaping up.

But I sure was hungry. I ate a quick breakfast, although it was lunchtime, showered, and put on a pair of shorts. I slipped into my loafers, sockless. The day was already warm.

I hummed, basking in the glow of accomplishment, as I dressed. The dappled light filtered through the leaves onto the porch. What a beautiful day. And, to match it, my music danced like the sunshine, leapt in my heart, and sang like my soul. I sat down and did more work, putting a few last amazing touches into the music with no effort.

My experiences with prior compositions had taught me I could keep working on this piece forever, but at some point I would have to decide to quit writing it. A composition is never really done, it just gets done well enough to leave alone.

I laid my pencil down and shoved the keyboard aside at long last, and let my mind dwell directly on Daryl. If the truth were to be made known about the burning of the cabin, he might be able to put it behind him completely, and begin to forget.

I wonder if there's any way I can help him. I stopped myself with that thought. *Little Miss Fix-It, that's me.*

I closed the door behind me as I went out, meaning to inspect the site of the burning again, but something fluttered in the breeze at eye level. There was a note taped to the door.

Since Daryl had left his note inside, I was puzzled. Did he leave another one out here? I pulled it off the door and opened it to see Len's handwriting.

Weak in the knees, I stumbled back inside and sat down to read it.

"Dear Cressa," it said. "I want to talk to you, but I can see that's hopeless. You won't listen to me, so I'll write it down for you, Bitch."

I shivered as I heard his voice in my mind. That voice that used to make my heart leap, but now made my stomach lurch.

The note continued. "I can see now that you don't deserve me. That other creep can have you. It sounded like you had a good time last night."

He heard us last night? He was outside the porch when the louvers were open. My God! I crumpled the note and threw it on the floor.

That was no good. I had to read the rest of it. My palms prickled as I picked it up and smoothed it.

"I wanted to tell you I took a job in Australia and I'm leaving in two weeks. You'll never see me again, and I never have to see your ugly face, or my nagging wife's face, either. You've both been replaced by someone better. I've been emailing a viola player in Sydney. I know she'll work out better than you did."

This means he had been following me last night. And now he was finally gone. I'll continue to look over my shoulder, though. I can't believe he's truly gone.

The note was signed "Len" with no closing. No "Love" or "Yours truly" or "Cordially" or even "Hatefully."

If my phone had any reception I would have called Neek. But I had no such luck. Ivan was back to being The Terrible.

I strolled down the road past Eve's empty cabin, past Hayley's sad-looking blue shutters, and stopped, surveying the site of the burned cabin.

Bushes had grown up all around the edges and screened it from view of the road. I found a set of concrete steps that led down to the level place where the cabin had stood. Aside from the cement foundation little else remained. None of the cabins here had basements; all were built on slabs. Two large, dead trees overhung the space that was once the roof of the cabin. Their trunks were coal black. Even the sunlight glimmered only dimly in this place. There were no clues here. I hurried back to the road and up the hill to my own cheerful cabin.

Finally feeling strong again, the time had come to read the message from Gram. I reached inside the armoire and found it where I had left it. I'd been half-hoping it would have disappeared, but it was there, waiting for me. Deciding this was an "occasion," I poured a glass of iced tea—I didn't have any champagne—and took the envelope out onto the back porch, lit some scented candles, and settled into the wicker rocker.

The rocker creaked as I pushed it back and forth with my toes. Gram used to rock at the end of the day, her toes touching the floor, her heels bobbing up and down in a serene rhythm.

The envelope held several sheets of paper. The top one was a short note from Gram to me dated two days before her death.

My Dear Cressa,

I've had this letter from your parents for many years. They wrote it just before they died. After you read it, you will no doubt wonder what I did about this. I want you to know I hired two different private investigators, but neither of them found anything in addition to what the police report said. The deaths were ruled accidental.

I hope we've made up our quarrel by the time you read this. I almost mailed it to you and may still. If I don't see you before your summer break, I'll give it to you then. It's about time you had it. I'm rambling on, aren't I, dear Cressa?

I don't think there's anything more you can do, just wanted you to know about this.

As much love as always,

Gram

P.S. I've put this cabin in my will for you. I think you'll like it.

I caressed the paper between my fingers, because she had held it. How wonderful to know she wrote her love to me two days before she died. And she knew. She knew I would decide to come see her over my break. And I had. I had come, but hadn't been able to see her one last time. I would treasure this scrap of paper always. One lone tear trickled down my cheek.

Then I turned to the other sheets in the envelope. There were receipts and reports from two different private detective agencies. As I skimmed them, I saw, as she said, they had investigated the deaths of my parents. The findings of both were that no foul play was involved in their deaths.

But the letter from my parents was not included. She must have meant to stick it in, but hadn't gotten around to it.

Now what? Gram was murdered and must have suspected my parents were, too? But everything pointed to an accident. I knew the circumstances. They had finished playing a New Year's gig in a Minnesota ski resort and were on their way back to their cabin at the resort for the rest of the night. Their car slid on an icy patch and rolled down a steep hill. Their sound equipment and instruments flew in all directions and it wasn't clear if they had died of the impact, or from the cases hitting them.

All these facts were familiar to me; they'd been told to me at the time, though I hadn't known about the PIs.

I gently folded the papers and put them back into the envelope to keep. These were big chapters of my life that were over, songs that had been sung. Still, I knew I would get these sheets out and re-read them often in the future.

How silly of me to dread opening this envelope, I thought, as I put it back on the armoire shelf. It was as good a place as any for it.

I only had one thing on my mind now; I needed to see the letter from my parents. I examined every place I had looked in for my necklace, and then some, becoming more and more annoyed. Sweaty and angry, I sat back on my heels on the floor after searching the cabinet under the sink. The letter from my parents wasn't in the cabin. My stomach clenched. I would never know the basis for Gram's concern if I couldn't find that letter.

I pawed through the cupboards again, unmade the daybeds, threw the mattresses to the floor, even moved the items in the refrigerator aside. Still no letter.

Have to get a grip, Cressa. That letter is NOT here.

In the little bathroom I threw water on my face, then sat down at the counter with another glass of iced tea. The cabin was a mess. How daunting to have to clean this up. Later.

The empty mousetraps lay inside the door, where I had left them days ago. Although I had decided to stop catching the poor little creatures, I still didn't want them living in the cabin. Maybe Mr. Anders in the drugstore would have a better solution, one that wouldn't kill them, just keep them out. A trip into town would delay straightening up my cabin.

And this cabin *was* mine now. My cousins would never get it. I had grown fond of it. I would have to close up the cabin and leave in the fall, but wanted to come back some day; I didn't want to return to an infestation, whenever I decided it was safe to return. Whenever people stopped dying here.

-43-

Calcando: "Pressing"; hastening the tempo (Ital.)

n the way to my car I heard angry shouting from the Weldons' trailer. As I slid into the driver's seat Sheila stormed out, slammed the flimsy screen door behind her, thundered down the steps, and stalked off.

Wayne shoved the door open and called after her. The filthy thin slacks he wore must have been the same pair he had on at Grace's funeral yesterday. He was barefoot, and the familiar red plaid shirt was untucked and half-unbuttoned.

His words were slurred with drink, but it sounded like he said, "I can too get them all." It came out more like "Ikin too gimall."

Sheila whirled around, her enormous orange housedress flapping against her chubby legs, and told him to shut up. She shook a hammy fist at him, then kept walking.

I pretended I hadn't seen them and drove to the .

What do you suppose Wayne is talking about? Is he the killer, wanting to kill them all? All the Toombses? Could he have just been swatting flies. Or trapping mice?

Wayne as the killer didn't make any sense, though. It was true, Toombs fired them, but that should have been a welcome development since they didn't like working here. For that matter, why had they stayed all this time, taking his abuse?

I went in to talk to Mr. Anders about mice abatement. But first I asked him exactly what he knew about the famous fire at the lake.

"The Lake Fire." His slow pronunciation gave it capital letters. "I remember when that cabin burned. Everyone does. Poor Norah lost her life that night. You know, most folks thought young Daryl Johannson set the fire. He was just a kid. He was even accused, but then he was acquitted."

He assumed his stool behind the cash register, rubbed his shiny dome, and propped his knobby elbows on the counter. I leaned on the counter, anxious to hear his take on things.

"I never thought he did it. Norah was awfully kind to him when he was going through his hard times." I breathed easier than I had since I read Gram's letter, glad someone else thought him innocent.

"He worked for me for quite a few summers. I know that boy. Honest, hardworking, he'd do anything for a friend. Lots of kids wouldn't be friends with him, though.

Their parents all told them he set the fire that killed Norah Grey and to stay away from him."

The tinkling bell interrupted us and he waited on a woman towing a sniffling kid and recommended an over-the-counter cough syrup. After they left, he climbed back onto his stool behind the counter and continued to spell out the history of The Lake Fire for me.

"That Norah, now, she was one of the best-looking women who ever stocked shelves in this store. She only worked here the one summer when she was a youngster. Same summer Al worked here. They had a romance going, leastways he did." Mr. Anders's chuckle was dark and humorless. "He would corner her back in the stockroom and they'd kiss. I caught 'em a couple of times and put 'em back to work. It was a short romance, though." *Al? Al Harmon?*

Here he frowned. "She showed up several times—two or three, I guess—with a black eye or bruises. The last time, she broke down and cried. She told me Al had done it and she didn't want to be his girlfriend anymore."

This didn't sound like the Al I knew. Or did I know him at all?

"Right after that, she quit working for me and got married to Hank Grey. I guess Al stopped pestering her then, for awhile. He got married, too, the next year. His wife left him after a few months, though, and he started bothering Norah again. Her husband even called the cops on him a few times."

A teenaged girl stuck her head in from the back room and asked what to do with a box of light bulbs.

"Leave it," he told her with a kind smile. "There's enough on the shelf. You'd better run along, you're wasting daylight."

She scurried over with the light step of youth and gave him a quick hug before she left.

"When Al got married to his second wife," Mr. Anders went on, "it seemed like he quit bothering Norah. It wouldn't surprise me, though, if it was him that burned the cabin. I'm not saying he meant to kill Norah, but I'm not saying he didn't, either. I wouldn't put it past him."

I tried to absorb what he was saying, and barely remembered to ask him about the mice.

"You can either try to seal all the places they're comin' in and get an exterminator for the ones that're in there now, or you can get a machine that lets out a high-pitched noise, too high-pitched for us to hear, but it drives the little critters out. I don't have one here. Might be able to find one in New Windsor. It's called a high frequency emitter. The only exterminator around is in New Windsor, too, for that matter."

I thanked him for the advice, got the number for the exterminator, and got into my car to return to the lake. I didn't feel like driving to New Windsor right then. My car meandered into the lake complex and up the hill.

Al—I should have asked him who Al was. The only Al I can think of is Al Harmon. The person Mr. Anders described doesn't sound a bit like Al Harmon, though.

There was Al, sitting outside his cabin fiddling with his fishing equipment, when I drove by. His family had left and he was alone.

He waved and I parked and came over, still carrying my purse with its pepper spray handy in the unlikely event he was the killer. I sat on the bench, out of reach of his long arms.

I asked politely what he was doing and he said he was having a sandwich for lunch and stringing poles, but he didn't have much appetite.

He looked down and my loafers caught his eye. "Where did you get your shoe so muddy?"

Gulp! I guess I didn't clean one side after my trek. The trek where I saw Al looking for his knife.

"I… I don't remember. Maybe when I found Toombs."

Wanting to change the subject, quickly, I asked him if he and Grace were both from Alpha. Maybe that would tell me if he were Mr. Anders's Al.

"Yep, both born and raised here. We left after we got married, you know. I worked at three different colleges in my career, including DePaul. But we've always wanted to come back here to retire." His gaze took in the towering trees, the clear sky, the peaceful lake. A light breeze stirred the leaves of a nearby lilac bush.

"We were glad to see Ida move in, too. Just sorry your grandfather wasn't still alive. Ida missed him something fierce."

"I know. It was my fault he died."

"How was it your fault he fell down the stairs?"

"I didn't replace the light bulb. If he'd had enough light he might have… wait. Wait a minute." My fingers tightened on my purse strap. I pictured us finding him, Gram rushing down to gather up his broken body, the light casting her shadow on him. I'd pictured this scene hundreds, maybe thousands of times in my head. It was always the same. But I'd never talked about it out loud. Since Gram cast a shadow, there had to be light!

"There was light at the bottom of the stairs. There *was* a new light bulb. It *wasn't* burnt out. Gram must have changed it."

Why had I never been able to figure this out before? *There's a time and a place for everything.* I would ponder this later. The ethereal part of Rossini's *William Tell Over-*

ture, the part with flutes and trills, floated upward in my mind, taking a huge chunk of guilt with it.

"Were you in town just now?" he asked.

"Yes. I talked to Mr. Anders, the pharmacist, about my mice problem. He's an interesting man. Did you work for him when you were a teenager? He says almost everybody in town did at one time or another."

Al set his fishing pole aside and rubbed his worn hands together. "Yeah, he's a character. Old as the hills, you know. A lot of us worked for him. Grace and I both did, but not at the same time. She was three years younger. I had to wait for her to graduate from college before we could get married. She was worth waiting for, though." He gave a sad half-smile. "I'll always miss her, Cressa."

A fly whizzed by and he shooed it away from his half-eaten sandwich.

"Mr. Anders spoke of an Al who worked for him one summer. It didn't sound like you, though. Grace was your first and only wife?"

"First, last, and only. She was my sweetheart, the love of my life. We were married forty-seven years. And I wasn't called Al when I was a kid. My nickname was Smiley. I tried to drop it when I went to college, but Grace still called me Smiley. It was her private pet name for me. No, Al would be Al Toombs. He's Albert, I'm Alvin. I've always thanked God I didn't have the exact same name he did. He's always been called Al. He's quite a bit younger than I am, too."

"Mr. Toombs is named Al?" My mouth gaped at that revelation. "That makes more sense. Mr. Anders was telling me about a guy named Al, but the person he described didn't fit you at all. Toombs was married briefly before Martha?"

"Married the youngest Nelson girl. She got enough of him real soon, though, and ran off somewhere after a few months. Just disappeared. She's never been back, even to visit. None of her family is left here. The one he always liked was Norah, even after she got married, but she had sense enough never to encourage him, except for a short fling they had when they were teenagers."

"That was the summer they both worked for Mr. Anders. He told me about that. He wonders if it was Al who burned down the cabin and killed Norah Grey." This would mean *Toombs* set the fire and then blamed Daryl. And killed his first wife?

"He does, does he? I suppose it's possible. But Daryl Johannson probably did it. All the evidence pointed to him, even though he got off. I have nothing against the boy but his mother had just died and his father wasn't paying too much attention to him. I'm sure he didn't mean to kill anyone."

Hot anger rose inside me. "He says he didn't do it."

"Of course he says that. What would you think he'd say?"

"I believe him. I don't think he did." I was speaking rather loudly.

"Well, it's old news anyway," he answered quietly, trying to defuse my anger. "It was big excitement for a long time, but not as big as what we have now."

"The murders, you mean."

Al Harmon didn't say anything, he just picked up his pole and continued stringing line.

"Did Martha ever talk to you about her husband?" *Did she tell you he killed your wife? And did you retaliate by killing Toombs, then Martha?*

"Martha? Toombs hardly let her out. I haven't said two words to Martha in years."

Al set his equipment down and slumped. "I'm tired, Cressa. Think I'll go inside for a nap." His voice sounded weary. He rose slowly, collecting his fishing poles and gear.

The sun was gathering strength and the day was getting downright hot. My purse was heavy on my shoulder.

I called after him. "Could I use your phone for just a minute?" I wanted to tell Daryl I had finished my composition last night.

"Sure," he said, then put his things in the house and returned with the phone. "Go ahead and use it. Just leave it by the door when you're done."

Okay, it doesn't look like Al Harmon killed Martha or Toombs. If Al Toombs is the one who set fire to the cabin, and if someone besides Mr. Anders also thinks so, then someone else would know Al Toombs killed Norah Grey. That person might want to avenge her death. By killing Al Toombs. But all these years later? Norah's husband is dead, Mr. Anders said. But Daryl mentioned a daughter.

I checked my cell phone one more time before I used Al's, but there was still no signal from good old Ivan. Daryl had put his number on the note he left this morning, saying to call any time. I tapped in his number from the note and he answered after two rings.

He said it was great to hear from me. He'd left because he was expecting an important phone call early this morning, but wanted to see me again as soon as he could.

"Great. Tonight's fine. I wanted to tell you I finished up my piece."

"Way to go, Cressa." His voice had a smile to it.

"I think I have what I want. I'm very happy with it. By the way, I need to ask you something. I hope you don't think I'm prying into something that's none of my business. I was thinking there might possibly be a connection between a couple of things."

I spied something shiny on the ground and wandered toward it, away from Al's, a little toward the Weldons' trailer.

"What things?"

"The fire—"

"I knew you'd say that."

"—and Al Toombs's murder."

"What? Okay. Go ahead, shoot." A dime shone in the dirt. Had I dropped it, or was it another omen? I'd have to check with Neek about that.

"Mr. Anders thinks Al Toombs set the fire. I was just figuring, if that's true, maybe a member of Norah's family would have a reason to kill him." I stooped to pick up the dime. A blue jay flew by, warning me of something with his shrill, "*Jay! Jay! Jay!*"

"Norah's family. You mean Norah's daughter. That's all that's left."

"Norah's daughter? Who is that?"

"Sheila Weldon."

"Oh, damn." It all fit. "Toombs went over to fire them the night he was killed. And at Grace's funeral Wayne was shouting about Sheila's mother being able to rest easy in her grave. It was hard to make out, but as they were leaving I thought he was saying he'd taken care of it. And Eve thinks she saw Wayne and Sheila load the body and drive the tractor to where they dumped it, where I found it. It all makes perfect sense. Wayne and Sheila must have—"

My words were tumbling out, but stopped short when I noticed, out of the corner of my eye, someone stealing up behind me. I glanced over my shoulder. Wayne Weldon, still drunk, rushed at me.

"Oh shit. Not you," I whispered.

Wayne grabbed Al's phone and threw it. I ran. He snatched the strap of my shoulder bag. Whipped me around. I slipped my shoulder out of the strap. Evaded his grasping hands. And ran. He flung my purse to the ground and took off after me.

No one was around.

"Al!" I screamed, but he didn't appear.

Wayne wasn't carrying a weapon as far as I could see, but he looked mad enough to kill me with his bare hands. He was between me and Al's place, so I instinctively ran toward my own cabin.

But what sort of shelter could it offer? The front door can easily be burst open from the outside. It swings inward. It only locks by the doorknob. There's a deadbolt on the porch door, but not on the front one.

My thoughts were going a hundred miles an hour.

My flying footsteps swerved around the cabin. I pounded down the earthen stairs. I made better time in my loafers than I would have in sandals, but sneakers would have been best. *What a stupid thing to think about at a moment like this!*

Wayne was losing ground. He wasn't sober and ran clumsily. As I reached the bottom of the steps I looked up and saw Wayne, unsteady, picking his way down. I ran out onto the dock. Knocked one of the loose boards off into the water with a splash. Slipped the loop of rope off the post. Shoved the boat off with a loud grunt.

I jumped into it, grabbed the oars, pushed one of them against the dock, then rowed as hard as I ever had. I was a good twenty feet into the water by the time he got down the hill and reached the dock.

He stood glowering at me for a few minutes, made up his mind to do something, and started back up the steps.

My mouth was dry from panting. The rough oars shredded the skin off my fingers. But I kept rowing until I was in the middle of the lake.

Please, Daryl. Please realize I'm in trouble. What did I say just before Wayne took my phone? I don't remember what I said. I should have screamed.

"Please, Daryl," I whispered over and over, my mouth parched with fear.

-44-

Allargando: Slowing down, usually accompanied by a crescendo
at a climax (Ital.)
Al Fine: To the end (also Ital.)

I listened, trembling, to the soft trickling of the trail left by the oars that I had tipped into the boat—I had nowhere except the middle of the lake to go, and I was already there—and pictured the look on Wayne's face when I had turned to see who was behind me.

I'm sure he heard what I was saying on the cell phone. I couldn't have indicated more clearly that I think Wayne or Sheila killed Toombs if I had written it with a sky plane. What an unfortunate place to pick for my conversation, right outside his trailer. Just because I wanted to see what that shiny dime was.

The look on his face had been pure anger. No, anger *and* hatred. He was so very strong when he grabbed the phone from me. I had tried to hang onto it. Then he jerked me almost off my feet when he took my purse from me. I imagined those hands, strong from years of manual labor, around my neck. My rough shudder shook the whole boat and the oarlocks jingled, sounding like a mockery of a death knell.

What if he gets a boat and catches up with me? What if he tips my boat? I haven't gotten around to digging out a life vest yet. I don't want to sink into this water again.

My bizarre logic was that, if I died out on the lake with a life vest on, at least my body would be recovered right away.

My breathing slowed so that a small, distant, buzzing sound intruded upon my thoughts. I stared at the bend in the lake, where the sound was coming from, frozen, until I saw a boat appear in the distance. It drew closer and closer, its trolling motor sounding more and more distinct, skimming through the water toward the spot where my boat floated idly, as if in slow motion. I could see it was Al Harmon's boat, and Wayne Weldon was in the back with one hand on the rudder, his plaid elbow cocked in the air, steering straight toward me.

I couldn't move. *Where can I go? How can I outrun an outboard motor with oars? Well, I will have to try.*

His motor was small, a trolling motor, the only kind allowed on the lake. I had no idea what my chances were, but they were the only ones I had. I jerked the oars up. Jabbed them into the water. Started pulling.

My mind swung into action. I waited until he was fairly close, thinking I could use his proximity to my advantage. I would try to cut back past him, heading in the direction he came from. As close as he was, it would take him awhile to switch directions to cut me off, using the motor. From farther out, it would be easier for him to swing over into my path and intercept me, so I had to wait until he drew nearer.

When I had steered my craft onto a path perpendicular to his, I plunged my right oar deep into the water and pulled with my left, twice, hard. It was easier to turn sharply with oars than it was with a motor.

I pulled, the oars making great watery plunks, heading back past him. He reached the spot where I had been and started making a wide arc, as I knew he would have to, skidding through the water, the motor churning, whining.

I had a good thirty-five or forty feet on him by the time he was headed in my direction. I decided to make for the boat docks past the beach area. Maybe Hayley or Mo, if one of them was at the yellow house, would notice my plight. Or maybe Al Harmon would. If I made it to shore ahead of Wayne, I could run to Al's cabin. I should have gone there in the first place, I realized, quite a bit too late. Or should I have gone to Martha's where there was a phone? Assuming anyone was there.

No, the house was still taped as a crime scene and was probably locked up. I knew Al was home. That's where I should head. *Good, I have a plan.* It didn't make me feel much better, though.

I made it around the bend and lost sight of Wayne. My aching arms quaked from my efforts, making the oars shiver as I drew them through the water. Over. And over. And over. My hands would soon be rubbed raw. I sat facing the rear of the boat as I rowed, which meant I'd be able to see Wayne as he appeared around the bend.

I'm not near enough to the docks yet. I have to go faster.

I pulled still harder, my breath ragged. I hardly noticed the tears joining the slick sweat on my face. I managed enough breath to yell for help, but my calls were met with echoes, then silence. No one was in sight.

The buzz of the motor crescendoed through the stillness. He closed on me and there was nothing I could do about it.

In horrible fascination, I watched as Wayne easily pulled up beside me, Al Harmon's little motor whining at top speed. He cut the motor before he reached me. A sudden quiet fell as his boat drifted next to mine and tiny sucking waves lapped between the boats. My breathing rasped loudly in my ears and my head and heart were pounding in asynchronous rhythm, as though my heart had moved into my eardrums.

Wayne lunged for the side of my boat, but I poled away with a jab of my oar.

He glared at me, malevolence shooting from his narrowed eyes, then stood and sprang. He was too far away, but he managed to grab the side as he hit the water and went under, tipping my boat upside down. Had he been taller, he might have made it into the boat.

I was catapulted over the side and plunked into the lake at the bow of Wayne's boat. I reached up and grasped it, treading water, and looked around. There was my boat, floating turtle fashion, but Wayne was nowhere to be seen.

Now I was doubly grateful I had worn my loafers today. I kicked them off in the water and found it much easier to stay afloat.

Goodbye loafers, I thought, inanely. A hysterical laugh exploded from my throat, sounding more like a sob.

I peered downward, trying to see Wayne, spitting the fishy-tasting stuff back where it came from, but it was too murky to see more than a few inches.

Should I try to get into Wayne's boat? I don't think I can without tipping it over, too. Should I swim for shore?

Exhausted, I didn't know if I could do that either. I reached into Wayne's boat, Al's boat really, and pulled out one of the oars. The oar lock rattled off the end of the shaft and slipped into the water.

I guess I owe Al Harmon an oar lock. I hope I live to pay him back.

I wanted to use the oar to help me stay afloat while I made for the shore. With despair, I saw I was a long way out.

But it was my only chance. So I started kicking my feet, thrusting the oar in front of me.

My feet stopped. They were caught. I was dragged under, but kept hold of the oar.

I saw, through the thick brown water, Wayne clutching my legs. I tried to kick free. Couldn't. He had to let go and come up for air sometime, didn't he?

At that moment I wanted to kill Wayne Weldon. He deserved to die. He could take the punishment for everything that had gone wrong since I came to Crescent Lake.

With a mighty spurt of adrenaline I kicked free and tried to whack him on the head with the oar. Damn! It was heavier than I thought. It was light when it floated, but, treading water, it was all I could do to lift it above the surface of the lake a couple of inches.

"What are you trying to do, you bastard?" I screamed.

"Get rid of you. What do you think, you goddamn bitch?" he sneered. He didn't seem as drunk as he had.

"It wouldn't be a good idea, idiot. I know you used the tractor to carry his body. And you hid the cushion in the bushes."

"Do you have it? Where?"

He thinks I have it? Is that a good thing?

"It's in my cabin."

We both gasped as we shouted at each other and splashed our hands in front of us to stay afloat.

"Good. When they go through your things after you're dead they'll find it. They'll assume it was you who murdered Al Toombs. Why would you put it in your cabin, stupid girl?"

Good question. That didn't scare him. It wasn't good to tell him it's in my cabin. Maybe I'm the idiot, not him. But if I'm going to die here, he's coming with me. I swear to God.

He grimaced, sucked in a mouthful of air and dived under for my legs again. I filled my lungs before he pulled me back under.

Hunh. I realized I hadn't panicked and gulped in water this time. I had other things to panic about.

He'll have to come back up for air again. He can't drown me from beneath me without drowning himself.

I fought terror as I was pulled farther and farther down into those dark depths. I lost my grip on the oar and it jumped up toward the distant sunlit surface. I tried to use my arms to counteract Wayne's weight and propel myself toward the top. My tired arms pushed the water as hard as they had pushed the oars, but it was no use.

Think, I lectured myself sternly. *He's going to need air soon. Then what?*

I was ready this time. As soon as his grip loosened, I kicked myself up, but not straight up. I tried to go at an angle—I still had enough breath left—so I would surface far from where he would.

The light was dim. An ocean of water between me and the surface. Lungs cried for air.

Maybe I don't have enough oxygen left, after all.

I kicked harder. Cupped my poor blistered hands. Pushed the water down. Daylight approached, the surface neared.

Kick, stroke, kick, stroke.

At last I burst forth into the sweet air and filled my burning lungs, looking around to see where I was.

I had done what I wanted to do. I had even judged the direction right when I was underwater. Wayne was still in the middle of the lake and I had come at least twenty feet closer to shore. I swam exultantly, as though I were fresh. It didn't matter that I had no breath, that I had no strength, I swam as though I did.

Wayne came after me. Halfway to shore he started yelling hysterically.

"You can't get away! I'll get you eventually! Sheila will help me! You're not going to tell anyone about us! You can't tell anyone!"

I forced down the delirious laughter welling in my throat; I had to concentrate on swimming.

Keep yelling. The louder you yell, the less energy you'll have for swimming. I kept quiet and kept stroking. *Thank you, Gram. Thank you for keeping after me until I could swim.*

"He deserved it," Wayne kept shouting. "He was gonna fire us. He bragged about taking care of Sheila's father. Fixed his wagon, he said."

By killing the man's wife and breaking his heart. I swam toward the still-distant shore, then realized I was closer to the diving deck that stood in the middle of the lake.

I changed direction and headed for it, giving quick glances behind me to make sure I knew where Wayne was. I wasn't certain I could make it to shore, but knew I could make it to the deck. He was falling behind. I was a strong swimmer and younger than Wayne, and he had been drunk when the chase started. He had sobered up quite a bit, but he wasn't gaining on me.

I reached the deck well ahead of Wayne, grabbed the ladder, and rested my aching arms, legs, and lungs. Could I possibly keep going?

As the pounding in my head subsided somewhat, I was able to hear the splashing of Wayne swimming toward me. I swiveled my head. Fear.

He's almost on me! Too long—I've rested too long.

Summoning strength I didn't know I had, I scrambled up the ladder. I stood at the top of the ladder, ready to push him off it as he reached for the top. I kicked viciously at his knotty knuckles as they came into view on the rung above the level of the deck, but his grip was iron and I was barefoot. His hands didn't loosen. His body must have been pumping as much adrenaline as mine. I searched the shore, but the beach was deserted. I gave a shout anyway. No answer.

I bent down and pried his fingers off the rung. His look of surprise probably mirrored my face. Neither of us would have predicted my hands were stronger than his.

He slid back into the water.

I hope I've recovered my breath enough to make it to the shore. I have rested and he hasn't. That's one good thing.

I took a run and jumped in without thinking of my fear of being underwater.

It occurred to me that finding a dime was probably *not* a good thing, in spite of most dimes being lucky.

I kept imagining I felt the start of the sudden downward pull of Wayne grabbing my legs every time a weed brushed against me, so I thought I'd better check to see where he was.

I despaired to see he wasn't far behind and was headed right for me.

He started shouting again between his rasping breaths.

"He killed Sheila's mother! He set that fire. I killed Toombs and I killed Martha and I can kill you. You would have killed him, too, you know. Anybody would of."

On shore, people were running down the steps from the Toombs place, out onto their boat dock. Daryl was there, and Chief Bailey from Alpha and Sheriff Dobson from Cambridge, his shock of snowy hair glowing in the sunlight beside Daryl's auburn head. Finally! Daryl unhitched the paddleboat, the only craft that was floating at Toombs's dock, and started pedaling it toward me. Chief Bailey had taken a boat from the docks on the other side of the beach. Sheriff Dobson helped him shove it into the water and two other men jumped in.

I didn't dare turn my head again in Daryl's direction, but I could hear the slap of the paddleboat approaching. Two uniformed troopers were also coming toward us in the motorboat Chief Bailey had found. Wayne didn't even hear.

His face distorted with hideous anger, he made one last lunge, caught my hair, and dragged me under one more time.

The last time. I swear.

I twisted until I was facing him—my hair ripping out—and wrapped my fingers around his neck. His nasty expression turned to surprise. We both popped up above the water, but I didn't let go. His hands were strong, but after years of playing piano for hours every day, so were mine. He flailed, tried to pry my fingers off his throat, then his eyes rolled back.

The boat that held the two policemen pulled up beside him just as he went limp. They reached down and hauled him up by his shirt. He came to as they pulled him into the boat. He resisted them, but was easily subdued by one of the burly officers.

Daryl, hovering nearby in the paddleboat, watched as Wayne was taken away. Then he turned to me. "Wanna lift?"

"You bet. But can I get on that thing from here?" He pulled and dragged until I was sitting on the other seat. My laughter released the tension in every muscle, every bone of my body.

"I've never been so happy to see anyone in my whole life," I said before collapsing like a wet rag. Daryl did all of the pedaling back to the dock.

Sheriff Dobson himself helped me out of the paddleboat, his cold blue eyes as warm as I'd ever seen them, then snapped handcuffs onto Wayne where he stood with his head down, between the two younger policemen.

Daryl helped me up the steps. My legs were made of seaweed. That thought probably occurred to me because there was a good bit of it clinging to me, even streaming down from my hair. A paramedic looked me and Wayne over and pronounced us fine. Wet and bruised, but fine.

Sheila stood, handcuffed, up at the road, guarded by another trooper. Silent tears coursed down her huge baby-soft cheeks.

The other officers brought Wayne up to the road and one of them read the Weldons their rights.

"We don't need an attorney. What you arrestin' us for anyway?" said Wayne, his voice hoarse. "She tried to kill me. See, there are marks on my neck. Why don't you look in her cabin?" He tilted his head up and gave a sly look to Chief Bailey, then pointed his handcuffed hands toward me.

"Wayne," said Sheila with a touching tenderness. "I already told them."

"Told them what?" he snarled. "What did you do that for? She's got the bloody tractor cushion in her cabin." He turned to Sheriff Dobson. "What does that sound like to you?"

"Another stupid move," he said softly. "And can you tell me, what does a tractor cushion have to do with anything?"

I was glad that cushion wasn't actually in my cabin. If it had been in the bushes when I went back to look for it…

"It's all covered with his blood," yelled Wayne.

"I see. Whose blood? And how would you know a thing like that?"

Wayne clamped his mouth shut and jutted his chin out.

"It's probably my old yellow cushion," said Sheila, still trying to calm Wayne. "We thought we'd lost it in the bushes over there, remember? Wayne, I've already told them everything. About you using Al Harmon's fishing knife, and dragging him over there."

"He was firing us." Wayne wailed. "He walked into the trailer and fired us. Sheila said he couldn't do that. He said he could, too." Wayne sobbed. "He said he could do anything he wanted to. 'Your precious parents were so much better than me,' he said. 'Well, I turned out better than them in the long run, didn't I? I'm the one who burned your cabin down.' He said that. He told Sheila he killed her mother! And that just about killed her father, too, for losing her."

"Yes, I know," said Sheriff Dobson with a weary sigh. He scratched the top of his head and his hair stood up in a swirl. "Your wife has told us all that. Including the part about you murdering Martha. Why on earth would you kill poor Martha?"

"I knew you should'nt've called to tell 'em Martha was dead." Wayne's eyes implored Sheila, too late.

"I had to. I couldn't just let her lay there."

"Martha told her," Wayne jerked his head in my direction, "she knew who killed her old man. I heard her say it when they were at the beach. She woulda gotten us caught. Damn you, Cressa, for finding him so soon. I wanted the ants and the flies and the possums and the 'coons to eat him. I wanted him to rot!"

Wayne's shoulders slumped and he deflated. Then started sobbing. "I didn't know everything would go so far. I didn't want to kill Martha, but what could I do?" He raised his tear-streaked face to Sheila. "What happened to us, Sheila?"

"Didn't do you much good killing her, did it?" Dobson said.

"I'm so, so sorry," Wayne blubbered. "Sheila, babe, what are we gonna do?"

"You're both going to the Henry County jail. You come, too, Miss Carraway," he added to me. "I'll need a statement."

"Could I get dry clothes first?" I thought to ask.

Daryl pointed to my feet. "She doesn't even have shoes on."

"Sure," he said absently, leaving with the others. "Don't be too long."

Daryl propped me up on the walk up the hill to my cabin and came in with me.

"Thanks for saving me again," I said.

"Looks like you had already saved yourself. Again. Wayne was almost a goner by the time the cops got there."

A drop of cold water ran down my back. I was glad I hadn't killed him. I knew I had tried, though. That was going to bother me for a long time.

We shared a quick embrace, then I went into the bathroom and warmed up with a hot, fast shower. As I finished dressing, Daryl walked in through the front door carrying a large canvas.

"I was going to bring this over to show you this afternoon. It was in my car. I want you to see it after you get back from the sheriff's office."

I smiled. I had caught a glimpse of the front of the painting before he turned it to the wall. It was a portrait of me.

"Wait here," I said as I picked up my car keys, wincing at my skinned palms, and, after a soft kiss, started out the door.

"I will not," he said. "I'll drive you."

-45-

Coda: A "tail"; hence, a passage ending a movement (Ital.)

I stood at the window and looked out from air-conditioned comfort at the dusty city sidewalks and wilted trees. The heat wave had begun two days ago and promised to keep up for quite awhile. The gentle days of early summer had now given way to an unseasonably hot July.

"Do you take sugar?"

I turned around and smiled.

"No, thank you. Plain." I tried to sip the iced tea, but glugged as though I hadn't had a drink for hours.

"I don't know why I'm so thirsty. It's only a forty-five minute drive in from Alpha."

"But it's a hot one today. The AC makes me thirsty." Daryl's father heaped a spoonful of sugar into his own glass and swirled the mix with a soft clink of his spoon.

"Have a seat," he said, leading the way to the dining room, furnished with antique spindle chairs and a massive sideboard. "Any friend of Darry's is a friend of mine."

I suppressed a chuckle. Here was someone who called him "Darry" with no repercussions.

Daryl and I took seats at the table, set for the three of us probably early in the morning.

Olaf Johannson's hair was gray, but his complexion didn't look like he'd ever been a redhead. Daryl must have inherited his coloring from his mother.

"We got news here in Moline of the murders, but maybe you can fill me in," said Olaf, passing me a plate heaped with cut sandwiches. "Daryl didn't want to worry me with the details. He didn't tell me anything." He gave his son an affectionate look.

"I knew you'd fuss about me, Dad." Daryl smiled at his father. It was as wide as the one he'd given me this morning in bed on the cabin's porch. Daryl saw me hesitate with the platter in my hands. "Those are Dad's special concoctions, rye bread with pimento cheese and ham, and tuna for good measure."

I noticed they also contained leaves of lettuce and slices of tomato. I took two halves and was pleasantly surprised when I bit into the first one.

"What was all that confusing business with Eve Evans and poisoning?" asked Olaf.

I told him what I had put together from the authorities and the locals. "It turned out she had been hospitalized for acute depression after her children's deaths and her husband's arrest, but hadn't ever gotten over the fact that he poisoned and killed their children. How could you ever get over that? She started fantasizing her children had needed to be killed. That was her way of dealing with it. But eventually, she got to thinking all the kids, Hayley's, and Freddie and Pat's, were hers, or something. She was really very, very confused."

I continued with the sandwich and helped myself to some pickles and olives from a dish in the middle of the round wooden table while the men polished off the rest of the sandwiches.

We moved back to the living room. I stole several glances at the artwork, framed and raw, that covered the walls of Olaf Johannson's small apartment. A photograph on the bookshelf caught my eye. Yes, Daryl had his mother's looks. A laughing young woman glanced up at the camera with warmth and affection. She had curly red hair.

Daryl and I sat on the couch. After making sure we were well supplied with more iced tea and store-bought chocolate chip cookies, Daryl's father took what was obviously his favorite chair, flanked by a small table that held the TV controller and a few magazines. He propped a pillow behind his back, shifting his weight and settling in with a satisfied sigh.

"Someone said Eve lost track of what year it was?" Daryl's father lifted his grizzled eyebrows.

"Pat Fiori told me she thought Eve was reenacting her children's murders, in a muddled way, by attempting to murder the other children," I said. "The Fiori kids are outgoing, not a bit shy, and ate a lot of the poisoned cookies she gave them. Hayley's girls were such timid little things they only took a few bites and didn't become ill."

"The sick ones are better, aren't they?" asked Olaf.

"Oh, yes," answered Daryl. "They recovered completely. It remains to be seen whether charges will be filed against Eve. Since she was locked up in the mental hospital anyway, after being permitted to attend Grace's funeral, and I doubt anyone will bother."

"What a business." Olaf shook his head with a sorrowful look. "Eve was always a delicate woman. She deferred to Henry in everything. He was a strange man… secretive. He moved here from California and no one really knew him. After Eve got married, he didn't want her to see any of her old friends, so she mostly stayed home and raised those kids. She sure got a bum deal." He stirred his tea absently. "Say, I heard Smiley Harmon was in the hospital, too. Is he okay?"

"He's out now," I said. "He just went in overnight. He had a bleeding ulcer. Used to have one years ago, he said, and it flared up again.

"He went to the doctor shortly before Grace's murder and the doctor actually told him he ought to leave the lake area and do some traveling. He started obsessing about their future there and their conflicts with Toombs." I remembered how I had suspected him because of his fiery temper. But only slightly. "Then, when Grace died and no one investigated at first, that aggravated his old ulcer all over again. Now that he knows what really happened to his wife, he feels he can deal with everything else. I saw him last night. He's back to fishing and making fires at night."

A bright abstract, swirls of blues and greens, caught my eye and I rose and went over to it.

"I don't know why," I said, "since I can't tell what it is, but this appeals to me."

"It's the color of your eyes," said Daryl.

"My mismatched eyes." I laughed.

Olaf's chest swelled and he came to stand beside me. "That little gem won a blue ribbon." He glowed with pride. Daryl had inherited his smile from his father.

"Dad, it was only the local fair," protested Daryl.

"But it's an indication of things to come. Mark my words, son." He turned to me. "So tell me, according to the news reports, you practically caught Wayne single-handed."

"More like, he almost caught me." I laughed and turned from contemplating Daryl's work. "I was talking to Daryl on the phone just as I figured out who killed Toombs, then Wayne came up behind me and tried to kill me, too."

"I called the cops as soon as the connection broke," said Daryl. "I knew something was very wrong." He put an arm around my shoulder.

"Thank God you did," I said, snuggling against him. "I couldn't have lasted in that water much longer."

"More like Wayne wouldn't have lasted much longer with you strangling him. Geez, your hands are strong!" He caught my palms in his and squeezed. I laughed and squeezed back, my blisters from June mostly healed. A tremor ran through me, in spite of my joy at being together with these two delightful guys. I had wanted to kill a man.

"But how did you know it was Wayne and Sheila?" Daryl's father asked me.

"Well, it was pretty confusing, since Toombs had been poisoned *and* stabbed. The autopsy analysis on the poison didn't come in for a long time. I was pretty sure Eve had poisoned the children, therefore I thought she might have poisoned Toombs, too, but I didn't know why she would. Of course, I didn't know why she'd poisoned the children, either." Daryl and I returned to the couch.

"Eve told me, though," I continued, "she saw Wayne and Sheila late at night transporting something with the tractor to where I found the body the next day. She figured all along it was them. But I didn't know whether I could believe her or not. She's so… off."

"I guess that's as good a word as any for her," said Daryl's father, rising to refill our glasses, then settling back into his big stuffed chair.

"I did see tracks from the tractor tires over there, though," I said. "And then I remembered seeing the tractor cushion near where the body had been. And I noticed the Weldons had bought a new red one." I shook my head. "Martha told the police she poisoned him. But later the coroner's report said he had died of stab wounds, not poisoning." I sipped the cool tea. Daryl's dad made good tea.

"What really told me it might be Wayne and Sheila," I said, "was piecing together the facts that Al Toombs had been obsessed with Sheila's mother. Also that he had been on his way to fire them that night. I wasn't absolutely positive, though, until Wayne overheard me on the phone with Daryl and began to chase me. He told me all about it while he was trying to kill me."

"Boy, you just never know, do you?" said Olaf. "I guess you were lucky Darry showed up with the cops when he did."

"Those cops drove me crazy," Daryl said. "The first thing they did was drive to the trailer and question Sheila. I was going nuts thinking Wayne must be somewhere with Cressa." He squeezed my hand again. "I kept asking if we could go look for you. Finally they sent me out with a detective, then we spotted you pretty quickly."

"I don't know quite how to say this," I said slowly, "But I have mixed feelings about the whole thing."

"What do you mean?" asked Daryl. "I know exactly how I feel about the whole mess."

"I agree with how Martha felt about Toombs being dead. But I'm not glad Martha's dead. I wonder what would have happened if we could have figured it out sooner. Maybe Martha would still be alive." I turned to Daryl and he nodded, considering what I'd said.

"She might. But she would have faced attempted murder charges," he said. "And you can't change the past."

"If only. I'll never, ever be sorry Toombs is dead," I continued, raising my voice slightly. "Even if that makes me a bad person. He was a murderer himself. "First Norah Grey, then my grandmother, then Grace. Maybe more, who knows. Like maybe his first wife? She was never seen again. I probably would have been happy Wayne killed him, if Wayne hadn't killed Martha and tried to kill me."

"And," added Daryl, "it's such a great thing to find out after all these years who really set that fire."

"I'm glad it's over." I could finally relax at the lake. When I had started out to surprise Gram that day, I had been looking forward to a peaceful interlude.

"More tea?" asked Daryl's father.

"No, Dad. I've got to get back to Alpha. I'm expecting a phone call."

"You still trying to set up that exhibit in Chicago?" he asked with obvious pride in his voice.

"Still trying."

Daryl and his father exchanged a quick embrace.

"Good luck, son," he called as we left. "Bring Cressa back to see me sometime."

"Will do," Daryl promised.

We left together and Daryl walked me to my car.

"I only have one more question," he said. "Your mention of seeing the tractor cushion in there made me think of it. What was Wayne talking about when he blubbered something about that cushion?"

I laughed. "That was the craziest thing. I was sure it was a real clue. And he thought I had it and I thought he had it."

"Who did?"

"Little Rachel and Rebecca had moved it and taken it to a place in the woods where they play house. They liked the yellow color and thought the brown blood splotch was from the dirt. The police retrieved it from there, and it proved to be the cushion with Toombs's blood on it that was on the tractor when they transported his body."

There was one more thing I needed to do. Daryl and I had taken separate cars so I was alone in mine on my way back to Alpha.

Just before I got to the town I turned left into the Alpha Cemetery. After I cut the engine I sat for awhile. I fished my locket out of my purse and fingered it, putting off my task. After Daryl managed to retrieve it for me, I threw away the chain Mo had stolen. He had broken it, and I didn't like the thought of his hands all over it, anyway.

A shade tree played leafy patches of shadow across the hood of my car. A robin *cheerio*-ed from a branch. Even the breeze was perfect, bringing a touch of coolness up from the valley beside the grave site.

Gram's headstone glinted in the sun. I got out of the car and knelt to trace the carving: her name, Ida May Swenson Miller, and the dates of her birth and death.

"Gram," I whispered, my tears starting to flow. "At least I know who killed you. Thank God the police were able to match the fingerprints on the lenses of Grace's glasses to Al Toombs. They had his prints on file from two domestic disturbances filed by his wife years ago. You probably know all about those.

"I sure got in trouble with Sheriff Dobson. He told me, once again, that the chain of custody was compromised by both Al and me transporting the glasses. But at least he agreed the combination of the fingerprint evidence and the testimony Martha gave me before she died points to him as your killer."

The quartz in Gram's headstone sparkled in the sunlight.

"Grace's killer, too, of course. I don't know if justice was served by his death or not. A rough justice maybe." I listened to the breeze stir the leaves of the nearby maple.

"These people aren't really evil, Gram. Toombs was the closest to that, I think, but the others were just doing what they thought was right for them. Eve Evans isn't a bad person, just a casualty of circumstance and precarious mental balance. Even Toombs's awful acts stemmed from his love for Mo, his desire to protect him, I think.

"But wait till you hear the debut of your piece, *Affirmation*. It's a song of life. I think you'll like it."

I returned to my car and retrieved my keyboard. After switching it on, my fingers flew over the keys. My piece floated over Gram's grave and wafted through the leaves of the maple, then up to the heavens. I closed my eyes, still streaming tears, and leaned into the music. The notes felt exactly right.

"Did you like it?" I asked when I'd finished. I was sure she had.

A red-winged blackbird sang his agreement and flew off, flashing his bright red shoulders.

To my intense relief, I found I needn't have feared my errand. These tears were different. Not bitter, but cleansing. I tucked the locket back into my purse and picked up my keyboard. I had begun to come to terms with my loss and hoped to soon lay my guilt to rest. I hadn't made a conscious decision to move on; it had just happened. As Gram used to say, "Life goes on."

Back at the cabin, I related the meeting with Daryl's dad to Neek over my new cell phone, named Edmund the Magnificent in hopes he'd live up to his name. I now had a P.O. Box and all my bills were paid.

"His dad looks so much like Daryl—there's one guy that could never deny paternity."

"They say you should look at a guy's father to see what he'll become."

I laughed. "And a woman's mother, don't forget." My mother never got to be very old, though. "I'd say it would be okay if Daryl turned out like Mr. Johannson."

"So you think things are going to work out for you and Daryl?"

A cardinal sang, *"Pretty birdy, pretty birdy,"* in the blue spruce.

"We'll see. It's a good possibility. By the way," I remembered to ask, "what does finding a dime mean?"

Neek's gasp came over my cell phone loud and clear. "No! Not a dime! That's terrible!"

"You're telling me."

"Actually, it can be really, really good, or really, really bad."

"I guess it was both. I survived it."

Epilogue

Postlude: A piece played at the conclusion (Eng.)

The sun felt marvelous. I scrunched down into a bunch of cushions at the prow of the boat, soaking up the heat. Daryl lazily fished off the back. The motor was tipped up out of the water. We drifted, silent, on the lake through the warm July day.

In the past year I had done a lot of thinking. After he'd moved to Chicago, Daryl and I had written each other constantly and seen each other occasionally. He was in Evanston, on the North Side, and I was at DePaul, so it wasn't easy getting together. Our phone bills were high. The longer we knew each other, the more I could feel an empty spot inside of me being filled up with his essence.

I was spending another summer at Gram's cabin and getting a great deal of composing done. Daryl had taken a week off from teaching his private students in Evanston.

I was funny about never wanting to get into a boat without a motor. Daryl humored me. My trauma from last summer was beginning to fade, however, just as Daryl's obsession with the fire from his childhood, now that he could discuss it openly, was dwindling.

We could see the cabins along the shore as we floated by. My red cottage could be glimpsed through the greenery riffling in the light breeze. The boat dock still had missing boards, but I would get it fixed soon.

The cabin next door, the one that used to be Eve's, housed a middle-aged couple who took care of the grounds now. The man had taken early retirement from a factory in the Quad Cities and was delighted to find a job in the country. They had bought some of Eve's furnishings when they purchased her cabin, and they visited her in the rest home in Rock Island occasionally, bringing her news of the lake people.

Our boat floated on down the lake past the cabin with the light blue shutters. It was still for sale.

Daryl pulled in his line and began to row. We passed the site of the burnt cabin. The lot had been sold and a young couple was building a summer house there. The blackened trees had been taken down and the house was half-finished. The buzz of a power saw vied with the racket of the katydids and locusts. We waved at the couple, out working on the window frames, as we drifted past.

A fish leapt in the shadows near the shore and sent thick, shining rings our way.

Around the bend, the Toombses' yellow house was empty. Hayley visited the lake with her girls and stayed there almost every weekend. They were starting to act less frightened, to run and shout, like Freddie and Pat's children.

"I got a letter yesterday from Mo," said Daryl. "He's finished boot camp and is waiting for his orders."

"I hope they send him far away," I answered, fingering my locket, hung around my neck on a new chain.

"At least he told me about your grandmother and Grace. He confirmed what Martha told you."

"I guess that's good." He had told Daryl essentially the same story as Martha's about his father drowning the two women. Daryl eventually confronted him about my locket and chain and, when Mo handed him the necklace and a set of rings, Mo told Daryl the rings belonged to my Gram. For some reason, he had never fenced them.

Al got Grace's earrings back, too. He was saving them for his granddaughter.

I felt like a big chapter of my life had closed, except for the missing letter Gram had mentioned, the one my parents left for her to give to me. That story wasn't done yet. Somehow, I would keep trying to find out what they'd wanted to tell me. I didn't know how, but I would.

Mo was seeing things straighter with his father gone, according to his letters to Daryl, but I didn't want to have anything to do with him. He had left the lake the day of Grace's funeral and bummed around several states before joining the army.

Daryl turned the boat and rowed slowly back the way we had come.

"I'm so glad Pat and Freddie decided not to prosecute Eve Evans," I said as we passed her cabin again.

"It might have been a different story if their children hadn't gotten better," said Daryl.

"Yes, that's something to be thankful for. I ran into Freddie last week at Southpark Mall in Moline. I asked him to come out sometime and fix my boat dock. Did I tell you?"

"No, you didn't."

The woods rang with bird song and I replayed passages of last summer's opus in my head. I had nicknamed my piece "Song of Life," but I would also always think of it as a Song of Death.

"Let's go in. I'm starving."

"Okay," said Daryl. He wheeled the boat toward the cove. There was a motor, of course, but he liked the feel and the sound of dipping the oars into the water, the oars dripping their way back for the next stroke.

"Someone's there," I said, sitting up. "On the dock."

Daryl turned around. "Looks like Freddie. Maybe he's ready to fix your dock."

Freddie helped pull the boat over as we floated in, bumped the dock, and tied up.

"How's your carpentry business going, Fred?" asked Daryl, stepping carefully over a space where a board was missing. He gave me a hand to help me out.

"Great guns." Freddie grinned his huge warm grin. "I'm so busy I hardly have time to eat. But Cressa said she needed work done, so I decided to drop everything and do it. I owe a lot to you, Cressa. I don't know what would have happened if Hayley had gone ahead and sued us for spreading lies about Toombs and her girls. Pat didn't mean to cause trouble for anyone, she was mostly mad at Toombs for not paying us for all the work I'd done that summer. Do you know he was threatening to kick us out for not paying rent, on top of everything?" Freddie shook his head, knelt, and pried up a rotten board with a ripping sound.

"Oh, I don't think Hayley really wanted to sue you," I said. "She was upset about her mother's death and was lashing out at whomever she could. After Wayne and Sheila were convicted, she felt much better."

"Well, Pat thinks you're the one that talked her out of her lawsuit. And then that money from Eve. I think you had something to do with that, too." He started hammering pieces of new lumber into place.

It turned out Eve had a huge bank account balance when her affairs were looked into. Even though she was committed to a nursing home and diagnosed as mentally impaired, she was considered competent enough to bestow a large sum of money on the Fiori family. Maybe it was considered as reparation in place of prosecution. She had a few lucid moments now and then when she was horrified at what she had done and wanted to make up for what she had put that family through. She told me, during one of my visits, she didn't have any living relatives after her husband passed away last winter in prison.

Shouts rang out from the woods on the hillside above us. "Ready or not, here I come!" A scream of pure joy soon followed, along with scrambling sounds through the brush.

"I brought the kids along. They miss the place," Freddie said. "Hayley says 'Hi,' by the way. Pat talked to her a few days ago. Nursing school's going great for her. Pat gives her all the encouragement she can."

"I'm so glad Hayley has decided to take care of herself," I said.

"So, Daryl. When do you start your new job?" Freddie asked through the nails in his mouth, whacking another board into place.

"Next semester, this fall." Daryl brought him another board from the stack on shore.

"You two will be teaching at the same college?"

"Some of our classes are even in the same building," Daryl answered. "Did you know Al Harmon used to teach at that college, too?"

I laughed. "He told me he wanted to turn this complex into a retirement home for DePaul University professors someday. I can't picture it myself."

"Can't say that I can, either," said Daryl.

Freddie stood and stretched his back. "There. That ought to hold you for awhile."

"Freddie, thanks so much," I gushed. "What's your charge?"

"Absolutely nothing. I said I owe you." He ignored my protests and gathered up his equipment. "That art show you had last winter sure got the write-ups," Freddie said to Daryl. "I saw photos of your paintings in the paper, but I just don't understand them. Except that one you did of Cressa. I like that."

"Thanks. I guess it's that picture and that show that got me the job working at Cressa's college."

"Wow. Hope you both like teaching there."

"I know I will," said Daryl. He threw me a wink with his brilliant green eyes.

The sun threw a bright shaft onto one of Freddie's new planks. I passed through the warm light to Daryl's side.

"I hope I will. We'll see," was all I could say. If anything deeper developed between us, I was going to make sure it was on my terms, as well as his. I had learned something from Len.

We linked arms and followed Freddie up the steps. I had cookies in the cabin the Fiori kids might like. There were no dark flecks in them.

THE END

KAYE GEORGE

Kaye George is a short story writer and novelist who has been nominated for Agatha awards twice. She is the author of two mystery series, the *Imogene Duckworthy* humorous Texas series and the *Cressa Carraway* musical mystery series. Her short stories can be found in her collection, *A Patchwork of Stories*, as well as in *Fish Tales: The Guppy Anthology*, *All Things Dark and Dastardly*, *Grimm Tales*, and in various online and print magazines. She reviews for *Suspense Magazine*, writes for several newsletters and blogs, and gives workshops on short story writing and promotion. Kaye lives in Knoxville, Tennessee. Find out more at her website, www.kayegeorge.com, or through Twitter and Facebook.

ABOUT
BARKING RAIN PRESS

Did you know that six media conglomerates publish eighty percent of the books in the United States? As the publishing industry continues to contract, opportunities for emerging and mid-career authors are drying up. Who will write the literature of the twenty-first century if just a handful of profit-focused corporations are left to decide who—and what—is worthy of publication?

Barking Rain Press is dedicated to the creation and promotion of thoughtful and imaginative contemporary literature, which we believe is essential to a vital and diverse culture. As a nonprofit organization, Barking Rain Press is an independent publisher that seeks to cultivate relationships with new and mid-career writers over time, to be thorough in the editorial process, and to make the publishing process an experience that will add to an author's development—and ultimately enhance our literary heritage.

In selecting new titles for publication, Barking Rain Press considers authors at all points in their careers. Our goal is to support the development of emerging and mid-career authors—not just single books—as we know from experience that a writer's audience is cultivated over the course of several books.

Support for these efforts comes primarily from the sale of our publications; we also hope to attract grant funding and private donations. Whether you are a reader or a writer, we invite you to take a stand for independent publishing and become more involved with Barking Rain Press. With your support, we can make sure that talented writers thrive, and that their books reach the hands of spirited, curious readers. Find out more at our website.

WWW.BARKINGRAINPRESS.ORG

Barking Rain Press

ALSO FROM BARKING RAIN PRESS

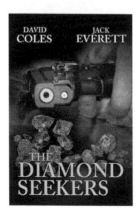

VIEW OUR COMPLETE CATALOG ONLINE:

WWW.BARKINGRAINPRESS.ORG

Made in the USA
San Bernardino, CA
22 July 2014